NORMAL

BENJAMIN LANGLEY

Published by Crystal Lake Publishing—Tales from The Darkest Depths

Website: www.crystallakepub.com/

Copyright 2020 Benjamin Langley
Join the Crystal Lake community today
on our newsletter and Patreon!
Download our latest catalog here:
https://geni.us/CLPCatalog

All Rights Reserved

Cover art:
Don Noble—www.roosterrepublicpress.com

Layout:
Kenneth W. Cain—www.kennethwcain.com

This is a work of fiction. Names, characters, businesses, places, events and incidents are either the products of the authors' imagination or used in a fictitious manner. Any resemblance to actual persons, living or dead, or actual events is purely coincidental.

No part of this publication may be reproduced, stored in a retrieval system, or transmitted in any form or by any means, without the prior permission in writing of the publisher, nor be otherwise circulated in any form of binding or cover than that in which it is published and without a similar condition including this condition being imposed on the subsequent purchaser.

WELCOME
TO ANOTHER

CRYSTAL LAKE PUBLISHING
CREATION

Join today at www.crystallakepub.com & www.patreon.com/CLP

To Nicola

Best wishes!

B. Long

For my girls,

Malibu and Georgia

ACKNOWLEDGEMENTS

I'm privileged to work at a school that has a specialist hearing support centre onsite, and from the amazing staff, I've learnt a bit of sign language. Any mistakes in this aspect are very much my own. Likewise, information on heart conditions came from the NHS and if anything in this book is wrong, it's my misinterpretation.

Once more Don Noble has produced an amazing cover. Thank you, Don, for doing such a fantastic job. Thank you also to those at the Ely Writers group who read parts of this in its infancy. As always, I appreciate my family for putting up with me when I'm deep into several projects at the same time. Some things never change.

Thanks to everyone who has taken the time to speak to me at an event or buy one of my books. I cannot tell you how much I appreciate those that also take the time to leave a review. It's not only great to hear what people think of my work, but it also helps others discover it, too.

I'm so glad this novel has a second chance with Crystal Lake Publishing. That you Joe and all that helped make this possible.

I hope you enjoy the novel.

1: TED

When Ted gasped, his lungs burned as if he'd breathed in a cloud of sulfur rather than the fresh countryside air, and his ribcage buckled to the point of bursting as his chest expanded. He tried to open his eyes, but his vision failed, and a throbbing pain surged into the back of his head. He squeezed his eyes shut again, left with only the memory of blurry shapes. Where was he? Certainly not in his bed. How was that possible?

Before panic could curl her spiteful fingers around him, Ted focused on his breathing, slowly in and out, reminding his body to do something which it had been quite capable of doing automatically for the last fourteen years. It wasn't good for his heart to race. He couldn't allow himself to lose control, but he'd practised calming techniques: inhale, count, exhale, count, repeat. With his breathing regulating, Ted became aware of the other signals his body reported. He lay on his side, and a breeze licked a cold tongue over his bare back. He felt... wet? With his fingers, he felt grass beneath him which wasn't right. Where was his bed? Where was his bedroom? He tried to open his eyes again, but as his retinas detected the tiniest amount of light, the searing pain returned, and he scrunched them closed.

Was this a dream? No, Ted was conscious of the fact that this was nothing like a dream, and yet he felt like he'd been stuck in a dream for a long time.

Ted scrunched the grass again in his hands. He pulled a clump to confirm its existence. While the grass snapped easily, the muscles in his hands and arms tingled. He kicked out his legs and heard a splash. Water. His feet were in the water.

He figured he must be at either a riverbank or the edge of a lake. Trying to fathom why was too painful, and he assumed he must have been there for a while as he couldn't feel his feet.

2 NORMAL

He rolled onto his side and pulled his feet out of the water and tried to rub some life back into them. They were freezing, but aware of the sensation of touch. After the exertion of movement, he had to stop again, to concentrate on his breathing as he felt the vice in which his brain had been placed tighten. On the edge of passing out, he had to control it. He drew a low, slow pull of air through his nose. He couldn't hold it for as long as he liked–his lungs were like balloons that had expanded against a row of sharp, metal teeth and if they held their position any longer, they'd pop. When he released the air through his mouth, the pressure in his chest subsided and the cold metal clamp on his head released, but only a little.

As the minutes passed, Ted noticed the sounds around him: the water lapping at the bank, the breeze rustling the leaves of a nearby tree, and farther away, the sound of cars. He managed to sit, and his vision restored enough for him to make out the shape of his limbs–all present–and realised he was almost naked; he wore only a pair of black underpants, sodden and baggy. Had he been entirely underwater? He felt the top of his head: dry, his hair warm from the sun.

He looked at the grass, ran his fingers through it and felt his fingers tingle as if the sensation of touch had long been alien to him. He looked a little further afield, careful not to raise his head too high and let in the light which threatened to blow a hole through the back of his head. This looked much like the path alongside the River Wissey. The cars could be on the A10, which would put him close to his home in Wiseham: 16 Riverview Terrace. If he had his full vision, he might have been able to see his house which backed onto the river. But that didn't answer how he'd got into the river. He tried to focus on some of the shapes he could make out on the horizon. The blurry shape on one side could be the water tower. Could that be the spire of the church?

Thinking of the church threw him into a painful spasm, and he was hit by a blurry vision of the creatures carved into the stone blocks above the church's door and on the nearby vicarage.

He shook the vision from his head and closed his eyes. If he tried to focus on anything, pain squeezed the back of his head. He felt at his gut, and then his legs. While he was never particularly big, he felt thinner than he remembered.

As the hot sun dried the water from his flesh, he remembered that it hadn't been this hot when he'd gone to bed, just another drizzly November day, but sitting on the path beside the river, Ted would have sworn it were summer. If he sat in the sun for too long, he thought, he'd burn. As a fair-headed child, he's always been susceptible to burning. Even the slightest bit of sun would bring out the freckles, another thing they mocked him for at school. No, he couldn't sit here. And what about if they found out that he paraded around in his underpants in public? Had they done this to him? No one hated him enough at school to play such a cruel prank, and no one would have the resources to do something quite so... elaborate. But thinking only confused him, made everywhere ache. Instead, Ted tried to push himself up onto his feet. He could feel the muscles in his arms quivering as he tried to work his body into position, and when he tried to put weight on his legs, they spasmed and he collapsed back into the grass. He'd never felt so weak. Had he been drugged?

He wasn't going to be able to make it home alone, so he tried his voice. When he tried to yell, only a squeak emerged, and his throat felt dry, like ancient stone. A second attempt produced something that sounded like a word. He swallowed to alleviate the pain and the dryness in his throat, but he had no saliva, so he sat and continued to breathe slowly. One last attempt. He tried to call out again. It sounded like he'd said, "Help." Hopefully, someone was nearby.

Just when he thought his attempt had been worthless, he heard a bark.

2: SIMON

Simon tried to keep the frustration from his voice as he talked the awkward customer through the process of rebooting their system. Customers like this moron made him long for a drink. He licked his lips and imagined he could taste Old Navy. Maybe he could. A taster had helped him out of the house. Just a little: not even a whole shot. On days like today, he wished he was on-call and visiting customer premises, or even better, off-shift altogether.

When his personal mobile rang, he put the moron on hold to check the caller ID. Yes, it was unprofessional, but every call could be someone responding to the appeal. Every call could be news about his boy. Every call could be the one that confirmed it was all over... for better or worse.

Alan Macintyre, his line manager, eyeballed him. Simon had been in trouble before for what Alan called his "lax attitude to customer service," but this was important, or it could be. Alan, or A-Mac as some of the younger team members called him, had only been in the job a few months. Had Simon not been preoccupied with his missing son, he would have gone for the role, and, given the years of experience he'd given the company, he'd likely have been promoted before A-Mac. When it came, he didn't look beyond the header of the email. Ever since Ted disappeared, after burning through his parental leave and then his annual leave, he'd done his shift (whether that be office or field), and then headed straight home, no overtime, no matter how much his superiors frowned upon him.

Before Ted went missing, he had a handle on his drinking. Today he wasn't sure he'd completely sobered up from last night, especially after the little taster. A-Mac was on to him, too. If A-Mac suspected he'd been drinking on duty, he'd be straight out of the door, but it hadn't come to that, not yet.

It had been different under his former boss. He'd understood Simon's situation and had allowed him as much time as possible. A-Mac, on the other hand, had the compassion of a cardboard coaster and the charisma of one too.

But when Simon saw Megan's name on his phone, he took the call, staring at A-Mac as he did so, daring him to confront him. She was probably calling to say she was working late again. Where Simon had worked as little as possible, sinking every hour into the search for Ted, she'd taken on extra hours, had stayed late to complete reports, and was running training courses left, right and centre. Simon had confronted her about it months ago, about the same time A-Mac came along and started applying the thumbscrews. It was a distraction, she'd said. There was nothing more she could do to help find Teddy, so she had to do what she could to take her mind off it. While Simon understood, he couldn't let go. Maybe combing the bedroom one more time would turn up a clue that had somehow been missed in the previous thousand searches. Every time he searched his son's room, he discovered something new about Ted and was hit with a pang of guilt about not knowing his son better. He'd discovered lyrics from songs by The Cure in a notebook and wondered how Ted had ever got into one of his favourite bands. Alongside those lyrics were some that Simon didn't recognise. He knew Ted played guitar, he'd yelled at him to keep it down enough times, but did he write lyrics too? Alas, there was nothing that indicated to Simon where his son might have disappeared to. If only he knew him better, he might have figured it out.

"Megan. What is it?" Simon said, his disappointment preloaded.

At first, it was quiet. Emotion dripped down the line. Simon could hear Megan's presence, unable to talk, stifled by sobs. Was this it? Was this the call he'd been waiting for? Dreading?

"They've found Teddy," Megan said, her voice on the verge of breaking again.

So, it was over. No further need to appeal to the public for answers. No further reconstructions. No further rifling through the sock drawer trying to find that missing piece of evidence. They'd found him, and it was over.

"He's alive," Megan said.

The phone slipped from Simon's hand, bounced on the cheap carpet tiles, and landed face up, undamaged.

He was alive? How? Where? As much as he wanted the call to come, as much as he wanted the stage of unknowing to be over, as much as he hoped, no part of him thought he'd ever hear that his boy was okay.

He scrambled for his phone, picking it up on the third attempt to hear Megan calling his name, asking if he was still there.

"He's alive," Megan repeated. "Thank God."

God had nothing to do with it. Simon had no doubt about that. He knew it was no good waiting for God's intervention. He'd learnt long ago that if there was anyone out there, he was uninterested at best, and at worst a cruel and sadistic observer.

"Where is he?" Simon started for the door.

A-Mac stood up as Simon disconnected the call. "Where do you think you're going?"

"They've found him," Simon said. "They've found Ted."

A-Mac held out a hand to stop Simon, but before it resulted in a confrontation one of the senior managers across the room spotted the look on Simon's face and knew he was not to be stopped.

"Are you okay, Simon?" he called across the room.

"They found my boy. I'm going to see him."

"Macintyre, get this man's work covered."

And Macintyre, his eyes full of resentment, shrunk back into his seat.

3: MEGAN

It was him, her Teddy Bear, the son she feared she'd never see again, lying in the bed attached to the drip and the monitors.

"Can I wake him?" she said to the doctor.

"It's best not to at this time," she replied before leading Megan back out into the corridor.

Megan glanced again at the name tag, hoping it would stick this time. "Listen, Doctor Hodder. My boy's been gone for the best part of seven months. I need to know he's okay."

Doctor Hodder reached out and rested her hand on Megan's shoulder. "I understand, Mrs Wallace, but he's very weak. It would be best if he were left to sleep and wake naturally."

Megan turned toward her Teddy. She'd never seen him so skinny. His hair had grown, but it was thin and messy, his skin pallid. He never had much colour, but now, he barely looked alive. "I just want him to know I'm here."

"That's understandable, Mrs Wallace. As you can see, Ted is very malnourished, but there is no sign of physical trauma—no broken bones, a few bruises, so that's good news."

"What about his heart?" Megan asked, thinking back to the first time she'd seen Ted. The blue tinge to his skin had at first taken her aback, but she didn't want to say anything, to accept there was something wrong with her newborn son. But while the midwifery team were checking him over, they were also concerned by what they referred to as cyanosis and sent him for more tests. Later, it was confirmed that Ted had a septal defect—what's commonly called a hole in the heart, and several operations had lessened the severity of the condition, but not repaired it completely. With the growth spurt, Ted had undertaken back in October, he was scheduled for another round of check-ups and, if necessary, another operation. Before that happened, he'd disappeared.

8 NORMAL

"His heartbeat is stable. There are more tests to run, but no unexpected abnormalities have been detected so far."

The detected abnormality he'd been living with his whole young life was already quite enough to deal with; it had made him different from the other children as he could never take part to the same extent. She'd feel he was safer if back home with her.

"When can he come home, Doctor?"

Doctor Hodder sucked air between her teeth. "It's too early to say. We need to monitor him for a period. He needs to gain weight, so we need to see him eat."

"But then he can come home?"

"We will have to assess whether he is emotionally ready, too. It might take time to adjust."

Megan nodded. She had so many questions but didn't know where to begin. She looked again at Teddy, and, alongside the relief that he had been found, another emotion resided within her: anger. All of the time Teddy was gone, Megan couldn't find a way to cope. She was angry with the police for having so few leads. She was angry with herself for being so damned powerless. Worst of all, she was angry with Teddy for going missing, however little sense that made.

She'd hoped seeing her Teddy Bear in the hospital bed, alive, if not entirely well, would allow her anger to dissipate. Still, it remained, but now, stronger than ever, Ted was its source. She was angry he was sleeping, and therefore not communicating with her. Asleep, he couldn't tell her what happened, and therefore she could not absolve herself of any blame.

As Megan gazed at her child, trying to comprehend what Doctor Hodder had suggested about Ted's mental health, Simon arrived. He went straight to her side, placed a hand around her waist, and stood with her, looking at his son.

Megan turned to her husband and saw only love and relief. If anything, he'd always been the one who was harder on Ted (when he wasn't too busy at work), but the way he spoke about him after he disappeared was as if his son were some kind of angel. She looked at the sense of wonder he wore, like a man struck by a miracle. Why couldn't Megan feel that same overwhelming sense of gratitude? Again, anger boiled inside. If Simon had done more, would he have found Teddy sooner? Then the anger turned inwards. Why was he able to look at his son with so much love, when all she had was rage?

Simon started with the questions, the same ones that Megan had asked. Of course, he wouldn't take her word for it; he had to hear it from the doctor, but before Doctor Hodder had a chance to repeat herself, they were interrupted by a gasp from the bed.

Ted had woken.

4: LOLA

"It's okay, Mrs Thakur, I'll walk," Lola said, shoving her French book back into her rucksack. "I'm sure someone will be home by now."

Her friend Jas had her piano lesson, and while Mrs Thakur had offered to drop Lola home en route, Lola knew there was a chance she'd find it deserted, and she didn't want Mrs Thakur to see that. Not again. By half-past-five, Dad should have been home. He finished at four this week. Her Mum's hours were all over the place. Walking home would also get her away from Jas sooner. They'd been friends since they were placed in the same form at secondary school, and Lola would often go to Jas's house to complete her homework, but it felt more and more like a chore. Besides, Lola wasn't learning from the experience, simply copying Jas to avoid trouble. Jas was smarter than her, and watching Jas do homework often left Lola feeling stupid. Still, how was she supposed to concentrate on French verb endings with everything going on in her life? Her brother disappeared out of the window one night.

She said goodbye, nodding that she wouldn't forget her PE kit when Jas reminded her and gave Mrs Thakur a wave. The Thakurs lived at the opposite end of Wiseham, in the houses behind the Spar shop. She had no idea what the food situation would be like at home. A rushed ready-meal? Take-away? Told to fend for herself and hunt first through the freezer and then the cupboards for something that would constitute a meal. Maybe she should stop by the shop...

After reaching into the bottom of her rucksack for her purse she realised she only had a few pennies anyway, so going in would be pointless. She avoided Downham Road, the main road that passed through Wiseham, knowing that if Mrs Thakur passed her, she'd insist upon giving her a lift. Instead, she cut through the passageways that linked one cul-de-sac to another. Passing Ted Hatcher's house, with its ramshackle fence, peeling paint on its window frames, overgrown plants, and rusting Land Rover on the drive, she couldn't help but think of her brother. Kids used to mock him for sharing a name with the village looney, a man that had been given the moniker Ted Hatcher: Child Catcher. She hurried past his house, keeping one eye on the living room window, expecting to see the yellow-with-age lace curtain twitch. So focused was she on Hatcher's house, she didn't notice other things going on around her: the gentle breeze that caused the leaves to rustle in the trees that covered the nearby passageway, the tweeting of the birds, the yowls of a pair of warring cats, and the car hurriedly reversing toward her. Maybe if she'd been wearing her hearing aid, the one that restored partial hearing in her right ear, it would have been more noticeable, but perhaps the stories of the Child Catcher's depraved acts collided with concern for her brother, concern that hadn't eased in the seven months he'd been missing, and all her senses were unable to tune in on the noise of the rest of the world. Had Lola been walking any faster, she would have been in the path of the reversing vehicle, a blue Golf which had seen better days. Instead, the car passed a few inches in front of her and came to an abrupt stop. The window buzzed down and the driver, Mrs Wright, barked at her in her thick Caribbean accent, "Why don't you look where you're going?"

Lola stopped and stared at Mrs Wright who shook her head and then continued on her way. She was always in such a hurry, but Lola could sympathise. Mrs Wright had suffered too. Like Ted, her son, Julius, had also disappeared. Like Ted, there were no leads, but unlike her family, Mrs Wright had to put up with all of the nonsense about Julius having run off to join a gang or having been recruited by drug dealers. No one had speculated anything like that about Ted.

Aware of how close she'd come to an accident, Lola put her hearing aid back in. It had never been a problem when she was younger. All of the trips to the doctor and the hospital had been exciting and everyone had made such a fuss over her, made her feel special. Other than the few times Ted had had to go in for an operation on his heart, all her parent's attention was on her. Now she was more aware than ever of what was meant by special—somehow deficient, lacking. But with Ted gone, the attention was gone too. All focus was on Ted, which she understood. There was no time for Lola and her magical hearing aid anymore. The check-ups had become an inconvenience. That was why she'd had to miss the last couple of appointments. That was why she hadn't bothered to mention that her hearing aid wasn't as effective as it once was. Her left ear was fine, she just had to be careful about where she positioned herself with others so she could hear; that way, no one would need to make a fuss.

She headed through the passage at the end of the street and emerged opposite the village green. A number of kids from her school year sat around the pond, some of the boys lobbing in stones, probably trying to hit the fish. They looked over at her and she could see them talking. She considered joining them. She could sit and chat. She'd gone to Wiseham Primary School with most of them. Some were in her classes at Fenland Village Academy, and they all got on the same bus in the morning. They weren't exactly friends, but she had no problem with them, and, as far as she was aware, they had no problem with her. But no, she thought she better keep moving. If anyone was home, they might worry if Lola didn't make it back at her usual time.

But as she turned the corner part way down Riverview Terrace, she noted the absence of both Mum's and Dad's cars. Typical. She opened her rucksack and hunted for her key. She always put it in the small pocket, but it wasn't there. Maybe she'd put it elsewhere? She spent five minutes hunting before concluding that she was locked out. Next, she took her phone from her rucksack and called Mum... Voicemail. Dad's phone rang but with no answer and no point leaving a message.

Once again, Lola had been forgotten. She wondered where her parents might be: police station? Support group? Doing another stupid appeal video where they urged Ted to come back? No doubt doing something for the child who was long gone rather than the one that was right there, sitting on the doorstep with no way of getting into her home.

She figured there was no point waiting for what could be hours, sent both parents a text asking them to call her when they arrived home and headed back to the green.

5: TED

He could see. There were still blurs at the edge of his vision, but he could make out much more than when he'd woken by the river. He could see the facial features of the people standing around him. Mum was there, and Dad too. Every time Ted blinked, his vision was slow to restore, as if he were seeing the world not only through an unfocused camera but one with a two-second delay and dirt smeared on the lens. His fragile voice, little more than a strained whimper, sounded alien and unlike his own.

Mum sat in the chair closest to his head and stroked his hair. Ted couldn't help but flinch at first but soon felt comforted. He turned his head slightly toward her. She looked older. He'd never considered his mum as old before, but now he could see the clear lines around her tired eyes.

"How are you?" Dad said, but as Ted opened his mouth, he quickly shushed him. "No, don't try to talk. Sorry."

Dad looked different too. His hair, peppered with grey, was longer than he'd seen it, a scruffy mess on top of his head, and where Mum's face had thinned, his father's had grown thicker, his cheeks sagging and grey.

How long had he been gone? He wanted to speak, to ask questions, but there were so many that his head throbbed, and the thought of opening his mouth to speak exhausted him. The heat in the hospital and the way Mum and Dad were dressed made it clear it wasn't November anymore. There was nothing but a gap between going to bed last night (only, it wasn't last night) and waking by water.

He couldn't fight the weight of his eyelids any longer and let them close, welcoming the absolute darkness. His other senses took over the primary objective of working out what was going on. His sense of hearing first of all tuned into his heartbeat. The palpitations were something he'd trained himself to listen for; often, when he relaxed, he'd experience a flutter or a missed beat so much so that the regularity of the rhythm–the lack of disharmony–unnerved him. He tuned back into the conversation instead.

"But why is he so weak?" Dad asked.

There was a new voice. It must have been a doctor. "Ted went missing on the second of November, is that right?"

Both Mum and Dad muttered in agreement.

"We don't know where Ted has been for over seven months. Until Ted can tell us that, what he's been doing, what he's been eating, we won't know why he's in this condition."

Ted groaned. Seven months? And he was just as in the dark as they were. He knew no better than they did where he'd been.

"The muscle atrophy here is similar to what you see in a coma patient. He has moved very little in the last few months. The malnourishment and dehydration suggest he has not been regularly fed–though he must have been fed at some points otherwise he would have died of thirst or starvation."

Mum started to ask a question, but the words didn't form into a full sentence, trailing off into a panicked whimper.

"Can he come home?" Dad said.

"Certainly not tonight, and tomorrow is doubtful, too. But if we can get Ted to eat properly, if we can be sure he's passing water and that his bowel movements are regular, that will be the first step. Obviously, with Ted's history, we have to make sure his heart is as healthy as it can be, but it may be he will be able to recover just as well at home."

Ted felt relief. He didn't want to be in the hospital. He wanted to be back home; he wanted to be back in his room. He struggled to picture it; only flashes hit him, like screenshots on a quickly moving slideshow that he couldn't go back through.

He opened his eyes wanting to see his parents again. They were still in conversation with the doctor, but they were speaking much lower, and Ted didn't have the strength to strain to hear them or bring them into clear focus.

16 NORMAL

As he watched them, the room darkened. He turned toward the window to see the bright light still shining through. Turning back toward his parents he realised that the room itself had not darkened; a shadow had fallen between him and his parents, only thicker than a shadow and with toxic substance. A dread swelled inside him. His chest tightened, and his flesh chilled. Despite this, he could feel each bead of sweat form on his brow and run down his forehead. The black curtain seemed to thicken and move toward him, and he made the loudest noise he'd managed since his awakening when he screamed.

6: LOLA

Something thick and nasty tasting clung to the back of Lola's throat and a sense of dizziness made her place one hand flat on the grass for stability. At least everyone hadn't laughed too much when she tried her first drag on a cigarette. Lauren had been one of her best friends at primary school, but since they were placed in different forms at Fenland Village Academy (possibly at the request of Lola's mum) they didn't see each other often and drifted apart. Lauren was always her fun friend, the one that sneaked biscuits from the kitchen, cut her own hair, and climbed to the tops of trees while her mum begged her to come down. Now Lauren was happy to share a cigarette with Lola, and as she always did, Lola acquiesced. It wasn't because Lauren pressured her; Lauren made it okay, made it the right thing to do.

The boys, Mitchell and Tyler, had run out of stones to lob into the pond and had instead crept over to chuckle at Lola as she took another drag on the cigarette, again coughing like she was trying to turn her lung inside out.

Mitchell and Tyler were in year 9–a year older than Lola, but they'd been in the same primary class on alternate years. Tyler was short, and his complexion pale. He had a scruffy mop of blonde hair, shaved at the back and sides. Lots of kids had that haircut, so for reasons Lola couldn't understand, she assumed it was fashionable. Mitchell was black and tall for his age–he always had been. His hair was short, much tidier, better looking. Back at primary school, they were always clinging to a football, and the teachers always seemed to call on Mitchell for special attention, either for a telling off or singling him out for praise, something which he always responded to with a shrug. At some point, they'd grown out of doing stuff (proclaiming doing stuff a waste of time for losers) in favour of hanging around.

"Here, Lola," said Mitchell.

Lola noticed a notch shaved out of his eyebrow, something Lauren later confessed that she'd inflicted upon him. She tried to answer Mitchell, but with the need to cough still sitting in her throat like an unwanted party guest that wouldn't leave, she nodded at him.

"What's going on with your brother? He hasn't been at school in ages."

Lola sighed. Couldn't she get away from Ted even here? "Dunno." She looked over at Lauren and waited for her next drag on the cigarette.

"D'you reckon he ran off with Julius?"

Lola shook her head. "No, Julius disappeared weeks later."

Tyler leaned forward to join the conversation. "I thought Julius went missing first?"

Maybe Julius was a more notable individual than Ted, Lola thought. "No, definitely Ted first. Plus, Julius's disappearance was different. He went out after school and never came back. Ted disappeared overnight."

She could feel the eyes of the group on her, and ran one hand through her hair, tucking it behind her ear.

"What's that?" Mitchell asked, pointing at the side of her head.

Lola pulled her hair free, again hiding her hearing aid. She stared at the ground.

"It's her hearing aid, duh," Lauren said.

"What, can't you hear us without it?" Mitchell had raised his voice.

"It's single-sided," Lola said. She pointed to the ear. "This boosts it."

"That's cool," Mitchell said, dropping his voice back to its normal level. "Hey, Lauren, are you coming out at the weekend?"

Was that it? No further probing about her disability? No one shouting at her to make her feel included? No being made to feel different, like an outsider? Lola smiled and again tucked her hair behind her ear, where it felt comfortable.

When her phone rang some minutes later, she was still sitting on the grass, still feeling queasy, but having had more of a laugh than at any time in the last seven months. She looked at the screen, saw it was Mum, and answered the call.

"Lola!" her mother's voice was strained, the tone unreadable. Had she been crying? "Lola, we're at the hospital. They've found Teddy."

Lola didn't know what to say. Good felt too underwhelmed, but as it was all she could think of, she remained silent. "He's in the hospital. Are you going to be okay at home on your own for a while?"

She could have said that she was locked out, but what good would it do? Mum didn't sound like she wanted to be dragged away from her beloved Teddy in a hurry. Calling her home would only send her into one of her uncontrollable moods, and that's the last thing she wanted.

"Okay. I might go out for a bit."

"Where to?"

"Just out with Jas." Lola knew her mother approved of Jas.

"Is there anything you want me to pass on to your brother?"

Lola swallowed, the taste of nicotine still making her feel sick, and she pondered for a second. "No. I'm glad he's okay." And she was, but when Lola hung up it was also with a sense of guilt. She should have been ecstatic that Ted was safe; she did love him, after all, but something held back her relief. She'd remain invisible to her parents while they'd baby Ted and made sure he had everything he needed.

Who needed parents anyway? "Lauren," she said, putting an arm around her friend. "Have you got another cigarette I could have?"

7: SIMON

Simon wanted to stay for the night, but the hospital would only let one parent sleep in the chair next to Ted's bed. In the children's ward, they had pull-out beds that an adult could sleep on, but there were no such luxuries here, and the doctors were reluctant to move Ted as it had taken so long to stabilise his heart rate and breathing after what the Doctor Hodder referred to as his 'episode'.

Simon wanted to remain by the side of his son to make sure he didn't disappear again. He was out when Ted went missing. He'd been on a night shift at work. It had been a particularly tiring shift, having been on a conference call with the technical specialists from the supplier to try to resolve a tedious software issue, and that journey home had felt particularly perilous, with the early morning sun reflecting off the wet roads and shining in his eyes. A couple of times he'd felt himself veering from the lane and had had to drive most of the way with the window open. The cold November air had done its job of making him alert enough to pull into the drive. He'd passed Lola in the kitchen. She was sitting at the table eating a bowl of Cheerios. He'd not seen Ted and assumed he was not yet out of bed. Megan would wake him, he remembered thinking as he trudged through the house and up the stairs (a Herculean effort) and collapsed onto the bed.

He must only have been out for a few minutes, no more than twenty, but in that time the fog of sleep had smothered his brain. Megan had screamed in his ear, and at first, he thought it was an alarm going off, but then came the words, "Ted's gone." Simon couldn't make sense of it. Gone where? Megan had dragged him into the bedroom to survey the scene. The window gaped open, and his bedding lay on the floor between the bed and the window. Megan called his name repeatedly, while Simon wandered over to the window and looked out. It was a first-floor window, too high to simply drop to the ground below and there was nothing to climb on. He couldn't have gone out of the window; that would be impossible.

While he gazed out, time slipping away from his sleep-deprived brain, Megan had gone downstairs and phoned the police. Simon hadn't slept properly since.

Part of him feared that if he left Ted's side, he'd disappear again. It was ridiculous, and he knew it. Ted would be safe with Megan. Looking at the way his wife stared at their son while she stroked his sleeping body, he knew he couldn't deprive her of this time with her Teddy Bear.

Besides, someone had to check on Lola. He'd pick up her favourite takeaway, and then tell her all about Ted when he got home.

Simon made his way back through the hospital. As he passed through the concourse, he felt an arm on his shoulder.

She was talking before he'd even turned around. "What's he say about my boy?"

An overwhelming desire for knowledge pinched Alesha Wright's face. Simon and Alesha had spent a number of evenings together in recent months, comparing cases, hunting for similarities in the manner of the disappearances of Ted and Julius, sharing the lack of leads with despair. Both of their boys had seemingly been plucked out of existence within a couple of weeks of one another, Ted from his bed, and Julius from the village. But now Ted was back. Somehow, Alesha must have heard. Simon understood her position. If their roles were reversed, he'd have done the same thing, but the news he had to share was not good—it would barely count as news at all.

"I'm sorry, Alesha, but he's said nothing."

Alesha's stare bored into Simon. He could feel her agony, could sense her suspicion.

"When he's able to speak," Simon said, looking into Alesha's eyes, trying to show some kindness, some understanding, "we'll ask about Julius. We'll find out what happened. We'll find out if they were together. Okay?"

"I need to speak to him now. He must know where my boy is." With this last sentence, Alesha's voice broke into a sob, all the hope that had brought her there faded, all strength sapped.

Simon placed his hand on Alesha's arm. "Ted's weak at the moment. He's barely managed to get a word out. He's malnourished and dehydrated. His head's a mess." Simon guided Alesha toward one of the nearby vacant chairs. "But when he's a bit more lucid, a bit more with us, we'll ask about Julius, okay?"

Alesha nodded.

"Until then, go home. Wait for our call."

Again, Alesha nodded but showed no sign of movement.

"I'll be in touch," Simon said before turning away and heading for the exit. When the balmy evening air hit him and the gentle breeze rippled his clothes, Simon sucked in a deep breath. Relief washed over him, but not completely. Alongside his elation that was something else, a nub of guilt for feeling this way while Alesha still suffered. Did he deserve to feel this swell of relief when others still wallowed in misery? Unanswered questions swirled around his head. How could someone be missing for so long and then turn up again like that? Why couldn't he tell them where he'd been? There was something wrong with the whole situation, and when he reached the hospital car park and saw his car, he was hit with an immense feeling of relief, not that his boy was safe, but that he could get away from him and all of the confusion for the rest of the evening, and perhaps sate himself with a little drink.

8: MEGAN

Megan may have dozed during the night, but she was not conscious of an extended span of sleep. She couldn't stop looking at her Teddy Bear. Perhaps it was being back in the same hospital where he was born (albeit in a different ward) but she couldn't help but remember when she first held him in her arms. The pregnancy had been a breeze, and she hadn't suffered from any of the complaints the midwife warned her of. The birth, on the other hand, was horrendous. So content was Ted inside her that he seemingly never wanted to leave. At a week late, they started to talk of inducement, but it was another week before that happened. The labour had lasted a gruelling fourteen hours, and while Megan had blocked most of the memories of the specific difficulties (otherwise she could never have had Lola), she remembered the absolute exhaustion she felt when it was over and the overwhelming love she felt for the tiny human they placed in her arms. She remembered looking into Ted's blue eyes for the first time and wanting to squeeze him so tightly to her, wanting him to still be a part of her, never wanting to let him go.

Then the complications came.

While Megan was coming to terms with what it meant to have a son with a hole in his heart, Simon handled it with booze. He'd come so far with his drinking since the early days of their relationship and had become someone that only drank on social occasions, and rarely to excess. This news tipped him over the edge of his ability to cope, and with it, he tipped the bottle, too. In his younger days, it was pint after pint of lager, the stronger the better, but this event turned him on to the spirits. His dad had been a rum drinker, and at his funeral, a bottle of Wood's Old Navy had done the rounds. Simon had insisted on having a bottle in the house ever since and would only drink from it to toast to his father on the anniversary of his birth and of his death, but Ted's heart problems were cause enough to reach for the bottle. Megan had felt like she was coping with Ted's condition alone, and it was only after she'd packed a bag for Simon and told him to sort himself out that he'd put the bottle to one side.

He'd stayed off it until shortly after Lola's birth. When her hearing problems were detected, he'd again reached for the bottle, muttering that he couldn't cope with having another bloody problem child. As much as Megan resented him for saying something so horrible, much of that hatred she had turned inwards, for she had let a similar sentiment settle in her mind. She felt a pang of guilt for having abandoned Lola for the night to stay with Ted. Lola was far from a problem child; she knew that now. She'd coped so well with all of the difficulties when Ted disappeared.

Now that Ted was home, Megan hoped for some stability again. The Old Navy could sail back into the cupboard to rest until a proper occasion called for it. She looked down at Ted, trying to drive that feeling of relief into the primary position among the emotions that wrestled for attention inside her mind. Since his earlier screaming fit, Ted had been out cold. Doctor Hodder had suggested they should both go home to get some sleep, but Megan couldn't leave her boy.

She leaned in close to smell the back of his neck, expecting him to smell as he did when he was a baby again. Instead, he smelled sterile, as if every natural scent had been scrubbed from his body. There was perhaps a hint of the river coming from him, but that was probably the clothes he'd been found in, now sitting in a carrier bag on a chair. Again, Megan was struck by a considerable feeling of loss. Ted was right there beside her, safe in the hospital bed, but something was wrong, something was somehow different. Those lost months could never be recovered.

Anger roiled in her gut again, displacing relief, beating love and compassion into submission. She thought having Ted back would be enough, but she wanted more. She wanted to know who had taken him, and she wanted them to suffer. She never put any faith into the theory that Ted ran away. After the police had been, they'd asked her to check the house to see what he might have taken. She still bought all of Ted's clothes, and all of his favourites were either in the wardrobe, the wash basket, or strewn on the floor. Neither his school bag nor any of the rucksacks, holdalls or suitcases had been taken. His wallet was on his bedside cabinet with money in it. If he had run away, surely, he'd have taken something other than the underwear he slept in with him?

No, in Megan's mind, it was always a faceless person that had abducted Ted. She had no idea how, but someone had reached in through the bedroom window and plucked Ted from the room without leaving a trace. Megan hated that faceless man. In her mind, she'd tortured him in many ways. She'd slashed at his throat with a pair of scissors, smashed the back of his head in with a sledgehammer and plunged a hot poker into his guts. Even though her boy was back, she still had no face for his kidnapper. There was no outlet for the anger which she couldn't release.

She'd have the answers she needed soon. When Ted had recovered enough, he could describe the man. Megan would have a face then, a face that she would put her fist right through to appease the anger that wracked her. She'd sit by Ted until he gave her the answers, and then she might finally find peace.

9: TED

When Ted woke, for a second he thought he was in his own bed. A pillow beneath his head, a duvet over his body, it was all so normal. He opened his eyes (with only the slightest delay in his vision clearing) to see Mum sitting in an uncomfortable chair beside him, but then the nearby machine bleeped, and the sterile hospital smell hit him. His head still felt spongy. His mind was a mess of memories and imagination blurred together compounded by the knowledge that seven months were missing.

Mum sat up when a nurse bundled through the curtain carrying another bag of fluids. He quickly removed the empty bag and connected the full one to his IV, pressed a button on the machine and then left again, too exhausted to speak.

"Hey," Ted managed to say to Mum, who poured him some water into a paper cup and held it to his lips. Ted moved to lift his arms, but felt it was too much effort so moved his head forward instead to sip the water. As the icy coldness trickled down his throat, he imagined it reaching and reinvigorating the parched parts of his throat, but it wasn't long before the water reached his gut and sat there uncomfortably.

"How's my little Teddy Bear this morning?" Mum asked. She brushed his hair away from his forehead. She hadn't called him Teddy Bear for years, not since he was six or seven, perhaps around the time he'd cast all of his teddy bears from his room. He could remember the day clearly. He'd seen something on TV in which a character had been told it was time to put away childish things, time to grow up. He couldn't remember the name of the show (there were lots of things he couldn't remember) but it had had such an effect that he'd gone straight to his room when it finished, and taken each cuddly toy from his bed, and walked it into the hall. That was the last he saw of them until he ventured into the attic many years later and saw them bagged up together. Clearly, Mum hadn't wanted to throw them away, hadn't wanted to accept that he was growing up.

As he lay in bed, devoid of stamina and short of words to say, he was happy to be her Teddy Bear again. "I'm," he said, pausing to find there was no pain when he spoke. "I'm okay. Tired."

Mum stroked Ted's head again. The smile on her face, though weak, suggested she was glad to hear him speak. "The doctor says you need to get your strength back. We've got to get you eating and drinking." She again offered the water.

Ted considered it, but disliking the discomfort in his gut, which felt over-full despite having only had a sip, he shook his head.

"I suppose you're getting all the fluids you need through that thing." Mum nodded toward the IV.

Ted looked first at the cannula in the back of his hand, and then at the pads attached to his chest. "Why have I got these... on me?" The longer sentence was a struggle.

"They're monitoring various things. They need to make sure you're well."

Ted looked at the wires attached to his chest and followed them to the machine. It had an output, but nothing he could understand. He assumed it would capture what it needed and report a problem if it found one. He certainly didn't feel well, but he didn't think it was his heart. He couldn't remember ever having been so weak that he could barely move, even with the worst sickness bug he'd had, but worse than the weakness was the blankness in his head. "Mum," he said, unsure if he even wanted an answer. "What happened to me?"

As Ted watched Mum bury her head in her hands and heard her weep for the first time since his great-grandmother died, he felt more confused than ever. What had happened to him that caused her so much upset? Why wouldn't she tell him? What was everyone trying to keep from him? "Mum," Ted said again. "What is it?"

28 NORMAL

She lifted her head and pulled a tissue from her sleeve. She looked at Ted with a look full of sorrow. She shook her head. "I was hoping you were going to tell me."

As Ted stared at Mum, her skin started to turn grey and she froze as if turned to stone. Beside her, the machine continued to beep periodically and spat out numbers onto its digital display. Beside it, the frame from which the bag of IV fluid range wobbled, drawing Ted's attention to the bag. Instead of the clear saline solution he expected to see, the contents were brown, muddied. He watched the liquid in the line turn dark and run up the tube toward his vein. If he had the strength to lift his arm, to tear out the cannula, he would have done, but he was powerless to stop the filthy fluid from entering his bloodstream. If he could have done, he would have screamed, but instead, he screwed his eyes tight, denying that it could really be happening.

"Ted?" Mum's voice called.

Ted took a second to process the tone of her voice: wavering, but relatively calm. Chaos could not be descending all around them. He opened his eyes. Some of the colour had returned to Mum's face, and she was again more animated. He followed the line from his hand, thankful it was clear again, all the way up to the bag of fluid which, despite rocking gently, was perfectly normal.

10: SIMON

Six days later, Simon sat down, joining his wife, opposite the consultant, Doctor Max Donaldson and Doctor Hodder. Hodder talked through Ted's progress, confirmed he was eating and drinking as well as could be expected, and claimed to be pleased about his returning strength. Bed rest was no longer what he needed, and therefore hospital care was no longer the best solution. Expecting this situation, Simon had bypassed Macintyre at work and gone straight to the senior manager, arranging to work more flexibly for the next couple of weeks: call-outs, late shifts and night shifts only so that he would be home during the day. Megan had made similar arrangements with her work so that she would be starting earlier so that there would almost always be someone home with Ted.

"Do you think he'll ever get his memory back?" Megan asked.

Simon sighed. This was a question she'd asked before and she was unlikely to get the answer she wanted this time either.

Donaldson cut in before Hodder could speak. "With this kind of trauma, memory can be problematic. If Ted is subconsciously shutting out his experiences, forcing him to recall them may cause greater problems."

Simon turned to see Megan nodding, taking in the same information she'd already heard.

Donaldson continued: "That's not to say that those memories will never come back. When Ted is strong again, both physically and mentally, it is likely that his subconscious will let the guard down so that Ted can understand what he has been through."

Simon was much more interested in the scientific side rather than the emotional. "What about the tests? Did anything unusual show up? Is there anything we should be aware of?"

Donaldson looked at Hodder. Something hung in the air between them, the detritus of a previous heated conversation.

"There were some... anomalies," Hodder said. "Now, it could be from injuries sustained naturally while Ted was missing, but there is evidence of a puncture wound at both the top and bottom of his spine, which has left very minor scarring, and deep scarring around the navel."

"What caused that?" asked Simon, leaning forward with interest.

"It's impossible to say. The wounds have healed well, leaving only the scarring, but it suggests that there was more than one insertion at these points."

Simon's brow wrinkled. "Insertion? Of what?"

"Again, it's hard to say. Some kind of epidural injection could have been administered, or a lumbar puncture..."

"You think someone operated on our boy?"

Megan's hand, which had been resting on Simon's knee, dug in.

"These are only possibilities Mr Wallace..."

"Was he... interfered with... in any way?"

"There was no clear evidence of any activity of a sexual nature, but again, it's not possible to confirm."

Simon felt the pressure from Megan's hand grow stronger on his leg.

"And what about his heart?" Megan asked.

"Ted was due for a check-up shortly before he went missing," Donaldson said. "We were expecting some degradation and believed Ted would need a further operation."

"Is that still the case?" Simon said as Megan grabbed his hand.

"Yes and no."

"What do you mean?"

"As previously discussed, with a hole in the heart, one of two things can happen. Growth can lead to the hole repairing itself—sometimes only partially, sometimes in its entirety.

Alternatively, as the heart grows, the size of the hole can grow with it. It is the latter of these two possibilities which has occurred with Ted."

"So, he'll need another operation?" Simon asked. He felt an urge for a little drink to take the edge off. He'd deserve it if he had to go through another round of operations.

"Usually, yes. But there are signs of some of this work already having been carried out."

Megan stood. "How's that possible? Who could have done it?"

"We've been in touch with every hospital in the country that has the expertise to carry out this type of operation, Mr and Mrs Wallace. None have any record of recent operation on a boy of Ted's age or description."

Simon put a hand on his forehead and rubbed hard. This made no sense. "So, are you saying that whoever had Ted carried out some kind of operation on his heart?"

Donaldson exhaled noisily through his nose. "It's a possibility... but the important thing is that Ted's heart is currently stable. We'll need to go in and investigate further once Ted is back up to full strength."

"Is there anything we should be keeping an eye out for?"

"Strenuous exercise is still a no-no. Monitor what he eats. Provide a healthy diet, plenty of rest."

"What else do we need to do?"

"As we said, make sure you bring Ted back to all of the scheduled follow-up appointments, and he'll need further blood tests."

Simon mentally recalled the list of dates on the card, one for each month for the rest of the year. "Is it normal to have to have so many blood tests?"

"Well..." started Hodder.

"Very little about this situation is normal, Mr Wallace," said Donaldson. "Now if there are no further questions we can proceed with the discharge."

Donaldson stood, and Simon did likewise, but Megan lingered, a question seemingly sitting on the tip of her tongue that she couldn't quite put into words. She too stood, her eyes constantly on Donaldson.

Once they were through the door, Donaldson quickly closed it behind Simon, Megan and Hodder.

"Ted's medication should be ready now," Hodder said, "so if you're ready, and Ted's ready, it's time to go home."

Ted waited on the edge of the bed, casually swinging his legs. When he saw Simon and Megan, he smiled. The colour had returned to his skin, and he looked brighter, happier even.

"Ready to go home, buddy?" Simon asked.

Ted grinned.

Simon couldn't help but notice the protruding mole on the side of his son's neck. That hadn't always been there, had it?

11: TED

Ted stood by his bedroom unable to enter. He couldn't even bring himself to open the door. He imagined the far wall obliterated as if some mighty being had punched a hole through it. He pictured the curtains still hanging from the rail, rippling in the wind, but no window for them to cover. His room would be a scene of devastation, his belongings strewn all over the floor and coated with dust from neglect.

It was only because the edges of his world started to blacken, only because his legs began to quiver that he reached for the door handle—for support, not to gain entry. But now he was so close, why not go one step further? He turned the handle, pushed the door open and prepared himself for the worst.

Everything was as he remembered it, and in truth, it felt like he'd only been away for a couple of days, and yet something stopped him from placing his foot onto the navy-blue carpet.

"What is it, son?" Dad climbed the stairs behind him, holding the small overnight bag they'd brought to the hospital a couple of days earlier.

Ted couldn't answer. Exiting the hospital had exhausted him, the walk across the concourse and through the car park too much for his shrunken muscles. In the car, he'd fantasised about getting home and flopping onto his bed. He wanted nothing more than to lay back and play some of his favourite music. He knew his guitar would be right there propped against the chest of drawers, but he had no illusions that he'd be able to pick it up and play like he could before. While not on the verge of becoming a huge rock sensation, he'd mastered a few complex riffs, but even thinking about it exhausted him now. He imagined himself playing The Cure's 'Just Like Heaven', a song that had taken him forever to learn. How come he could still remember every hand movement required to play that, but not a single event in that seven-month window? Before he let himself become frustrated about his inability to remember, he recalled what Doctor Hodder had told him: "Don't get worked up about what you can and can't recall. When your brain's ready, it'll let you in."

He'd also been warned that the brain was much like a Chinese finger trap in some ways: the more you tried to pull information out of it, the tighter it held on to it, and it would only release when you relaxed, explaining why the name of a forgotten song pops into your head, hours later, when you're doing something totally different. He thought he'd get home, climb into bed, and wait to see what popped into his head, and while he was waiting, he could listen to all of the tunes he wanted to.

But when it came to entering the bedroom, he simply couldn't do it, and he had no idea why. There was nothing in there that scared him: same Boys Don't Cry poster on the wall, with the guitar and amp against the drawers beneath them; his PlayStation by the TV, a few of the games neatly stacked up, the rest on the shelf (that wasn't how he left it, but not a problem); the bed, neatly made with its navy bedding that didn't quite match the carpet.

Dad leant round to look him in the eye. "You okay?"

Ted had to force himself to breathe, and he put a hand on Dad's shoulder for support.

"It's okay," Dad said, "I've got you."

But when Ted let him take some of his weight, he felt his body being shifted into the room. No doubt Dad thought he was being helpful, getting him into bed, but the dread that came with that only deepened. "No Dad," Ted said, trying to disguise the panic in his voice. "Can I go downstairs and sit in the living room?"

"Sure, buddy. No problem."

Ted never saw Dad as a particularly strong man; he wasn't as tall or butch as some of his other friends' dads, so he was surprised when Dad chose to carry him back down the stairs, awkwardly craning his head and staring, making Ted feel self-conscious and as if he had a strange growth sprouting out of his neck.

Once placed on the long sofa (so he could stretch out and have a nap if he wanted to), Ted looked around the living room trying to spot seven months' worth of changes. Much of it was the same. The large sofa was still at a slight angle from the wall, blocking access to the dining room. It had been like that for years, and Ted remembered Lola's lament at not being able to loop around the ground floor of the house in a continuous circuit: living room to dining room to kitchen to hall to living room. Repeat. Perhaps that was why, when the new sofa had arrived, it had been placed strategically to block such tedious activities. But no, there was nothing new in the living room. The biggest difference was the late afternoon sunlight that poured into the room. Before, it would have been practically dark after school, but that was November, seven months ago. That was going to take some getting used to. Despite it being summer, Ted felt chilly. This was something else Doctor Hodder had explained—the lack of fat made him susceptible to cold.

When Mum came in seconds later to check he was okay, he asked for a blanket. After going upstairs to the airing cupboard and returning to wrap a fleece around him, Mum plonked down on the single sofa next to the three-seater. "What do you want for your tea?" she asked.

Ted hadn't much of an appetite (Doctor Hodder's note #3 your shrunken stomach will give you a lack of hunger, but you must eat) and there was no choice at the hospital, so he'd picked at what was placed in front of him. But what did he want? "I don't know," he said. "Something easy. I'll have whatever Lola's having." He'd only seen his sister once while he was in hospital. It was awkward for people to go back and forward to fetch her after school during the week, but she had come in at the weekend to see him. Lola's appearance had shocked Ted so much more than seeing Mum or Dad had done, for Lola had had a growth spurt, possibly not noticeable if you saw her every day, but if you hadn't seen her in months, it was more than apparent. She looked more grown up too. She'd lost some of the baby fat from her cheeks. Her attitude had become much more like that of a teenager, too. He'd missed her birthday. That was in February. His was coming up in July. He'd missed Christmas. Did they have a Christmas without him? Again, the weight of trying to come to terms with the missing time and so many missing events hit him hard and a pulse of pain shot through his head and made him grimace. He wanted to ask about Christmas, but he didn't want Mum to get emotional about it. He'd ask Lola, later, when he could speak to her alone. "Where is Lola, anyway?"

Mum looked around the room as if expecting to see Lola sitting in front of the television. "I imagine she's with Jas. They do their homework together most afternoons."

Imagine? This wasn't normal either. Mum never used to let Lola out of her sight. It wasn't so much that she didn't trust her, but she was the baby of the family, and Mum always went overboard about looking after her, especially with her hearing problems and all of the appointments. Maybe she'd grown up a lot in those missing months. He didn't want to think about it anymore. The journey home had exhausted him enough, the reality of it almost overwhelming, threatening more spikes of pain. He closed his eyes, looking forward to sleeping in his house, even if he hadn't been able to make it into his bed yet, and dismissed the strange shapes flickering in his memory or his imagination as mere tricks borne of exhaustion.

12: LOLA

Lola *had* gone to Jas's house, but they'd not long begun their maths homework when Mrs Thakur came over to the table and said, "You must be glad to have your big brother back."

She'd mumbled in agreement. It was true that she was glad he was back, very glad. When she saw him in the hospital, she'd hugged him so hard that Mum had told her to go easy on him. When at home, or with Ted, she was so happy about his return, but she wanted to be more than just Ted's sister. She had it at primary school from every teacher— "Oh, I used to teach your brother," they'd all say, and she'd feel like she was already judged because of that. Not that there was anything wrong with Ted, but she wanted to be her own person. She didn't want to hear about Ted when she was at her friend's house. It was supposed to be somewhere to get away from it all.

"I've just remembered," she said, picking up her maths book and placing it in her rucksack, "I've got a dental appointment. I was supposed to go straight home."

She left the Thakur household in a hurry but, aware that Mum and Dad would be driving through the village at some point when they brought Ted home, she took the long route, using the passageways between cul-de-sacs. Passing Ted Hatcher's house, she stretched onto tip-toes to look through the windows of his rusting Land Rover, just in case he was sitting in there ready to pounce, and then as she passed the house, she peered into his windows.

Just because Ted had been found by the river, it didn't mean that the Child Catcher was innocent.

As she gazed at his house, the front door swung open. He stepped out and turned back to lock the door. He might have been a tall man, once, but his stoop took that away. Lank, greasy hair, long only at the back stuck to his neck. At the front, his hair had receded so far, that his forehead seemed endless. The low neckline of his stained t-shirt allowed tufts of wiry, white hair to sprout out. She hated the way his eyes seemed to bore into her, and his nose looked as if he'd spent his life pressed against glass.

Lola picked up her pace until she emerged at the back end of the park. Lauren, Mitchell, Tyler and a few others were by the play equipment. Mitchell and Tyler stood on opposite sides of the seesaw, trying to balance while the others sat on the grass lobbing stones at them.

Lola sat down next to Lauren and said, "Hey."

Lauren pushed half of her pile of stones toward Lola. "Go on, try to hit him in the head."

Lola giggled and then shrugged. She felt awkward. So much for hoping she could just slip into this group when she was uncomfortable elsewhere.

"Go on," said Lauren. She picked up a small stone and placed it in Lola's hand.

What did she have to lose? She gently tossed the stone toward the seesaw. It fell some distance short.

"You're not even trying!" Lauren said. She picked up a stone and hurled it toward Tyler. He had to lean back to dodge it, which put the seesaw off balance.

Lola laughed as both Mitchell and Tyler rocked back and forth, raising their arms to shift their balance. She picked up another stone and flung it toward Mitchell. She thought he'd see it coming. She thought he'd move his head. He didn't. The stone struck him just above the ear, and as he raised his hand instinctively to the place it had hit, his balance was lost, and he had to jump from the seesaw. Doing so caused Tyler's side to plummet to the ground, but he managed to stay on and raised his hand in victory.

"Was that you?" cried Mitchell, his annoyance clear. He was pointing at Lauren.

Lauren held her hands up. "Not me, boss," she said.

"Was it you?" Mitchell was closer. He pointed at Lola.

Lola's mouth dropped open. Her stomach clenched. Should she go? All she managed was to say, "Err."

Lauren laughed at her and gave her a playful shove.

"It bloody was you!" Mitchell grinned and sat beside Lola. "Look at her. Comes over here, looking like she's nice as pie. Turns out she's a silent assassin."

Lola shrugged again. "Sorry," she said.

"You don't have to apologise. We were just messing around."

Lola chuckled. "Okay."

"You have to kiss it better though."

The rest of the group oohed and turned to look at Lola.

"Go on, Lola, give him a kiss." Lauren again shoved Lola, pushing her closer to Mitchell.

Did she really have to kiss him? She hadn't kissed a boy before. This wouldn't count as a first kiss, though. Not kissing someone on the side of the head. Did the rest of them expect her to kiss him? What would they say if she didn't? Would they shun her and send her away? She turned to look at the side of Mitchell's head where the stone had struck. There was no sign of damage.

A chant, started by Lauren, went around the group: "Lola, Lola."

Lola's pulse raced. She didn't want to do it. She didn't like Mitchell. Not like that. But she had caused him to lose the game.

Mitchell stood up and shook his head at Lola. "Nah, I was just messing."

Lola laughed uncomfortably. It was a joke. Of course, she knew it was a joke. Two of the other boys climbed onto the seesaw, and to avoid further trouble, Lola kept her aim at their feet.

13: TED

Ted lay in his bed listening to the heavy rain beating against the window and cascading from the gutter. The occasional crack of thunder and flash of lightning would make it hard to go back to sleep. A further flash illuminated the whole room, the guitar casting an odd-shaped shadow which was there one moment and gone the next. The thunder cracked, making Ted jerk in shock.

Again, the room was illuminated by lightning, but not just a flash. The white light continued to pour through the window. The sound of the rain had stopped. It was as if the world outside had frozen. Inside, the curtain twitched in the breeze, which was impossible, because the windows were closed, and yet, the curtains continued to billow out noiselessly.

From the window, from behind the curtains, a shadow emerged, thick and black in the brightly illuminated room. Four more followed, parallel, but of different lengths. Wispy tendrils curled away from the main part, like thick hairs on a giant's knuckles. The shadows started to curl, and a fifth appeared, shorter, to one side. That's when Ted realised that it was an enormous black hand reaching in for him, coming to take him away, coming to take him back.

Ted jolted upright with a yelp and he was back in the living room, on the sofa, with Mum on the chair beside him.

"You okay, Teddy Bear?" Mum said, stroking his hair again.

"Bad dream." He pushed the blanket away.

Mum came over and felt his forehead. "You're soaking wet... and cold. Are you feeling all right?"

Ted tried to reply, but when he opened his mouth a slew of black filth tumbled out and came to rest on his abdomen.

"Teddy?" Mum said.

He looked down at the muddy substance on his midriff and then at Mum. She launched herself from the sofa and hurried from the room.

Inside Ted's mouth, his tongue felt fat, like it was pushing against the inside of his cheeks. Despite his mouth filling with water and the taste of mould and decay, he was certain nothing else was coming up. He stared at the black lump on his belly and slowly moved a finger over to it.

"Don't touch it!" Mum was back, armed with a bucket, a pair of rubber gloves and a couple of tea towels. She dashed to Ted's side. "Are you going to be sick again?" She positioned the bucket close to his head.

Ted swallowed back the water in his mouth, getting another taste of the rotting substance. As vile as it was, he felt better with it out of his mouth, and he shook his head.

Mum placed the bucket down, still within reach if required, and turned her attention to what had evacuated Ted's body with such force.

Ted saw her nose turn up as she sniffed at the substance.

She pulled on the gloves and poked at it, and then broke some away from the main body and rubbed it between her fingers. "Smells like... mud," she said, looking at Ted, lines of confusion, worry, or both forming on her brow.

She picked it off him and dropped it into the bucket, leaving a peaty-black mud stain on Ted's top.

She leaned over the bucket, probing the mass inside with her gloved fingers.

"What are you doing?" Ted asked.

"Having a look to see if there was anything else in there."

"Was there?"

"No, but I'll give the hospital a call—see if they want to take a look." With what looked to be an enormous effort, Mum tore her attention away from the bucket. "You sure you're feeling okay?"

Ted nodded. If the evidence wasn't sitting right there, stinking away in the bucket, he wouldn't believe what had happened.

"Well, we better get you out of those clothes," Mum said, looking at the mess he was in. It wasn't just the mud stain. It looked like he's sweated out about a gallon of water. She moved over to help him lift off his t-shirt but suddenly reeled back. "You smell just like the river," she said.

Ted wrapped himself in the blanket to keep warm as Mum ran the bath. "I don't think I can sleep in my bedroom," he said.

Mum nodded. "We can have you switch with Lola. I'm sure she won't mind."

"No, I..." Ted imagined the hand grabbing his sister. "I don't want her in there either."

Mum moved away from the bath and over to Ted. "Have you remembered something?"

"No, but... the dream. I was in my room. This huge hand reached in."

"It was a nightmare, Teddy, that's all." Mum returned to the bath and adjusted the taps.

"I have this horrible feeling about it. Could I sleep in the spare room?"

Formally the office, the spare room was located partly beneath the stairs between the living room and the kitchen. It had a faulty PC in it and was used to store various toys and games that were no longer played with and rarely used kitchen implements, things that had neither made it up to the attic for future recovery and use, nor to the future car-boot sale they always spoke of.

"I suppose we can do that. It'll be trouble getting your bed down the stairs."

"No, I can't sleep in that bed."

"You can't sleep on the floor."

Ted pleaded, "I'll sleep in a sleeping bag. It'll be comfortable enough. Please, I don't know what will happen to me if I go back into the bedroom."

"I'll talk to your dad, see what he thinks." She turned both taps off, patted Ted on the shoulder as she passed him to go to the airing cupboard and handed him a towel.

As Ted lay down in the bath, he felt at peace again. He liked the way the water covered every part of his body. It felt like it kept him safe.

14: SIMON

Simon surveyed the office. The self-assembly bed frame would fit along the back wall, but there was insufficient room to put it together with all of the crap mounted up in there. He shook his head as he considered the ordeal before him. He'd deserve a reward for finishing, and there was enough Old Navy left in the bottle for a proper celebration.

He started to shift boxes around. Some went straight into the back of the car, ready to go to the tip in the morning before returning to work in the afternoon. Some were pushed into the hall for relocation to the attic though he had no intention of trudging up and down the stairs with box after box until after he'd put the bed together. He considered other places to store things. Would that box fit behind the sofa? Whether he'd be able to find anything he'd rehomed ever again, he didn't know, but given that very little ever came back out of the room and into practical use, he didn't care.

The process took longer than it should have as many of the boxes were unmarked, so they had to be opened to check their contents. It was in doing this, that Simon discovered the box of photographs. Most of the pictures were from Simon's childhood, having fallen into his possession when his mother passed away, but they were from when Ted and Lola were young. She hadn't switched to digital photography until long after the rest of the population and had still sent films for development.

Simon picked up one photograph in which he held baby Lola in one arm. Ted was standing beside him, looking at his baby sister. Simon studied the picture, trying to find evidence of the mole. Nothing. It could be the way he was facing obscured it, or it may not have been there at all.

He pulled out his phone and searched when moles appear. Most appear in early childhood—so not having it as an infant was no big deal. What about when he was older? First, he checked the camera roll on his phone. Minutes later he sat there frustrated. Had he taken so few pictures of his son? There was one in which he wore a hoodie, but that was of no use.

Megan was the main family photographer, but he couldn't very well ask to check her phone. *Hey honey, can I look on your phone at pictures of Ted? I want to check if he had a mole on his neck before he disappeared because...* because what?

There would be some on the digital camera. Megan used to take that on all of the holidays. But where was it? He looked over to the PC. The pictures always used to be uploaded onto it. Maybe the camera would be nearby. He checked the drawers on the computer desk. One was full of wires and cables, including the digital camera charger. He tried the next drawer. Old webcam, computer speakers and, there it was, the Panasonic Lumix camera which had accompanied them on numerous holidays. He took it out and pressed the power button. Nothing. He opened the other drawer and untangled the charger, then remembered that he'd have to pop the battery out to charge that, so he couldn't boot up the camera while it was charging.

He plugged it in and checked the light indicated that it was charging. Maybe, while waiting for that he could boot up the computer. The kids had abandoned it because it had become too slow to use for homework. Now, they had their own laptops—Christmas presents from a few years ago. Simon no longer needed it once he could access emails and social media on his phone, but surely it would still function. He pushed the power button and heard it whir to life. He had to separately turn on the monitor with the flimsy button that seemed destined to get lost within the casing. Eventually, the blue background, the logo, and the words Windows 7 appeared on the screen. While waiting for his desktop, he shifted a few more boxes outside the room. Once it loaded, he hit the folder icon. The PC thought about it for a while before launching the window. He navigated to My Pictures and saw a row of folders, all dated and named after different holidays and outings. He tried 'Warwick Castle 2013'. They'd gone during the October half term. Surely Megan would have taken a few family pictures, maybe as they were watching the trebuchet demonstration or the jousting competition.

Simon looked at the thumbnails: images of the castle, a couple of family shots. He opened one of the pictures with Lola and Ted eating an ice cream. The shot was straight on, and Simon couldn't work out if he had the mole or not. He returned to the thumbnails and changed the setting to large icons and scanned through them again. Megan had taken pictures of the jousting while standing behind the kids. He opened the picture to see the horses approaching each other, knights wielding lances, but in front of that, Ted's neck, and on it, the mole.

So, he'd had it for at least eight years.

Simon shut down the computer, satisfied. What had he sought? Did he think the boy in the living room wasn't his son? Of course not. Ted was back, and relatively unharmed. That's all he ever wanted. Why couldn't he shake his suspicion?

He hated himself for thinking it. Part of him had come to believe that Ted was dead. That was the call he'd been expecting for months, so finding him alive was unbelievable. Good things like this, amazing things, incredible things simply didn't happen in Simon's life. When his mum had been diagnosed with cancer, he hoped for a miracle and didn't dare ask for any more than one more Christmas with her, but fate had taken her away before the first door on the advent calendar had been opened. When his grandfather suffered from dementia, forgetting everyone he'd ever loved, but not the horrors he'd experienced in the Second World War, Simon had begged for death to swoop in and put him out of his misery. Alas, the old man kept surviving in the home, looking greyer and more like death with every visit as the years ticked by. Every time, Simon's grandfather would stare at him, his lower lip quivering, the horrors of the past alive in his eyes. No, Ted's return was such an unbelievably great outcome and Simon simply didn't have the tools at his disposal to deal with good news. Part of him didn't want to climb out of the pit of grief in which he'd resided for so long, part of him clung to doubt because if he accepted that his Ted was back and okay, and then it didn't turn out that way, he wasn't sure that he could cope with the loss again.

Simon surveyed the office again. The task would be much easier if he had a drink.

15: TED

Ted slept soundly in his new bed. The most important aspect was that the office had no windows. He hadn't had access to his music as that was on his phone, and when he asked his mum to fetch it from his room, she told him that the police still had it. They'd taken his phone to see who he was in contact with when investigating the run-away theory. The detective inspector was coming to see Ted, and his phone would be returned to him after proving to be utterly useless for their investigation.

Mum had offered breakfast before she left for work, but it was too early for Ted. He got up to see her off while Lola sat at the table eating dry toast. Ted sat down opposite his sister. "What have you got at school today?" he asked.

Lola shrugged. "Usual stuff." She'd been quiet last night too.

Ted worried that she didn't know what to say to him and he could understand that.

"Don't you want anything on that toast?" Ted asked, trying to force conversation.

"No. When are you going back to school, anyway?"

"Soon, I suppose." Ted hadn't thought about it. There wasn't much to think about. A few minor friends might have missed him, and he'd be behind in all of his subjects.

"What do you want me to say to people?" Lola asked, raising her eyes from her toast.

"About what?"

"People keep asking me where you were and what happened."

Ted smiled. "Tell them it's top secret."

Lola rolled her eyes, but behind the façade, a smile broke. She put down the toast and stood up. "Have a good day," she said before grabbing her rucksack, shouting bye to Dad and hurrying out of the front door.

What would a good day be for Ted? Maybe Dad could get his guitar from his room, and the TV and the PlayStation. That would give him something to do. The doctor had told him to do exercise to work all of his muscles, so he'd have to do that, too.

While he was pondering, Dad came downstairs. "Want any breakfast?"

Ted supposed he should and nodded.

"I'm doing bacon and eggs, sound good?"

Ted shook his head. "I'll just have a bit of toast."

He had it dry, like Lola, and like Lola, he didn't manage to finish the piece before his stomach felt bloated and uncomfortable.

Ted retreated into his bedroom, the smell of food frying too much for his full stomach to take. He sat on his bed and read through his exercise instructions. Most were like the warmups he'd done during the PE lessons he was allowed to partake in (contact sports were always ruled out). He considered trying one of the exercises, but his stomach felt solid and painful after his meagre breakfast. He'd do them another time.

Ted must have drifted back off to sleep, because when Dad opened his door and told him he had a visitor, his mouth felt dirty and his head swam. It took a moment to climb off his bed and make his way into the living room.

Dad introduced Detective Inspector Heimlich, a tall man, probably mid-forties. The black dye in his hair (and possibly in his moustache too) was fooling no one.

Ted sat on the larger sofa, next to Dad, leaving Heimlich to glare at him from the other side of the room. He wasn't subtle about the way he checked Ted over, his eyes scrutinising him. He scrawled something in his notebook with a short pencil, cleared his throat, and spoke: "Ted, my job isn't to make you feel awkward or uncomfortable; I'm here to get to the bottom of this. So, if there is anything that makes you feel uneasy, let me know, and we'll stop."

Ted nodded. He wanted to tell him to stop staring, but as he already felt like he was being judged, he didn't want to give Heimlich a reason to see him in a negative way.

"We had the report from the hospital about your injuries, so you needn't tell us anything about them."

As Ted was unaware of any injuries other than the odd scar he'd spotted around his belly button, he was glad the policeman wouldn't be quizzing him about that.

"Can you tell us about the day you were found by the river?"

Ted recounted the events as best he could, telling Heimlich about not knowing where he was, his poor vision, the cold and dead limbs, and the man with the dog who found him by the riverside. He couldn't pinpoint how far along the river he was, but the rough idea he had about where the church and water tower were, told him he wasn't massively far from his house.

Heimlich scribbled down notes as Ted told his story but tried to maintain eye contact as much as possible. "I've been told you have no memory of the time between when your parents last saw you on the second of November and the day that you woke by the river, is that still the case?"

Ted thought for a moment, but those same feelings, like drills boring out from the inside, trying to escape his skull, hit him and he shook his head. "Every time I try to remember, it hurts," he said, raising his hands to either side of his head.

"Ted, I'm not asking you to try to remember if it's causing you anguish. I was only asking if anything had come back to you."

"No. Nothing." But it wasn't quite nothing. There was the black hand, like a shadow only of greater substance, that had come in through the window. But that was a nightmare, not a memory.

"Could you tell us about the night you went missing?"

The memory wasn't that distant. To him, it seemed about seven days ago, not seven months. It hadn't been a significant day in any way at all. "I went to school during the day, but that was pretty normal. I came straight home. It was raining, and my school clothes were wet, so I got changed and played some games for a bit. We ate pizza. After, I went back upstairs, played my guitar, and listened to some music. I don't remember when I went to bed."

"Is that all? Nothing else significant?" Heimlich shrugged.

Ted pondered for a moment. "Nothing unusual. It was a bit noisy outside when I got home because they were doing some work on the river. That's why I turned my game off. The droning noise was putting me off."

Heimlich scrawled something down though Ted didn't think he'd said anything important.

"What were they doing on the river anyway?" Ted asked. He remembered that it had annoyed him for a few weeks with the constant chug and drone of the machines.

Dad cut in. "They cut in a new channel as some sort of flood prevention system for the new houses."

"Thank you," Heimlich said. "Do you know a boy by the name of Julius Wright?"

Ted had already been asked about Julius by his father, and at the time he had no memory of the boy. Now, at least, he could remember who he was. "Does he go to my school?"

"He did," Heimlich said. He stared at Ted, offering nothing else.

"He's in the year above me, right?"

"Correct. Tell me, Ted. Have you seen Julius at all lately?"

Ted could sense the intensity growing in Heimlich. He looked across at his dad whose brow began to wrinkle.

Ted shook his head. "I don't think I've ever spoken to him."

"You see, Ted, you weren't the only person to go missing last winter. Julius disappeared only a couple of days after you did."

Ted tried to focus, tried to bring Julius' face into his memory. He had an idea of what he looked like; he could picture him shouting or screaming. Was that something he'd seen him do? Shouting out to his friends on the school field?

"We were thinking that wherever you were hiding out, we could find Julius too."

"But I don't know where I was."

Heimlich made a noise which was neither agreed with nor disputed Ted's remark. He kept his eyes on Ted, still trying to read something which wasn't there.

"What..." Ted had reservations about asking his questions. "What do you think happened to me?"

Heimlich raised his eyebrows and puffed out his cheeks. "It's an unusual circumstance when we locate a missing person, and they can't tell us where they've been."

"Could something have taken me out of my bed?" Ted again recalled the shadowy hand. It was never far from the edge of his conscious memory.

"We considered all sorts of possibilities when we began to investigate your disappearance. Our forensics team found no evidence to suggest anyone was ever outside your window."

"What about something inhuman?" Ted felt stupid as soon as he asked it.

Heimlich smirked. "We try to keep out investigations within the realms of possibility."

"Did you think I'd run away?"

"As there was no sign of a break-in, our conclusion was that you opened the window. However, there was no evidence that you left through it."

"Did you think I'd run away, Dad?"

Dad shook his head as he spoke. "I never believed that."

"We took our investigation on the route of greatest probability. With your return, we're no closer to knowing by which method you left the bedroom."

"So, what now?"

"I'm afraid there's little more we can do. Unless something in your memory comes back to tell us a crime was committed, we'll close this case. It's a missing persons case, and that person has been found."

Ted felt his brow wrinkle. Were they going to leave it like this? "But... you didn't find me. I just turned up by the river. Is that in your realm of possibility?"

"Ted, calm down. Detective Heimlich did all he could," Dad said, patting Ted on the arm.

"It's okay. I can understand your frustration." Heimlich took a large envelope from among his papers. "I understand this is yours."

Ted took the envelope and opened it to find his phone.

Heimlich held out a sheet of paper. "If you could just sign this to confirm there's no damage."

Ted checked his phone and scrawled his name on the sheet.

"You too, Mr Wallace," Heimlich said, offering the sheet to Dad.

"Are we done?" Ted asked.

"Yes," said Heimlich. "Thank you for your time."

Ted didn't respond. Instead, he headed to his new room and sat on the bed. How could they consider it over? He'd lost seven months of his life, and they were closing the case. It wasn't fair.

16: MEGAN

Megan arrived home from work at three-thirty to find Ted on his bed, headphones in, listening to music. She gave his foot a shake to let him know she was there, and he tapped the screen of his phone and removed the headphones.

"All okay?" Megan asked.

Ted explained how things had gone with the police.

"What time did your dad leave?"

"Half two."

"And you'll be okay on your own for a bit when your dad has to work?"

"I'm fourteen, Mum. I think I can manage an hour or two by myself."

"Have you done your exercises?"

Ted groaned.

"You have to do them to get your strength back. Come on." Megan took hold of Ted's arm and coaxed him off the bed.

"I'm not doing them with you standing over me."

"No. We're going to go for a walk. The fresh air will do you good."

Megan had been reading about amnesia online. Taking sufferers to familiar places could help to stir memories. If Teddy could remember where he was, and who'd taken him there, justice would be possible, one way or another.

"Do we have to?" Ted looked up with pleading eyes.

"Yes."

"Where to?"

"A little circular walk past the church and back along the river."

Ted froze. "The river?"

"I know it might seem strange, but one of the things Doctor Hodder said you needed to do is to become aware of how the world around you has changed, so you can accept those changes and that lost time."

Ted vaguely remembered lying in bed while they had this conversation. There was nothing wrong with his ability to remember anything since his awakening, but some conversations were less memorable than others. "On that subject," he said, "you owe me a Christmas. You know, so I can move on and accept that it happened."

"I'll give you a clip round the ear for Christmas," Megan gently cuffed him on top of the head.

"Lola said you didn't celebrate properly."

"How could we without you?"

Ted smirked. "So, we will have a catch-up Christmas?"

"Yes, but in a few weeks, when things are a bit more... normal."

Talk of Christmas helped cheer Ted enough to get him out of the house with no further complaints. He moved down Riverview Terrace at a fast walking pace first of all, but by the time they reached the end of the road, he had started to slow.

"You okay, Teddy?"

"Yeah, but..." he took in a deep breath, "it feels odd to be so weak and out of breath."

"That's why we have to do this. We have to build your muscles and your stamina back up."

They crossed the road. "We'll slow the pace down until we get to the church," Megan said.

Ted nodded, and as they made their way toward the church, Megan kept an eye on her son, noting how he was eagerly checking out different things in the village, and the way a smile almost formed on his lips.

Megan stopped when they reached the vicarage, and the gateway that led to the church, "We'll walk around the back of the church and follow the path to the river from there. Is that okay?"

Ted didn't respond. He stood, staring up at the vicarage, an enormous two-storey house with turrets at each corner, built in the early 1800s in the gothic style, similar in concept to Horace Walpole's Strawberry Hill house. Megan had always considered the building an eyesore and completely out of place in the village. She'd always meant to look up how it came to be, considering that it looked so different from its neighbouring church, which was typically Norman with its huge arches.

"Ted," Megan called to no avail. Still, he continued to stare up. Megan reached out and shook Ted's shoulder.

He jumped back, turned to her, and shook his head.

"You okay?"

"Yeah, sorry Mum, just zoned out." He glanced at the building again. "I'd never noticed the gargoyles up there before, that's all."

Megan gazed up. She'd not spotted the gargoyles before either, but now she saw them, she didn't think she'd forget them in a hurry. Their mouths were wide and littered with sharp teeth sticking out askew from one another. A dirty spout from the centre of the open mouth was used to divert water collected from the drains toward the ground. For Megan, those hideous creatures were another negative for the ugly building, and she dragged Ted away before he could become fixated upon them again.

Megan watched Ted pay more and more attention as they closed on the river and then started down the path that led home. As much as she hoped it would spark some kind of memory, she was also glad to see him taking in some of the fresh air. Being stuck in the hospital for so long with that sick air couldn't do anyone any good. Megan pointed out where they'd flattened the land on the opposite side of the A10 for a new village that was going to be called Fenmore. Some Wiseham residents had protested against it, but it was progress. She wanted somewhere for her kids to live when they grew up and couldn't see the point in complaining.

Ted looked along the river and back. "Where were they working when I disappeared?"

It wasn't something Megan had paid close attention to in the time before. She knew it had already been going on a couple of months with most of the river section widened and the bank built up, and it was the work on the additional channel they'd started on. She made a rough guess and pointed to the midpoint of the channel. She'd spent a lot of time outside immediately after Ted's disappearance, so she had a rough idea of where they were working then. But all of the work was done during the day, and they were a little too far away from the house (though visible, she'd studied the scene out of Ted's window carefully) to be involved. And what would a bunch of landscapers want with a fourteen-year-old boy anyway?

"Can we... Can we go to where they found me?"

While surprised that Ted had asked, Megan was more than happy to guide him there. They walked along the river, crossed the old footbridge (a new one was to be built that was cycle-friendly, linking Fenmore to the A10) and headed along the riverbank.

Ted spent the whole time looking into the water. "Is that why it's all so straight?" he asked. "Because it's man-made?"

Ted got about halfway down the path and then stopped. "Was it about here?" he asked. He glanced again at the church and the water tower.

"So I was told," Megan said. Again, no one had given her a specific location, and she hadn't thought to ask.

"How did I get here?" Ted peered into the water.

Megan looked in, too. The report had said that it was likely that Ted had been in the water. Could someone have held him for a long time, kept him drugged, completely out of it, and then, for some reason dumped him in the water? Instead of drowning, had Ted roused and struggled out of the water? Megan shook her head as she tried to picture the kind of person who could do something so cruel. How she longed to find that person and to inflict the same level of anguish upon them.

Ted continued to stare into the river, looking farther along both sides.

Neither of them heard the woman approaching from behind. "Where is he?"

Megan turned to see Mrs Wright moving past her and toward Ted.

Before Megan could move, Mrs Wright was upon Ted. She grabbed one of his arms and pulled him toward her.

"Where's my boy? Where's my Julius?"

Megan moved toward them, but it was like she was wading, each step barely closing the distance. She wanted to call out, but she found herself staring at Ted, helpless.

"I don't know where he is," Ted said.

"But it was here they found you?" Mrs Wright said, speaking so quickly it was barely intelligible.

Ted nodded. "Somewhere along here."

Megan could see he was flustered by the questions, could see his brow wrinkle in fear, but she was incapable of acting.

"Why hasn't he come back, too?" Mrs Wright was yelling now. Her face screwed up and tears ran down her face.

Ted stepped away from her. "If I could bring him back," he said, "I would. But I don't know anything about it."

The second Ted stepped away, Megan was conscious of her body again and able to move freely. She wanted to go over to Alesha Wright and shove her into the water. No one had a right to confront her Teddy Bear like that. "I know you're hurting," Megan said. "If anyone knows, then believe me, I do. But you do not speak to my son like that. Got it?"

Alesha Wright covered her face, her sobs becoming audible.

"Mum, I want to go home," Ted said, stumbling toward her.

She let him fall against her and wrapped her arms around him. It was another reminder of how much weight he'd lost, that someone had taken him from her care and then looked after him so poorly. If only she could lay her hands on them. If only she could have a minute to take out her frustration…

17: LOLA

During morning registration, Lola's form tutor told her she needed to see the head of maths at break time. No doubt it would be about the recent test which she was sure she'd done terribly in.

After surviving the first two periods of the day, Lola made her way toward maths. En route, she was accosted by a lanky boy with greasy hair, a year ten. She'd come across him before, the sort to loiter in corridors and make stupid comments to much younger kids. She remembered someone had once called him Larry—probably a nickname.

"Hey, when's your brother coming back to school?" Larry asked.

Lola signed. "I don't know." She continued walking.

"What happened to him?" Larry followed behind her.

"I don't know," Lola repeated.

"Was he taken away by aliens?"

Lola sighed and increased her pace.

"Did he get anal probed?"

Lola didn't bother to respond. She reached the steps and started to head up.

"We're gonna call him anal probe when he comes back."

"Good for you," Lola said, continuing up the stairs. Larry didn't follow. Too much effort.

At the top, she peered into the head of maths' classroom. Ms Fletcher was a tall woman with a booming voice; she'd taught Lola for a term in year 7 before they'd shifted the sets around. As Lola stood in the doorway, it was clear Ms Fletcher didn't recognise her. Can I help you?" she asked.

"Yes, Miss. I was told to come and see you. I'm Lola Wallace."

"Ah, Lola, yes. Things haven't been going quite so well in maths recently, have they?"

Lola shrugged. "Not really." Things hadn't been going so well anywhere, in truth.

"I've been speaking to your teacher and we've decided that you might be able to get on better in a slightly smaller classroom."

It wasn't just a word about how poorly she'd done in the test. They were moving her down a set.

Ms Fletcher placed her hands on her knees and leant forward. "How would you feel about that?"

Lola felt a cramp in her gut but said nothing.

"I have a letter here explaining the situation to your parents."

Lola nodded. "When will I be moving?" There might still be time to do something about it.

"Immediately."

Crap, thought Lola.

"That's why I wanted to see you now, as you have maths next. Don't worry, you're not moving far. Mr Levin's class is next door to where you used to be."

"Okay," said Lola. What else could she say? She left the classroom and headed back down the stairs and toward the canteen.

Larry, who had been slumped against a wall, stood upright as Lola approached. "What's that on your ear? Is that alien technology?"

Lola reached for her hearing aid and felt herself reddening.

Larry moved to her side. "Did anal probe tell you about his adventures in space?"

Lola kept walking. He followed.

"I bet he loved getting an anal probe."

Once in the courtyard, Lola tried to spy a friend, someone that could help her to ignore Larry's jibes.

"Does he anal probe you?"

Lola heard a laugh and turned to see a pair of Larry's cronies had joined him, one standing on either side, flanking him like they were the most hideous boyband ever put together. The boy on the left was a good foot-and-a-half shorter than Larry, with a face full of freckles. Dark hair hung limp over his forehead, doing a bad job of hiding his zits. On the right, the boy had a face like an eagle: a huge hooked beak of a nose dominated the centre of his face and made his eyes look like they were set too far back. Above those eyes wriggled a hairy caterpillar mono-brow. When he laughed, his mouth formed a tiny circle. "Anal probe," he muttered before breaking into a hee-haw laugh again.

Across the courtyard, she saw Jas and picked up her pace. Then she felt a finger jabbing at her backside. She turned around and yelled, "Fuck off."

Larry faked outrage, laughed, and hurried off, offering his finger to his minions to smell as he headed into the school building.

Lola's outburst had attracted attention. Everyone in the courtyard turned to look at her including one of the senior teachers, Mr Butcher.

He stared at her and beckoned her over with the wiggle of a finger.

Lola had no choice but to march over to him. At least he cut the distance by approaching her.

"What was that all about?" he asked.

"He poked me..."

"That kind of language will not be tolerated in this school, do you hear?"

So, he wasn't going to even listen to her side of the story. Great.

"I asked you a question, young lady." He stood so close that he had to place his chin on his chest to look down at Lola.

Patronising bastard thought Lola. "He tried to..."

"I don't care what 'he', whoever 'he' is, tried to or didn't try to do. Foul language of that nature will not be tolerated. Do you hear me?"

The bell rang for the end of break. Lola had no choice but to acknowledge him, and then, hundreds of pupils filed past her, including Mitchell who stuck his tongue out at her. Lola couldn't help but smirk, something which neither passed Butcher by nor amused him.

"I don't find this matter in the least bit amusing. Planner out. Now."

"Sorry, Sir," she muttered, stepping back and reaching into her rucksack to grab her planner.

She watched Butcher record the details of her lunchtime detention, sickened by the glee in his eyes at doling out punishment and thought what a depraved old bastard he was.

Clearly, he wasn't teaching next lesson, as he took time to issue another lecture about language and expectations.

By the time Lola got back up to maths, her new class had already gone in. Her old class were in the process of entering. Jas turned to look at her and mouthed, "Are you okay?"

Lola held out her hands, a gesture demonstrating her powerlessness and pointed to the other classroom.

Jas kept moving into her classroom, a puzzled look on her face as Lola walked past the end of the line and into the room next door.

Everyone turned to look at her as she entered.

"You must be Lola," said Mr Levin who must have been closer to one hundred than he was to her age. "Take a seat over there," he said, pointing.

For the first time that day, something felt like it was going right. She'd been seated next to Lauren.

Lola stuck to the usual after-school plan—homework at Jas's house. Lola and Jas chatted, but Lola was wary of Mrs Thakur listening in. She had no intention of giving the letter revealing that she'd dropped down a set to her parents, and she didn't want them finding out from a third party. Not that it would bother them, she thought. Then she realised that was why she didn't want to give them the letter. What if they weren't angry with her? What if it proved they didn't care?

"What homework are you doing, girls?" Mrs Thakur asked, peering over their books.

Lola could tell she was comparing their work, making sure she wasn't copying Jas. She didn't want her precious star pupil to get into trouble.

"English, Mum," Jas said.

Their letters were completely different, so Lola had nothing to worry about.

"Don't you girls have any maths homework to be getting on with? You know how important maths is."

As Lola said, "No," Jas said, "Yes."

"Well either you do, or you don't. Jas?"

"What Lola means is we don't have any due until next week."

"Don't leave it until the last minute. You'll end up rushing it. That's much more important than writing letters. Who even writes letters these days?"

"We'll do it next," Jas said.

And that's how Lola found herself doing homework she didn't even need to do about a concept that hadn't been covered in her class.

When Mrs Thakur left the room, Jas finally had a chance to ask Lola what had happened. She could have told her about Lanky Larry picking on her and getting a detention, but instead, she kept it to maths. "My test was so bad, I got moved down."

"Oh," said Jas, looking sheepish.

"How did you get on?"

"Ninety-two per cent."

"What's ninety-two per cent, dear?" asked Mrs Thakur as she re-entered the room.

"Oh, my result in the maths test."

"Hmmm. Could do better. How did you get on, Lola?"

"Eighty-two." She lied.

"Girls, you'd better be finishing up."

No doubt Jas had an extra lesson of something somewhere. Lola could no longer keep up. And to think once

Lola had attended clubs and activities after school: trampolining and musical theatre.

"I'll drop you home," said Mrs Thakur, looking out the window. "Or you'll get soaked."

Lola glanced up at the rain streaking down the window. Typical. It had been bright all day, but now she was free, it had started to pour down. So much for trying to find Lauren on the way home. No Mitchell either. Not that she wanted to see him. His stupid tongue had got her in enough trouble. Besides, with the rain, they probably wouldn't be out.

The rain running down the car windows as they drove through Wiseham made Lola smile sadly. She traced a raindrop from the top of the window to the bottom, picturing the dance routine to 'Singing in the Rain' that was to be performed in her dance and theatre company's winter show. That was to follow Lola's bit, singing a song from Mary Poppins, but when Ted had disappeared all that came to a stop, and now it felt like a distant part of her childhood too far away to ever recover.

18: SIMON

Working the late shift had its advantages, especially on a Friday. After six, only emergencies had to be actioned, so there were none of the dull support calls which plagued day shifts. There were fewer people in the building, especially managers, so the atmosphere was more relaxed. Sometimes he'd come in and inherit an awful job from the early shift, but today was not one of those days. In fact, upon his arrival, Simon was made to feel like a film star. So many people stopped him on the way through the building to tell him how happy they were that Ted was back, that he was a couple of minutes late getting to his department, despite being in the building in plenty of time.

Macintyre gave him an evil look as he entered, but Simon headed past him to his desk. He apologised to the early team, took a quick handover, and let them go. As he was getting logged on, he overheard Tracy (Toady Tracy, abhorrent witch) speaking to Macintyre. "Wish I had kids," she said. "Can use them to get loads of extra days off, switch to the best shifts."

Simon turned to give her a look, but she was gazing into Macintyre's eyes. How he'd love to give her a piece of his mind! The last seven months hadn't exactly been a walk in the park unless it was the park by the River Styx. He'd not exactly taken all that time off and switched shifts to shirk out of work. When the phone rang, it took a moment to shake off his annoyance and respond in a professional manner. They'd be gone in an hour. He just had to keep his head down until then and he'd be fine.

Midway through the shift, Simon had caught up on his emails. They'd got the work queue right down, and unless an emergency came in, they were unoccupied. They had their appraisals to write, but Simon wasn't in the mood for that. No one would mind if he did a bit of web browsing. It was the first chance he had since Ted's return. While he was missing, he'd plunged the depths of the web for stories about missing persons, half of which had terrified him when he considered the implications and half of which gave him hope. What he hadn't searched for though, was mysterious cases of reappearance. He hoped to find some commonality with Ted's case, hoped to find someone out there who had been through something similar. Maybe they could shine a light upon the situation. No such luck. He found plenty of accounts of alien abductions: victims caught in a bright white light and descriptions of short, humanoid creatures with bulbous heads and large black eyes carrying out operations. He found stories about people blacking out in bars and hotel rooms and waking up missing vital organs (and in one case with a note stating that he should go to a hospital as they'd taken three pints of blood). Where he could, he scoured images, looking at residual injuries and comparing them to Ted's scarring.

When he thought the stories couldn't get any weirder, he discovered a ridiculous blog called *Doppelgangers and Decoys* which told of people returning who weren't whom they claimed they were. Plenty of nefarious theories had been suggested, from aliens who were now living in host bodies as they awaited invasion, and creatures from alternate worlds who'd switched with their Earthly counterparts, to vessels to herald the return of the demon king. With a heavy sigh, Simon found the idea of writing his appraisal suddenly much more appealing. He decided to try one more link: *East Anglia's Missing Epidemic*. This was more like it—all sorts of facts and figures about missing persons showing that the region had a record for unexplained disappearances. There was even a map on which areas in which people had disappeared were circled. Due to the age of the PCs in the office which were limited to an older version of Internet Explorer, the map couldn't be zoomed in on to see further details. The message board on the website still worked though, and remained quite active, with three messages having been posted in the last week. Given the content of some of the messages, people asking for help to find their missing loved ones, Simon was surprised he hadn't stumbled upon it when looking for help to find Ted.

Another thread was of greater interest to Simon. The user claimed that his dad had been missing for two years, and when he came back it was like he was a different person altogether. An admin from the site had responded, citing other cases of returned imposters and asking for contact details so they could personally investigate further.

What harm would it do to leave a message on there? Surely someone would respond in a way that would set his mind at rest, or at the very least tell him how he could make sure it was Ted who had come back.

19: TED

When Ted and Mum got home from their walk, which finished with a dash out of the summer rainstorm, he was exhausted. It was such little exercise, but his body was screaming at him as if he'd run a marathon. Worse, his head was full to bursting point with questions. What had happened to Julius? Did it have anything to do with him, or was it entirely unrelated? He crashed onto his bed and slept.

Sometime later, a knock at the door woke him.

Ted took a minute to rouse himself from his sleep and sit up as the door crept open.

Lola stood in the doorway, holding on to the doorframe, drifting from side to side, looking anywhere but at Ted.

Ted smiled. "Are you coming in, or are you going to stand there all day?"

"Ted," she said, stepping inside, keeping one hand on the doorframe to anchor her in the hallway. "People have been talking about you at school."

"What have they been saying?"

Lola repeated some of the things she'd heard, staring at the floor as she said them.

Ted knew what the kids at his school were like—after all, he was one of them, but to hear such stupid stories still pulled at the pit of his gut. "Who was saying it?"

Lola looked up, her eyes meeting Ted's for just a second. "That kid they call Larry."

Ted knew the one. He knew his friends too, and whenever he could, he did his best to avoid them. He knew from experience just how rotten they could be. At the end of the school day, back when Ted was in year 8, he'd had to stop by the toilets before going home, or he wouldn't have made it. As soon as he'd entered, the smell of cigarette smoke hit him, and he'd coughed. With that, Larry had come bundling out of one of the cubicles, one of his mates following. It looked like they'd planned to run off, but when they saw Ted, they changed their minds.

"Don't tell anyone what you saw," Larry said, getting right in Ted's face, so close he could make out the individual heads of the spots on his nose, yellowish green, like the seeds of a disgusting face strawberry.

Ted had struggled not to cough again as Larry breathed smoke over him.

His mate had then grabbed Ted's arm and twisted it, forcing Ted to turn around and then slammed him into the wall. He continued to push the arm up and hissed. "What do you say?"

With the pain in his arm, Ted struggled to hold onto the contents of his bladder. "I won't say a thing," he said and when he felt like his arm would either snap or his bladder would give way, he was freed, and the two of them went off laughing. Ted had dashed to the urinal, and while there had been a little bit of leakage, it wasn't a complete disaster.

Yes, Ted knew they weren't the kind of kids he wanted to mess with, and it angered him that they'd been hassling Lola, but what could he do about it?

He looked at her again, standing awkwardly in the doorway. "Well, thanks for letting me know," he said, and Lola left without another word. So, seven months away from school had earnt him the moniker of anal probe. Great.

He hated how awkward it was with Lola. They used to have private jokes, but now she barely spoke to him. When they were younger, they used to walk around holding hands, but he didn't think she'd even touched him since he'd returned, not since that first hug back at the hospital. Was he in some way tainted by what he'd gone through? Had he contracted something contagious?

He looked at himself in the mirror. The trouble was it had been a while since he'd examined his body anyway, so how would he know if he was any different? With the torch on his phone, he looked in his mouth and at his teeth. They looked normal, but should he have a dental appointment to check them out? No doubt he'd missed one while away. He placed his phone back on his bed and studied his eyes, pulling the eyelids down. What about an eye test? He didn't need to wear glasses before, but his vision had been so bad when he awoke, should he get his eyes checked? He studied his fingers and then his arms: nothing unusual there, other than how thin they were. On his left arm, there were bruises—no doubt from where Mrs Wright had grabbed him. It wasn't normal for him to bruise so easily but perhaps it was because he was so thin.

He took off his top and looked at his chest: nothing abnormal. He held his hand there to feel the rhythm of his heartbeat—as irregular as ever.

He looked at the scarring around his navel. He'd yet to study it properly. He never felt pain there, and the doctors suggested it had healed, so must have happened early in the time that he was missing. He ran his fingers across the skin, tight in some places, ridged in others. The doctors hadn't been clear about what they thought had happened. It wasn't a routine cut; it was more of a swirling pattern. They'd suggested a burn, but again that didn't quite fit with the scarring they'd previously seen. He removed his socks and looked at his toes. The toenails were soft and thin. He remembered that they used to be much harder and would ping off the clippers. What about his bum? Had he been probed? He removed the last of his clothes, turned his back on the mirror, and tried to see his bottom. He spotted the marks at the top and bottom of his spine. He ran his fingers over them. He bent over, trying to get a better angle to look at his backside, but it was impossible. He grabbed his phone and took pictures and then checked them. He couldn't see anything peculiar. How would you know if you'd be probed anyway? Would it leave a mark? If the scar on his belly was painless, he wouldn't feel anything there either. He sat on the bed with his head in his hands. Was he normal? How could he possibly know one way or the other? He poked at the scar at the back of his neck and felt a sensation run down his spine. Was that normal? He touched the mark at the bottom of his spine, rubbing it to try to create a sensation. From the hall, the phone rang. It suddenly made him feel very conscious of what he was doing. He quickly dressed and sat back on the bed, staring at the wall and wondering.

20: MEGAN

Megan picked up the phone. Her relationship with it had changed entirely in the last seven months. While Ted was missing every call was hope, but also potential despair.

She'd yet to rid herself of this emotional attachment and felt her heart race as she spoke and awaited a response.

"Good evening, Mrs Wallace, this is D.I. Heimlich."

This was a rare treat. Over the past seven months, she'd found herself chasing for updates. Perhaps Heimlich wasn't the kind of man who thought it necessary to make a call when there was absolutely no news.

"Inspector Heimlich," Megan replied. "How can I help you?"

Megan had exchanged a series of text messages during the afternoon with Simon who had reported how poorly Ted had taken his meeting with Heimlich.

"Mrs Wallace, I'm just calling to ask if Ted is with you presently."

Perhaps he was calling to apologise for his earlier demeanour. "He's in his room."

"Can you check he's there for me?"

Megan felt her mouth drying. She licked her lips. "Do you... need to speak to him?"

"No. Could you please verify his whereabouts at this present time for me, and since I saw him this afternoon."

"I assure you, he's in his room." Megan could feel a buzz inside her head, a nagging doubt, an awakening worry.

"Mrs Wallace, this could be important. We have had a report..."

Megan dropped the phone and raced to Ted's new room. She flung open the door to see Ted sitting in the bed looking ponderous. He turned to her, his face glum.

"Just... checking," Megan said and strode back to the phone.

"Yes, he's in his room." Megan had become so tense that the cords in her neck stood out, and she couldn't relax them. "Why would you do that?" she hissed.

"I apologise if I caused you any concern."

Megan was not ready to take that apology. She had questioned where Ted was, and Heimlich's words had, for just a second, made her believe it was all beginning again. "What's this about?" she said.

"And where was he this afternoon?"

She spoke through gritted teeth, a jaw that wouldn't unclench. "We went for a walk."

"And what was the purpose of this walk?"

Memories of the walk both relaxed Megan and diverted her anger to Alesha for what she'd done. "Ted needs exercise. I hoped it might bring something back..."

"Something like what, Mrs Wallace?"

"A memory... why, what do you mean?"

"Something did come back this afternoon, by the river."

"What do you mean?"

"Mrs Wallace, this is very important. An announcement will be made shortly. Mrs Wright was walking down by the river—she said she saw you—and not much further down, that's where she found Julius."

"Julius is alive?" A memory of her own relief hit her, and she had to place her hand against the wall for stability.

"Yes."

"And he's okay?"

"Listen, this isn't going to be easy to hear." Heimlich paused and Megan heard him take in a deep breath. "He's missing an arm."

Megan gasped. She'd seen pictures of the boy, so happy, so free, so... normal, but now he'd have to live his life with a permanent disability. Shame quickly replaced the feeling of thankfulness that it wasn't her boy, it wasn't her Teddy Bear that would have to live like that.

"The wound has been sealed up, and like Ted, he's very malnourished, but there's something else..."

"What?" Megan couldn't imagine what could possibly follow the news of the missing limb.

"He keeps saying one thing, over and over."

"What's that?"

"He said your son's name, Mrs Wallace. He keeps saying 'Ted', again and again."

"Okay," Megan said. "Why?"

"I don't know, Mrs Wallace. But in a day or two, if the situation hasn't changed, we might ask you to bring Ted in. Together, it might get their memories working."

21: SIMON

The weekend had passed in a blur. Ted had spent most of it resting, despite the constant visitors. Megan's parents had come down from Yorkshire to see how Ted was which seemed to utterly exhaust him. Lola had spent most of the weekend glued to her phone, and Megan had continued to plague Ted with questions until her sister Claire arrived to distract her for a bit.

The reappearance of Julius had drawn the press back to Wiseham. While some interest was generated by Ted's return, the lack of details meant the story quickly faded. With a second boy back with a similar lack of knowledge it created mystery and speculation.

Simon peered out of the window. A yellow Saab convertible that looked like a relic from the early 90s with badly faded paintwork and significant rust on the wheel arches loitered on the pavement outside. It definitely didn't belong to the neighbours—he'd have noticed a car like that. The car wasn't typical of any of the journalists who'd flocked to the area like flies around stink, either, though the activities of the occupant (sitting and waiting) matched theirs. Simon had first noticed the car before he went to bed. It hadn't been there when he'd waved off the in-laws, so it had arrived after darkness had fallen. He'd been standing at the window, gazing out while sipping on a glass of Old Navy, when he'd spotted it. He was still there this morning. Had he slept in the car, or had he waited there like that all night? Simon squinted, trying to get a clearer view, but he couldn't make out many of his features from that distance, other than the fact that he wore sunglasses and, as his hands moved to the steering wheel, driving gloves. Simon shook his head and went to the door to pull on his shoes.

Megan made her way downstairs, ready to head off to work.

"Did you warn Lola not to talk to the press?" Simon asked.

"She knows better than that," Megan said.

"But did you tell her?"

"No, I've not seen her. Have you?" Megan grabbed her handbag from where it hung at the bottom of the stairs and peered in.

"Saw her having breakfast, but she said she had to head off early."

"And did you warn her?"

"I didn't think about it at the time." Simon turned and craned his neck to peer out of the window again.

"She's sensible. She doesn't need telling."

"I'd feel better if we'd have said something."

"Call her, then. Send her a text. I've barely been able to get her off her phone the last few days."

"Okay, will do."

Megan grabbed her keys from the hook beside the coat stand.

"Have a good day," Simon said, following her out of the door.

"Where are you going?"

"To speak to our friend." Simon nodded toward the Saab, which must have once been a sunny yellow, but had faded to the colour of bile.

While waiting for Megan to back out of the drive, Simon sent Lola a quick message advising her to be careful if strangers approached asking questions, and as soon as Megan's car had disappeared around the corner of Riverview Terrace, he approached the battered vehicle.

The window eased down as Simon approached. His initial assessment had been correct. The driver wore sunglasses, little round ones reminiscent of those John Lennon wore, and a pair of black driving gloves. He was balding and had combed over his hair from one side to try to disguise that. His face carried little weight, his cheekbones prominent. The lines around his eyes and his grey stumble put his age around fifty.

"Listen, Pal," Simon said as he bent down to the height of the window, "no one's going to speak to you. You're wasting your time if you think there's a story here."

The man removed his sunglasses and turned to look at Simon. His eyes were different colours: one green, one brown. "I'm not from the press, Mr Wallace."

"Then what are you doing here?"

"The name's Grant. I run a little website that investigates East Anglia's missing persons, and I have a question for you."

Simon paused for a moment before rising. "I'm not answering any questions." He turned to walk away.

Grant opened his car door and stepped out. "I only have one. How sure are you that the boy you brought home is your son?"

22: LOLA

As arranged with Lauren, Lola waited at the entrance to the passageway between Honeydew Way and Poplar Avenue. She craned her neck and looked both ways, hoping to see her friend coming. As she waited, her phone buzzed. She pulled out her phone and checked the message. She sighed when she saw it was a text from Dad. *Lots of press about. Be careful who you talk to.* Why would anyone want to talk to her? She knew how to be careful, and who to be careful of. While waiting for Lauren, she gazed down the street. Outside the Wright house, among all the extra vehicles, was a van topped with a radio dish. No doubt they'd heard about Julius, but he was still at the hospital. She craned her neck to look further down the street, to Ted Hatcher's house. Maybe they were there to investigate him, the creepy old bastard.

"Boo!" a shout coupled with hands on her shoulders made Lola jump, and her phone slipped from her hand, bounced on the pavement, and fell, screen-side down. She turned to look at her attacker.

"Shit, I am so sorry," said Mitchell. He bent down to pick up the phone.

Lola tucked her hair behind her ear and took it from him. She glanced at the screen, saw it was cracked, and stuck it in the side pocket of her rucksack. She didn't want to make a big deal about it. "What are you doing here?" Lola asked. She looked past him for Lauren, wondering if they'd come together.

"What do you mean what am I doing here?" Mitchell asked. He smiled.

"I mean why are you here?" Lola smiled back.

"Beginning to feel a bit of a mug, to be honest." Mitchell looked up at the sky and groaned.

Lola admired Mitchell's neck. "What?"

Mitchell made eye contact with Lola again. "You weren't expecting to see me this morning, were you?"

Realisation hit Lola like a smack in the face. "Lauren!" she called out, chastising her absent friend.

"Let me guess, she said she'd meet you here, right?"

Lola nodded.

"And you get the crushing disappointment of having to put up with me instead." Mitchell frowned.

"It's not so bad," Lola said with a smile.

"Not so bad!" Mitchell gave Lola a playful shove on the arm. "Anyway, nothing's gonna bring me down today."

"Why's that?"

"My boy, Julius, is back."

"I didn't know you were friends?"

"Are you kidding? He's a great guy. Always had my back."

"Have you heard what happened to him?" Lola peered over her shoulder in case anyone was nearby.

"What?"

"You don't know?"

"Don't know what?"

"About his arm?"

"What about his arm?" Mitchell's face screwed up with concern.

"Don't tell anyone I told you, but I heard my mum on the phone. They found him, but he was missing an arm."

Mitchell put his hands to his head. "You're kidding?"

"It's just... what I heard."

Mitchell sped off toward the Wright house.

Lola followed a few steps behind. She watched him bang on the door, knowing it wouldn't be answered. She spotted movement in some of the vehicles that lined the street and remembered Dad's message. With Mitchell preoccupied she took the opportunity to take out her phone. Yes, the screen was cracked, but worse, the was no picture. She held down the power button, but nothing happened. She slipped her useless phone back into her rucksack. When she looked up, she noticed The Child Catcher at his window.

"Come on, Mitchell," she called, suddenly desperate for some company. "He's not there. We've got to get a move on, or we'll miss the bus."

As they started to make their way toward the bus stop Lola craned her neck again trying to spot if anyone else was close. This time she hoped Lauren wasn't on her way yet.

23: TED

Ted tried to form an image of Julius in his mind, but it simply wouldn't come. He knew who he was, but only because he was at the same school. With a bit of invention, he could roughly picture his face. Julius had moved to the village at the age of twelve, so Ted didn't have the advantage of having seen him on a regular basis on the playground at Wiseham Juniors. He tried to remember some of the other boys. Larry came to him in an instant, but only because of his negative experiences with him and the fact that he was the sort always found slouching in the corridors and making himself known with his stupid comments. Julius wasn't like that. He wasn't the sort to hang around making trouble. A vague memory came of seeing Julius run one leg of the relay during the last sports day. He was sure he hadn't spent the last seven months with him. If that were the case, he'd be able to picture him vividly. He tried to imagine his vague idea of Julius without an arm... Mum hadn't been specific about how much of the arm he'd lost—hewn off just above the elbow? Plucked from the socket at the shoulder? Nothing stirred a memory.

As he tried to push something that wasn't there out of his memory, Dad came in.

"How you doing, son?" he asked, staring at Ted as he awaited a reply.

"I'm okay, I guess."

"Do you fancy a game on your PlayStation?" Dad practically bounced as he spoke, and his enthusiasm seemed false.

They always used to play together. It was a regular occurrence before Ted hit his teenage years and started to shut Dad out. "Okay," muttered Ted.

Dad picked up a controller and switched on the console. "What was the football one we used to play? FIFA?"

"Yeah."

"Have you got the disc?"

"It's digital."

"Digital, hey?" Simon turned to stare at Ted. "We didn't have that in my day." He laughed.

Ted looked at his dad. He had a strange edge to him. He seemed to be a little frantic—on the edge of mania. Maybe the news about Julius had upset him.

"You okay today, Ted? No strange emotions? Are you feeling yourself?"

Ted took his controller and loaded the game. "Feeling a bit better today," he lied. He didn't like his dad's manner and didn't want to say anything to set him more on edge.

The brightness of the screen hurt Ted's eyes, and he found his concentration drifting from the game. Dad, playing as Arsenal, scored the opening goal.

"I thought you were good at this," he said, again staring as Ted kicked off.

Another goal came quickly. "I've not even played this version, and I'm giving you a right good hiding. It's like you've never played before."

"It's a bit bright, that's all, Dad. I'm struggling to see it properly."

"You think we need to get your eyes tested?" Dad lay the controller down, leaving the ball at the feet of his motionless attacker.

"Might be an idea."

"I'll mention it when we're back at the hospital."

"Are you sure it's just that?" Simon stared at Ted again.

Ted nodded.

Simon placed a hand on his forehead. "Well, I guess I'll leave you to it for now."

"Okay. Thanks, Dad."

Dad looked at him quizzically and then left, hurrying out of the door. Ted sighed. Why couldn't everything go back to normal? Why was everyone and everything getting so much weirder and weirder? And did Dad have to remind him of the hospital? Back in November, he'd been dreading his forthcoming hospital tests for it may have been the precursor to another round of operations. He knew he'd had three prior rounds but could only remember the most recent one when he was eight. He'd had other operations when he was just a couple of months old, and again when he was two. On each occasion they'd operated on his heart, working to close the hole that refused to permanently seal. With any growth spurt, there was a chance that the hole would seal itself up, but so far, on every occasion of growth, the hole had only ever reappeared and therefore had needed re-patching. While he didn't remember the operation (obviously, he was not conscious for that) or even its build-up, he remembered the continuous pain he suffered in the recovery period. Every little movement had led to agony, as if his blood was full of thorns, lacerating the inside of his arteries.

He covered one ear and placed a hand on his chest, again listening to the rhythm. After a minute, he knew two things; the beat was not regular, and it was different from before. He hoped that the difference meant he wouldn't need another operation.

24: MEGAN

The uncomfortable heat of the hospital waiting room brought back a plethora of memories: Ted's and Lola's births, Ted's heart operations, Lola's ear operations, and most recently, Ted's return. She pictured him lying in his bed and smiled. For a long time, this was a sight she thought she'd never see again. But days had passed, and Ted still had no idea of where he'd been while he was away. He had no idea who had taken him, held him, operated on him. But maybe Julius would know something. Heimlich had asked her to come and had wanted her to bring Ted along to see if it sparked anything in either boy, but first, Megan wanted to see Julius for herself. She didn't want to place Ted in a room with him if she feared it would cause him agony.

Heimlich approached the waiting area armed with a coffee in a disposable cup. The heat of the hospital didn't agree with him either, his hair swept to one side and held in place with sweat. "Shall we?" he said.

Megan rose and before she reached him, he'd turned and was walking away. No doubt it was a power thing, forcing others to chase him. Megan quickened her pace to walk abreast of him. "Has there been any change?"

"From my last status report, the boy was unchanged. Stable condition. Got a little more meat on his bones than your boy, and it's your boy's name he keeps saying."

"And the arm?"

"Still missing." Heimlich picked up the pace again.

Megan increased her stride to stay beside him. Part of her didn't want to respond to such a glib remark. "I meant what's the wound like?"

"You'll see." Heimlich stopped abruptly outside a private room.

Ted never got a private room, Megan thought, and wondered if that meant there was something more going on here than she'd been led to believe. Before Heimlich opened the door, she understood. She could hear the boy's voice, a low, slow growl. If he was saying 'Ted', it certainly wasn't clear. The door opened with a creak. Inside, Julius imitated the creak, ending it with a clear 'd' sound.

Megan looked first to Alesha Wright sitting in the chair beside her boy's bed. It was clear she'd been at the hospital for some time and had spent the night. Then she turned to Julius. His eyes didn't meet hers; they didn't seem fixed on anything as his head slowly rolled from one side to the other. Maybe it was the drugs; she suspected he'd been loaded with painkillers and sedatives. With Julius in a catatonic state, he wouldn't be offended by a glance at the arm or lack thereof. The oddest thought that crossed Megan's mind was that it looked natural. The arm came to a stop perhaps six inches from the shoulder. Megan wanted to look at the stump—to see how neat it had been left. In a former job, she'd worked with amputees, her role assessing their entitlement to benefits and helping her clients to apply for any compensation or available grants. She wondered if she should say something to Alesha, point her in the right direction, but that wasn't her job anymore. Someone else would sort that out. For a second Megan felt a pang of guilt for going into work mode, for assessing the situation and thinking about what should be done instead of the human suffering apparent before her eyes. She looked again at Alesha, but she seemed almost as distant as her son.

A low growl formed in Julius' chest and he started to tremble. First of all, Megan thought that he was looking at her, but his eyes fixed on a point beyond her. She turned to look at the boy's mother. Alesha looked up, and, having no doubt experienced this countless times before sighed and stared at the floor again.

"Ted," Julius barked. He breathed heavily before saying it again, and then, in three short bursts, "Ted, Ted, Ted." He exhaled, almost with an air of contentment, and then went back to his former catatonic state.

"Mrs Wright," said Heimlich, who had been observing calmly for the whole duration, "would you mind stepping outside for a moment?"

Alesha looked at Julius, checking he was still there, nervous about leaving the boy, but then she nodded at Heimlich and started to rise.

Heimlich indicated to Megan that she should also be part of the conversation.

Outside, Alesha held on to the door, keeping one eye on her child. "Excuse me," she called out, peering over Megan's shoulder toward the nurses' station, "would someone be able to come in and keep an eye on my Julius?"

One of the nurses hurried over. "Certainly Mrs Wright. It's time we took some more readings."

Only once the nurse was by Julius's side did Alesha let go of the door.

"So, this is the situation," Heimlich said. "I've spoken to the consultant, and they can see no harm in bringing Ted in here because Julius, so far, has had no cognition of what's going on around him."

Alesha sighed.

"We're not expecting the presence of Ted to alter Julius' state at this time. The doctor says there's a chance it might, but my hope, and my seniors support me with this, is that if Ted sees Julius, if he sees he's alright, if he sees what they did to him, then he might finally talk about whatever it is he's keeping quiet about."

Megan stepped forward, staring Heimlich in the eye. "Ted's not deliberately keeping quiet about anything."

"That may be the case, it might not. This might be what forces him to remember. What do you say? Shall we get them together?"

Alesha still looked toward the door. She nodded and muttered in agreement, and Heimlich waved her off.

"Okay," Megan said. "We'll do it."

25: SIMON

Simon took the card from his back pocket, looked at the number, and punched it into his phone. He checked over his shoulder and then stopped. What was he doing? So what if Ted hadn't been able to play FIFA? Did that prove he'd been replaced by a doppelganger by a mysterious entity for some nefarious purpose? Simon rubbed at his right temple and then ran a hand through his hair.

He looked at the card again and considered tearing it up, but then he heard a cough from Ted's new room, and he jumped. Even if that was actually Ted in there (and it was, of course it was) it wouldn't hurt to have someone to talk it through with, would it? It wasn't like he could approach the topic with Megan, not when she was still carrying so much anger. Yes, he'd give the number a call, talk to Grant and see what he suggested. He wouldn't do anything to hurt Ted, not if they knew it was really him.

Simon turned to face Ted's room, his eyes fixed on the handle, his ears listening for any movement, and made the call.

26: LOLA

As the bell sounded for lunch, Lola started to pack away her maths equipment. "What are we doing this lunchtime?" Lola asked.

"Me?" Lauren said. "I've got a bloody detention, haven't I?"

Lola nodded. She didn't know this. She wasn't in any other classes with Lauren–though that might not be the case for long once the results of the tests in her other subjects came through.

"It's only twenty minutes. Get me something from the canteen and I'll meet you on the field, under the tree, okay?"

They exited the classroom together but then moved in separate directions.

In the dining hall, Lola saw no one she knew. Jas was sitting at a table eating her packed lunch with some of her other friends, but there were no spaces at that table. Funny how quickly she'd been cut from that particular group. She assumed she was still going over to Jas's after school to do homework, but she'd have to talk to her about it, and she didn't want to do so and run the risk of being rejected in front of other people. She dug her phone out of her bag to check it... only to remember she'd killed it by dropping it earlier. Instead, she got out her water bottle and took a sip. Realising they were making progress, she shuffled forward in the queue, unaware of a group of lads joining the line behind her.

Later, when Lola thought back on the event, she realised she should have been able to smell him and his gross mates that wandered around in the same cloud of B.O., barely disguised with a can of Lynx body spray. She should have had her defences up before it escalated to that level. She shouldn't have reacted—not audibly, not physically.

He had his finger on her before he spoke, so she felt him at the same time as she heard him.

"Oi, oi! Anal probe," he said, poking a finger through her skirt, into her backside.

Lola couldn't help but yelp as she turned to see Larry grinning at her. Her cry had drawn the attention of the whole dining hall and they all stared at her, laughing at her. The temperature rose to one-million degrees, she felt like she was going to vomit, and this hideous troll leered at her, his grin spreading across his face, showing off his yellowing teeth. She still held her water bottle in her hand, so she launched it toward him, sending a cascade of water into his face, but he didn't melt away into nothing and the laughter didn't subside, so she kicked him in the shins and the whole world slowed down as if the Gods were reviewing the moment to decide upon her punishment.

Larry moved first. He shoved Lola on one shoulder, pushing her back out of the queue, closer to the seating area. He stood over her. Beads of water clung to his face—in his eyebrows, hanging off the end of his nose, magnifying the zits on his cheeks. "What you gonna do?" he said, moving closer so that his face was only inches from hers. "What you gonna do?"

She could taste the foul stink of his breath, could feel the heat radiating from him, could see the anger roiling in his eyes. Looking around for help, she saw only grinning faces, and the cafeteria staff busily serving others, oblivious to the event or deliberately turning a blind eye to it. Where were the teachers who were supposed to supervise at lunch?

He pushed her again forcing her to take another step back. Lola was powerless now. She'd made her move and her strength had deserted her. Those that observe from above had made their judgment and decided not to intervene. They had decided to leave her to suffer her punishment, and it was her stupid brother's fault. She knew if Larry placed another hand on her, she wouldn't have the strength to stumble back. She'd crash to the floor, defeated and humiliated where she'd be taunted by the laughter of the dining hall and suffer for the rest of her days.

"Back off, mate."

Larry's face shrunk away from her. He was still mouthing something: she could see the saliva clinging he his lips as he was spitting ire.

Two bodies had come between her and Larry. She recognised Mitchell's haircut, and after a glance assumed his companion was Tyler.

"Wha's it gotta do with you?" Larry said. He tried forcing his way past Mitchell and Tyler, but they made a solid wall.

"Back off," Mitchell repeated, this time through gritted teeth. With that, Larry slunk off to rejoin his mates. Lola watched him wipe his face with his sleeve and then grin.

Mitchell put his arm around Lola. "You okay?"

But before she could answer Mr Butcher was upon them.

"Tell him what happened," Mitchell said.

Lola was taken aback. She never took Mitchell for a snitch.

Then Butcher looked at the floor and saw the pool of water. "Whoever is responsible for this mess had better clean it up promptly."

No, she'd get no help there. "I'm going outside," she said, looking at Mitchell, hoping he'd follow.

27: TED

For the one-millionth time on their journey to the hospital, his mother told him that he didn't have to do it if he didn't want to.

Did he want to see Julius? The idea generated no feelings either positive or negative. All he felt about it, about almost everything, was neutral. He wanted it all to be done with. He had a hospital appointment coming up, so he couldn't see why this visit couldn't wait until then. Maybe after that hospital visit things would be normal again. Yes, he still held on to his anxiety about another potential heart operation, but that was a feeling from before–even that was almost normal compared to dealing with the fallout from his disappearance.

"When can I go back to school?" he asked, thinking that might help restore some kind of routine to his life.

"We need to speak to the school to set a date." Mum continued to concentrate on the road.

"Can it be soon?"

Ted watched his mother shift her focus and stare into the rear-view mirror for a long time. She held the glance for so long that Ted glanced over his shoulder to see what was worrying her, but there was nothing there.

"We'll see what the doctor says at your appointment."

"But if I'm okay, I can go back, right?"

She turned her head to look at the side mirror and sighed. "I suppose so."

Minutes later, they arrived at the hospital. Again, Heimlich was to meet them in the waiting area.

"If you want to leave at any time, just say," Mum said.

Ted nodded. "It'll be okay."

Ted sat quietly listening to his mum take shallow breaths. He watched the way she moved her arms up and down her thighs in time with her jerky breathing.

"I'll be fine, Mum," Ted said.

Heimlich appeared.

Ted noted that he seemed taller here than he had at home. The sterile environment no doubt made his suit stand out and while everyone else either huddled into themselves in fear or pain, he stood erect. He held out a hand which Ted shook.

"Young man, I thank you for coming."

Ted shrugged. "That's okay."

"We don't want you to feel uncomfortable or as if you're under any pressure to do anything in there."

"Okay."

"And listen, I'm sure your mum has prepared you for this, but seeing Julius in this state–physically and mentally–may cause distress. Is there anything you want to ask before we start moving?"

Ted thought for a moment and then rubbed at the scar on his lower back. "Other than the arm, are there other injuries? Scars or anything?"

"That's a good question. Are you interested in becoming a police officer?"

Ted didn't answer.

"It's very different to your case. It looks like his body had experienced severe trauma beyond the loss of the arm. There's evidence of multiple breaks which had been set and are healing."

"What do you think caused it?"

Heimlich smiled. "Anything I'd say would be speculation. The only time I've seen injuries like these was when a little boy got hit by a truck. Let's get moving."

As they walked along the corridor, Ted had to be hurried along a number of times by Mum. Ted was lost in thought about Julius. It made no sense for him to have been hit by a car months ago, to then disappear, only to turn up with those broken bones mostly healed. As he followed, he peered down corridors, wondering what procedures were carried out in each of the departments with names he never thought he'd be able to pronounce. He'd never had much of an interest in hospitals, in medicine, in biology before, but maybe it was an area he'd like to pursue in the future—once he'd put this behind him. Ted had come to the realisation that there was little more he could do than put it behind him. The events of the last seven months were closed off, but if he had to jump through a few hoops to prove that to others too, so be it. Doubts remained about whether he could move on, whether he had a future to move on to. Everything seemed so pointless, so hopeless.

Ted heard Julius before he saw him, rhythmically moaning, "Ted," as he breathed. He mimicked the creak of the door with an elongated, "Ted". Ted's presence in the room had no effect on the frequency or pitch of the Teds. Mrs Wright sat in the chair beside Julius's bed but did not react to their arrival. Heimlich had Ted stand in various places, sometimes shining a bright light on him, sometimes cloaking him in darkness, but it made no difference to Julius.

"Okay," said Heimlich, and urged Ted and Megan to leave.

Back in the corridor, Heimlich took hold of Ted's forearms and bent down to look him in the eye. "Anything?" he said, continuing to stare.

Ted thought for a moment. Memories of Julius had returned to him, but nothing from the last seven months. The memories were of seeing him around school with his friends, laughing and joking nothing more. Somehow, that was more tragic. Julius was once full of life, but now he was in some kind of stupor, muttering for no reason. Worse was his arm. Ted remembered Julius sprinting on sports day as part of the relay team, taking the baton in his hand, and sprinting around the corner, arms pumping as he tried and failed to make up ground on the other teams. He remembered him handing over the baton and his attention passing to the new runner. Julius was no longer a factor in the race, and he might never be a factor in any kind of race again.

"Nothing," Ted said. "It's just..."

"Just what?" Heimlich asked, his stare becoming more intense.

"It's just sad."

Ted felt a tear roll down his cheek. As ugly as he felt inside, at least he was feeling something again. Feeling ugly inside was normal, and therefore it was very welcome.

Heimlich released Ted and turned around and cursed.

Ted looked at Mum, and when she saw the tears welling in his eyes, she pulled him to her.

They might have remained frozen in that moment forever were it not for a change in the noise Julius emitted.

Heimlich had started to get excited, asking Julius to repeat what he said, but he'd returned to his 'Ted' mantra. Ted had a pretty good idea of what Julius had said, but he didn't feel like sharing that Julius had said, "Go home."

As they walked away from Julius's room, Mum continually looked back over her shoulder at Heimlich. She was muttering the whole time about how unfair it was.

Ted started to think about what had happened. While he'd accepted the missing seven months in his life, others hadn't yet. Mum still wanted answers, and he'd failed to deliver any. Heimlich was in charge of the investigation, and he was no closer to knowing the truth than when they'd disappeared. But there was nothing in his head that came to him when he saw Julius. As they walked across the car park, Ted felt weary. He always did when the sun shone on his back as it had on that day he'd woken by the river.

After they got in the car, Ted looked at his mum. Her face bore a pained expression, and a frown so severe Ted half expected her to burst into tears.

"Are you sure you don't remember anything?"

Ted was tempted to lie to make her feel better, but if he gave her a thread to tug on, she wouldn't let go until it had entirely unravelled. "No," he said, his honesty sending shoving daggers of guilt into his heart. "It meant nothing to me."

Mum gasped and her mouth hung open for a moment. "Maybe Julius doesn't mean you when he says, 'Ted'," she said. "You're not the only Ted around here."

Ted forced a smile. If it gave Mum comfort, so be it. Even though seeing Julius had failed to spark a memory, he was certain that when Julius said, "Ted," he had meant him.

Mum smiled. She patted him on the knee. "That's right, son. You're my Teddy Bear, and there's no one quite like you, but there are other Teds."

She stared in the rear-view mirror again.

28: MEGAN

After dropping Ted home, Megan told him she just had to pop out. She drove around the corner to Poplar Avenue. She had to pull up on the kerb some distance from her target.

There was no point reporting it to Heimlich; he'd be as ineffective as he was for the last seven months. What would he say? Lack of evidence? They'd already investigated? You can't go around harassing members of the public? But her Ted wasn't the only one with that name, and a prime candidate was right there in the village of Wiseham. Bloody Ted Hatcher. He was the only person in Wiseham, where she'd lived for over fifteen years, that made her skin crawl. She'd always felt guilty about the feeling of revulsion he stirred in her, but there was something very unsettling about the man and the way he'd stare without saying a word. It didn't help that her first encounter with him had been so strange. She was pregnant with Lola and taking a walk through the village, guiding Ted on his infant trike. Ted Hatcher had an extravagant garden back then—planted full of lovely flowers, once alive with colour, but he'd recently let it go. He stopped weeding and pruning, and it became wild. At first, it still looked pretty, but after a while, everything started to droop. Just as she passed his house, Hatcher had emerged from behind a bunch of wilted hollyhocks. Megan hadn't expected that, and she'd cursed at the man. She let go of the handle on the back of Ted's trike and had to grab it again to stop him from veering toward the road. Hatcher muttered something she didn't understand, and it was only later that she realised he might have been saying something about his mother, for it was only days later what he'd done came out. Hatcher's mother had died some weeks prior, but he didn't report it. He just left her in her bed. Some argued that it was for fraudulent purposes and claimed he continued to draw her pension and intended to do so for as long as he could, but charges were never brought against him as he was deemed to not have the mental wherewithal to carry out such a ruse. He was close to being sectioned, but an investigation by the social care team found him capable of looking after himself—no doubt only because the state had insufficient funding to house and look after all those that truly needed care. In the end, the assessment was that the death of his mother had resulted in only an episode in which he was unable to function, and after the funeral, he was considered to have recovered sufficiently to look after himself again. And so he had. He'd stayed in the house, letting it fall into disrepair, and while some in the village argued that he used to be a lovely, kind man, for Megan he was always the man who hid in the garden, spying on Ted.

It was that tendency to materialise from within the overgrown mess of the garden, or from the shadows of his stationary Land Rover and to stare at the children that had earned him the title of 'Child Catcher', no doubt started by an adult in the community rather than a child, and while many parents chastised their children for calling an innocent, old man horrible names, Megan accepted it and preached caution against him.

Maybe he'd remembered Ted from that day. Maybe he'd had his eye on him ever since. Maybe, many years later, he saw an opportunity to take Ted away from his home. What would he say when confronted with the accusation? Would he deny it? Would he come clean? Would Megan finally have her chance for vengeance?

She started the car and drove away from the house, intent on returning on foot later on when there were fewer eyes in the area.

29: LOLA

On the school bus back to Wiseham, Lola made her excuses with Jas briefly, blurting the words in her face before going back to sit with Lauren without waiting for a response.

Lauren stared at her as she sat down again, red-faced. "How come you used to be able to get up on stage and dance around, belting out a song, but you can't say two words to a friend without turning into a nervous wreck?"

Lola shrugged. "I don't know. It's different face to face."

"Stop taking everything so seriously all the time. If you don't want to do something, like going around a friend's house to do homework, just say. It doesn't have to be a big deal all the time."

"It is a big deal," Lola said. "My mum arranged it."

"So? At the moment it's not working for you. You're trying something different. You're growing, becoming a different person."

"Am I, though?"

Lauren pointed at Lola. "Of course you are. You're a warrior queen for standing up for yourself like that in the canteen. I'm proud of you."

"I don't know about a warrior. I just threw some water on him and kicked him in the shins."

"Yeah, but that's some proper bad girl shit. Most people would have let him get away with what he did. Not you."

When the bus reached its stop, they disembarked and headed across the road to the park. Once out of sight of the road, Lauren took out a cigarette and lit it. She took a long drag.

"I don't know what I would have done if Mitchell and Tyler weren't there. I reckon Larry would have hit me."

They sat down under the trees at the back of the park, and Lauren handed Lola the cigarette.

"You know, you really should show Mitchell your appreciation," Lauren said, leaning back on the grass. She waited for Lola to take a drag on the cigarette and held out her fingers to take it back.

Lola knew smoking wasn't good for her. She's been in the science lesson where they'd talked about the damage that smoking caused to the respiratory system. She'd been in the assembly in which they introduced the Kick Ash programme, and at the time she never thought she'd be the sort to take up smoking, but having tried it and realised how it calmed her, she didn't think it could do so much harm. Lauren had told her that if she gave up by the time she was in her mid-twenties, her body would be able to reverse all of the negative effects of smoking anyway, so there wasn't any real risk.

"I did show my appreciation. I said, 'thank you'."

"Thank you?" Lauren said, her eyes wide. "He'll want more than a bloody thank you."

"What do you mean?" asked Lola. She stared at the end of the cigarette as Lauren took another drag. Lola nodded her head, indicating that she wanted it back.

Lauren handed it to her. "You know what I mean. Show him how grateful you are."

Lola took a toke of the cigarette as Lauren winked at her. Lola furrowed her brow at her friend and passed the cigarette back. "How?"

"You don't get what I'm saying, do you?"

"I really don't."

Lauren stubbed out the last remnants of the cigarette and took hold of Lola's hand. "Sex."

Lola clapped a hand over her mouth. "I'm not doing that!"

"What, don't you like him?"

"I do like him, but, I mean, I've never even kissed a boy before."

"Yes, you have, you liar!" Lauren picked a daisy and threw it at Lola.

Lola picked the daisy from her lap. "Have not!"

"What about that kid in year six? Will?"

"You mean Jimmy?"

Lauren grinned and pointed at Lola. "Yeah, him."

"We never kissed!"

"Yes, you did!"

"We only went out for around three days. I let him hold my hand, but that's it."

"You let him hold your butt and that tit?" Lauren rolled around in laughter.

Lola watched Lauren giggling and had to stop herself from falling into a fit of laughter, too. How had she and Lauren drifted apart? The two Ls, that's what people used to call them. Lauren and Lola, and here they were, together again and raising 'ell. She knew Mum never approved, but it was a long time since she'd laughed like that. Of course, Lauren had been joking about the whole sex thing, hadn't she? Lola took a second to compose herself. "Lauren," she said. "Have you ever... done it?"

"What, held a boy's hand or touched his butt?"

"No..." Lola said. She looked away. She couldn't even say the word while making eye contact. "Sex."

Lauren looked to the ground. Eye contact wasn't a thing for this conversation. "Yeah," she said. "Of course."

"No way! Who with?"

"Loads of people."

"Like who?"

"Loads of people. No one you know."

Had she? Lola didn't think so. They were only thirteen, but why would she say it?

"So... are you gonna do it with Mitchell?" Lauren asked.

Lola shrugged. She had no intention of actually doing it, but if Lauren had done it, she didn't want to seem like a prude.

Lola was starting to feel awkward. She looked up, and she was almost pleased to see Tyler walking over. Or she was until Lauren opened her mouth again.

"Hey, Tyler," she called out with him still some distance away.

"Wassup?" shouted Tyler.

"You're going to have to up your game if you want to get some action."

Tyler looked puzzled. He trotted over and sat down.

"Lola's gonna be rewarding Mitchell for his heroics, but you miss out."

"Is she? What's he getting?"

Lauren made a hand gesture, sliding a finger into the hole made by finger and thumb of the opposite hand.

Tyler laughed. "She isn't!"

Lola sighed and shook her head. "No."

"Well, she would say that now," Lauren said. "She's gone all shy."

"Whatever," Lola said.

"As Mitchell's backup, don't you think Tyler deserves something?" Lauren asked.

Tyler looked at Lola. He propped his head up on his fist.

The silence hung in the air, thick, palpable.

"Okay, close your eyes," Lola said.

Lauren gasped as Lola stood up and approached Tyler.

Tyler pouted his lips and tilted his head back.

Lola stood over him. A little bit of gunk had gathered in the corner of his mouth, and the wispy hair on his top lip suggested he was almost ready for shaving. Lola gave his cheek a little pinch. "Cheers, Pal," she said and sat back down.

Tyler opened his eyes and stared at her in mock indignation. "Cheers, Pal? Cheers, Pal? Is that all I get? Seriously, next time I won't bother helping." Tyler folded his arms across his chest.

"Honestly though," Lola said, "thank you for what you did."

"No problem," Tyler said. "The guy's a dick."

"On the subject of dicks," Lauren said, "where's Mitchell?"

"His mum's taken him to the hospital to see Julius."

"Shit, yeah. I heard he's turned into a bit of a fruit loop since he came back." Lauren circled a finger around her temple.

Tyler rolled his eyes at Lauren. "He'll be all right in a few days, I'm sure. Your brother's doing okay, isn't he?"

Lola didn't respond. She was staring into space.

"Lola," called Tyler. He reached down and put his hand on her knee, giving her leg a shake. "Your brother's doing okay, isn't he?"

"Um, yeah," Lola said. "I think so."

A pang of guilt hit Lola. Since his return, she'd not spent any time with Ted. They'd always got on well. They had some great shared memories and when they were much younger, they'd often played together, so why hadn't she bothered with him since his return? When he disappeared, it was hard for her. Mum and Dad couldn't tell her what was going on, and at the time it felt like they were keeping stuff from her. Their attention was entirely on Ted and it seemed that she dropped off the radar altogether.

Lola reached up and touched her hearing aid.

But it hadn't been Ted's fault that she'd been forgotten by her parents. He always used to look out for her. Even when she started at Fenland Village Academy, he'd come to find her on the playground and make sure she was okay and knew where she had to go next.

Suddenly Lola had fingers waving in her face.

"Come in, Lola! Lola, are you in there?" Lauren said.

Lola batted her hand away and smiled. "Sorry, I was just..."

"We know what you were doing." Lauren laughed. "You were thinking about what you were going to do with Mitchell."

"Lol shook her head. "No, it's not that... I've got to go, that's all."

30: TED

Ted wondered if he'd done something wrong. Mum had dumped him in the house, alone, when they got back from the hospital and dashed off. He stood for a moment in the hallway. The light poured in through the glass panel, making the whole thing shine. It made the hallway too bright, but he couldn't look away. Around the periphery of the brightness were feathers of blackness, like tiny fingers reaching out, trying to venture further into the light. Why was he so bad with brightness these days? Had he been kept blindfolded for all his missing time? Had he been stuck underground like a mole? He looked at the light again, certain hands reached out from within. Was there something else beneath the surface? Ted felt a tingling sensation coming from the scar on his lower back, and a jolt shot up through to the top end. It was like an electrical current being run through his spine, pulsing, making a sound like 'ted, ted, ted, ted' but then as quickly as it appeared it was gone. Was that what Julius was referring to? The sound that came with the paralysing sensation? Ted's stomach groaned and he could feel the world closing around him, tiny black hands pulling the light away. He stumbled toward his bedroom, each footstep jolting electricity through his nerve endings and up his spine. He threw himself on his bed and felt immediate relief at no longer having to control his body; he could let it rest.

He didn't want answers. Every time he probed for them pain wracked his body. Not knowing was better than this. Ignorance *was* bliss. This was surely his body's way of telling him that whatever he'd suffered, he didn't need to relive it.

But if he was home alone, he couldn't stop his mind from wandering and it always meandered back to those missing months. If he was going to lie there alone, he'd end up wondering, and that would bring the pain. He felt a rumble in his stomach, like something moved inside, burrowing deeper.

A wave of nausea washed over him, and then he felt it in his throat, something solid, moving up. The feeling of sickness passed, but an obstruction remained in his throat. He tried to draw in a breath and, as he inhaled, he pulled something down with it, debris flaking down his oesophagus, tickling it. His mouth filled with water; the taste of the river overwhelmed his senses. He coughed into his hand and out came a lump of blackness. What was it? It looked like mud. He grabbed the towel he'd left on the floor from his earlier shower and wiped his hand clean. What was happening to him?

He heard a key rattling in the front door and was hit with a feeling of euphoric relief. If Mum was back, he could chat with her. Maybe Dad had got the afternoon off? Was it time for Lola to have finished school?

"Hello?" he called out.

"It's only me," Lola shouted back as she made her way up the stairs.

"Don't go," called Ted. "Come back and we'll chat."

"Just a minute," shouted Lola as she continued thudding on the steps.

She's not coming back, thought Ted and he could feel those fingers gripping the base of his spine again, but before they took hold, his door opened, and Lola stepped inside.

"What did you want to talk about?" Lola said, swaying from side to side.

Ted could smell the perfume she'd put on. That wasn't like her. "Come, sit down." Ted patted the end of the bed.

Lola crept over, seemingly thinking about each step, and perched on the end. She turned her head to face Ted.

"So how are things with you? I feel we've barely spoken since... you know." Ted said.

"I was thinking the same thing. Things are... okay." Lola shuffled back on the bed a little further.

Ted's nose twitched. He was sure that his sense of smell had improved. He sniffed at the air. "Lola, have you been smoking?"

Lola gasped and then held a finger to her lips. "Shush, you can't say anything."

"Relax, there's no one else here. Seriously though, smoking? How long have you been doing that?" Ted wasn't sure whether he should be saying anything. He'd only just been able to lure Lola in to speak to him, so he didn't want to preach at her, especially as it was probably a habit she'd formed because he went missing.

"I've only done it a couple of times," Lola said. "In the last couple of days." Her cheeks had reddened, like they always did when she'd been caught out. "And Lauren says it has no lasting effect if you quit young."

So, she'd started since he got back? He didn't know whether he should go in hard and tell her what a foolish thing to do, or if he'd be better to laugh it off to keep her there. He hated the thought of being left alone again. "You know that's bullshit, right?" Ted grinned at her.

"Yeah, I kinda figured..."

"So, you're hanging with Lauren again?"

"Yeah—don't tell Mum that either."

"Don't worry," Ted said. "I won't say anything. But go easy on the perfume; Mum will suspect something right away."

Lola smiled.

"How is the." Ted reached up and grabbed his earlobe. There was a time, when Lola was younger and there were fears her hearing could also degrade in her other ear, when Ted had tried to learn a little sign language, just in case it was needed. It wasn't, but Ted still fell into the practice of signing from time to time. Between them, it was a secret code, a conversation they could have behind Mum and Dad's backs.

Lola shook her head.

"Not good?" Ted said.

Lola shook her head again.

"You don't need another operation, do you?"

"I don't think so. The hearing aid's not working like it used to. It probably needs adjusting. Maybe I need a new one."

"When are you getting it checked out?"

Lola shrugged.

"You're kidding? Haven't Mum and Dad booked you in?"

Again, Lola just shook her head.

"You haven't told them, have you?"

"Don't say anything."

"Lola, it's your hearing. It's important."

"I know, but they've been so worried about you… just give them a bit of time for things to get back to normal."

Ted huffed. "Normal, hey? You think things can get back to normal?"

"I hope so."

"Come here," Ted said, opening up his arms for a hug.

Lola leant in, but as soon as she touched him, she backed away again.

"You're cold," she said.

He didn't feel cold. "Well, never mind. It was good to chat. You wanna watch a movie or something?"

Before they could decide on what to watch they heard the key in the door again.

"I'll be back," said Lola, hopping off the bed and sniffing her clothes. "I better go change."

31: SIMON

A-Mac had stayed late to complete Simon's appraisal which meant half an hour in the stuffy meeting room with the torn seats and the wobbly desk–the one that was no longer used for external meetings with clients and suppliers.

It was an utterly redundant process. Simon had completed few of his extra objectives, and A-Mac knew why, but he went through the rigmarole of reading through each objective and making Simon explain whether it had been completed, partially completed, started, or not yet commenced. And no, Simon hadn't completed the analysis of the failure codes reported by customers in the final quarter of the last financial year. In fact, Simon could not give a rat's arse about failure codes, response times, or any of his other measures. He didn't care if he didn't receive his pay rise for the year. He didn't care if he was put on a performance improvement plan. The whole job seemed utterly pointless, but he stopped just short of saying so.

Instead, he listened to A-Mac suck air through his teeth, watched him shake his head and scribble notes on his copy of the objectives and felt the creeping heat of the room make him sweat. He wanted out of the room and back to his desk. He wanted A-Mac to clear off so he could get back to his phone and check to see if Grant had been in touch, but A-Mac was intent on dragging out the appraisal to the full length of time scheduled.

As it crept toward the hour mark, and A-Mac had scribbled something in the last box on the appraisal sheet, he linked his fingers and nodded at Simon. "And do you have any feedback for me as your line manager?"

Simon gulped. He could have launched into a tirade about incompetence, about a lack of compassion, about the micro-management that drove everyone crazy. Instead, he thought he'd play nice. "No," he said, before grinning as widely as possible, a smile that would look false and forced, "but I did want to thank you for being so understanding, and continuing to be so flexible, while my family and I have been going through such a difficult situation."

A-Mac's mask momentarily slipped. He looked ready to hiss at Simon and reveal his forked tongue, but he was able to resume the façade. "That's okay, Simon. If there's anything else you need, do let me know, and we'll make sure it goes through the proper channels."

"Will do," Simon said. As A-Mac headed for the door, Simon discretely gave him the finger. Proper channels? No, he'd go over A-Mac's head if he needed something else and speak to someone with a little humanity and understanding.

Before returning to his desk, Simon checked his phone. There was a message from Grant: *Can you meet at The Boar at 10?*

The Boar was a drinkers' pub. There was no need to spend a penny on the décor when you had a faithful clientele who would always prop up the bar as long as the prices remained reasonable. It wasn't a complete dive—it had had a coat of paint since the smoking ban came in over a decade ago to get rid of the nicotine stains. Around the same time, some of the seats had been reupholstered and most were still intact, but it had no pretensions about what it was. Simon had been in a time or two before. It was far enough from where he was brought up for no one to be able to recognise him, so he could get served when he was underage, but it certainly wasn't the kind of place you'd go to socially for any other reason. Back then a pool table drew people into the room at the rear, and, after he bought himself a Coke which brought a look of disdain from the barman, he made his way there, keeping an eye out for Grant. He wasn't surprised to find the pool table still in situ. The baize fabric of the table had faded and thinned, the D redrawn with a marker pen, and small tears in the corners showed its age. On the lone table beside the unoccupied pool table, one man sat alone. The lighting in the back room was designed to best suit the table, so he was almost entirely in shadow, but the tiny glasses told Simon that he was looking at Grant.

"Thanks for coming, Mr Wallace." Grant spoke in a low voice. He held out his hand for a handshake but didn't stand.

Simon took his hand and was surprised by his firm grip.

"Before we get to your son's situation, I want to ask you to think about a few things. I don't need you to tell me. What does it mean to be human? Think about that."

Simon shrugged and looked over his shoulder. He could see into the other room, could see some of the men slumped at the bar, either lost in thought or just plain lost altogether. Knowledge was part of what made someone human. He'd read somewhere that what separated humans from other creatures was knowledge of our mortality. Was that what made those men sit at the bar like that every night, knowing that there was something very wrong with their lives, and there would be no second chances, no chance to change it before their ultimate demise…? He thought about how close he'd come to being one of their kin, could almost taste the alcohol, taste the sweet appeal of a life of oblivion.

"Okay, another question for you. Can you tell when someone isn't human?" Grant sipped from the half-empty pint glass in front of him. It looked like he was drinking some kind of dark ale.

Not human. His first thought was of A-Mac, the reptilian bastard—a coldness, a lack of compassion, a lack of humanity. What kind of answer was that? What makes someone inhuman is a lack of humanity!

"I can see it in your eyes, Mr Wallace; you're a thinker."

Simon nodded. "Call me Simon, please," he said. Mr Wallace always felt like his father's title.

"I saw the way you looked around the bar. You're in touch with people. You understand people. Not everyone is like that." Grant took another sip from his pint.

Simon did similar, drinking his Coke.

Grant nodded. "If you know what to look for, there are all sorts of social cues that we, as humans take part in. For instance, I had a drink, you did too."

Simon looked at his glass. Of course he'd taken a drink. He was thirsty, and there was a break in the conversation.

"Some people, you'll notice, don't follow these same conventions. You might hear that they are introverts, or that they have social anxieties, and in some cases, that might be true. But what about if some of them aren't human at all?"

Simon felt himself deflate. What was he doing here with this nutter?

"I know you're not going to want to hear this, Simon, but there's a chance that your boy isn't your boy anymore."

Simon exhaled noisily and threw his arms out. He wasn't normally one for elaborate gestures, but it just came out. "What are you saying? He's been replaced by an alien decoy?" Simon drained the rest of his drink.

"Not aliens, Simon. We've managed to access hundreds of secret government files and not one of them contains any evidence of actual alien encounters."

Simon shook his head. "What are you saying? What do you want from me?"

"We're not talking about something extra-terrestrial here, Simon, but a sub-terrestrial threat."

Simon wanted to get up and leave. He'd heard enough. But if he'd learned one thing about lunatics and fanatics it was that if you let them talk long enough, their entire argument tended to fall apart. If he listened to Grant spout nonsense for just a few more minutes, he'd come to realise just how ridiculous his argument was. Yes, when he'd sat down with this man, he had an element of doubt about Ted, but if this theory was the alternative, he was well and truly on the road to recovery from his delusion.

"So, something underground?" Simon rubbed his chin.

"See, I know you're human," Grant said. He leant forward and adjusted his spectacles. "I can see your doubt and the discomfort it has put you in. You can't just get up and leave though, that wouldn't be normal, and that's what most of us are. Normal. Those that aren't, they're forever struggling to imitate what's normal, to do what a normal person would do. I can read people. It's what I do. I know when someone's normal and when they're trying to put it on."

Simon nodded. He'd seen this, too. The fanatics attempt to normalise themselves, to split the community into normal, and other. "So, what is it?" Simon asked, "This subterranean threat?"

Grant leant back. "You won't believe me, and I'm not expecting you to at this stage. You'll need more proof. I'll tell you what to look for. If your son is one of them, he will be drawn to the earth. Not only that, he'll struggle to control his temperature. Beyond that, it's all of the social cues that we've talked about. Pay attention; is he normal, or is he merely striving to be?"

Simon looked to the ceiling. Cobwebs clung in the corners. Again, he doubted his son. He looked at Grant. With his mismatched eyes, he was the one who wasn't normal. "You still haven't told me what these things are." Could he trust this guy who hadn't even revealed his full name? If anyone was out of sync with reality, it was him. "What are you saying that my son may be?"

"This is the point where I'll lose you. What I say next, you won't be able to think about it rationally. You'll get up and leave. You'll think I'm nuts. You'll probably report me to that policeman friend of yours, Heimlich, is it? But the doubts will come back, Mr Wallace. And when they do, I'll be here for you."

"Okay," Simon said. "Say it. Say whatever it is that's going to 'lose' me."

"I'm going to try to explain. I know you won't want to hear this, but I have to try. These things are as old as humanity itself. They're mentioned in the oldest texts in existence. I'm talking about what you've probably heard referred to as demons."

Simon rolled his eyes.

"And there it is. The eye-roll. That's the point. It's always the point."

Simon stood up. "Why do you do this?"

Grant stood too. "It's not biblical. It's not Good versus Evil. It's not God versus Satan, but it is real, Mr Wallace."

Simon opened his mouth, but there was nothing more to say. He shrugged and turned away.

"Don't lose my number," called Grant, and if he said anything else, Simon didn't hear it. He moved past the bar into the earshot of a couple of mumbling drunks and was soon outside in the night air.

He stood, looking up at the moon. He rubbed his face. Demons: red-skinned beasts with horns, half-man, half-goat creatures, tails. What a crackpot. He knew it was only a matter of time before rationality went out of the window. He tore the card with Grant's number on it in two and dropped it into the drain at the side of the road. At least he could go home and believe in his son again. He needed some refreshment first. En route home, there was a much nicer pub: The White Swan. It wouldn't hurt to pop in there to rid himself of some of Grant's nonsense. A drink or two would do him good, he was sure of that.

32: TED

A great thirst hit Ted as he woke. He struggled out of bed, his gut inflated to the size of a football. Had he eaten too much popcorn while watching *The Princess Bride* with Lola? He stumbled out of his room and into the hall. It was dark, and he had no idea of the time. Dad's shoes weren't in their normal spot, so he wasn't home from work yet... but it seemed later than that. He kept moving, placing a hand on the wall to help him balance as he made his way to the kitchen. Moonlight shone through the kitchen window. No one had bothered to draw the blinds. Was that because Dad wasn't home yet? But where was Mum? Didn't she used to stay up and wait for him? She should have been in the living room curled up on the sofa either reading a novel or watching a film. Had they changed their habits so much? Didn't she wait up for him anymore? Weren't they as close as they used to be? Had his disappearance caused his parents' marriage problems? He had friends whose parents had split up, and some of them blamed themselves...

His stomach cried out again and his throat was so dry that each breath sandpapered his gullet. A single glass stood on the draining board which he filled from the tap. From the kitchen window, he could see the river. A duplicate moon reflected there.

He took a sip of the water, but it tasted tainted; it tasted of chemicals.

The duplicate moon wavered. That was the water he wanted. He wanted to cup his hands into the river, catch a taste of the moon. The reeds at the water's edge waved at him, beckoning him toward them. The back door was locked, but the key was in it. Ted left the house and made his way down the path. The concrete paving slabs were too hard and too cold beneath his feet, so he took a step to the right to walk on the grass the rest of the way to the gate. The earth had absorbed some of the day's warmth and felt comforting beneath his feet, and the lush grass pleasantly brushed against the soles of his feet. The security light flicked on, and the moon in the river was lost, seemingly swallowed by the water. He could get it back. If he hurried, he could dive in and fish it out. He passed through the gate. A few steps later he was on the riverbank, the warm mud beneath him feeling like home. The breeze passing through the reeds carried their cheers, welcoming him as they held their arms aloft in elation at his return. He bent down, knowing the level of the water was too low to reach, but he could dive in, could take back to the moon. He could hear voices whispering through the reeds, calling his name, telling him to come home.

As he moved toward the water, he felt suddenly restricted, arms around his body stopped him from reaching his destination. They weren't like the arms that were calling him; they were strong, restrictive.

"What are you doing?" came a voice he recognised as his father's.

"Going home," he said, but then the pressure on his stomach was too much and a tide of whatever was inside him came out in a great torrent and the blackness washed over him again.

33: SIMON

They were both covered in filth and Simon couldn't get a word of sense out of Ted. His freezing body was covered in some kind of mud. He was sure he'd heard Ted vomit, but there was no sign or smell of sick, just river mud that stunk of stagnant water. Considering the river outside was always relatively fast-flowing, there was no reason why it should be stagnant water they stunk of unless Ted had been messing around in a pond... but where? Why?

"Ted," he called again. He wrapped him in a towel. His skin felt cold to the touch and like rubber... inhuman. No, he couldn't let thoughts like that into his head. He propped Ted up against the kitchen units, detoured to lock the back door and went upstairs to start a bath running.

While upstairs, he heard Lola's door creak open. "Everything okay?" she said through a haze of sleepiness.

"Nothing to worry about," Simon said, looking at his daughter. When had she got so big? "Go back to sleep."

Simon looked down at himself and saw the awful state he was in, almost covered head-to-toe in mud. Luckily Lola had been too dozy for his appearance to register, and she returned to her room.

On the way downstairs he took his phone from his pocket. The black mud had seeped inside somehow, and he had to wipe the phone on a clean part of his trousers.

He went to his contacts and called Megan. By the time he returned to Ted, the call had gone to voicemail. Where was she? He hung up.

"Ted, how are you?"

Ted's eyes were closed, but he was breathing normally. His temperature still felt too cold for Simon's liking. "Ted," he called again.

This time Ted responded but it was the kind of nonsense one might mutter in their sleep.

He looked at his phone again and scrolled through the contacts. Doctor Hodder had said he could call any time if there was an emergency. This felt like an emergency.

He spoke to her as he checked on the bath. She had more questions than he had answers. How long had he been outside? What state was he in when he found him? Was he talking?

She stayed on the phone, waiting for Simon to lift Ted up the stairs. Her advice on the next steps would be based on Ted's reaction to being bathed. If he woke and was lucid, then he could wait until his check-up the next day. If he remained in a sleep-like state, urgent care would be needed.

Simon checked the bath again. He needed to get Ted's temperature up, but he didn't want to scald the boy. Next, he had to decide whether he should strip him or not. For the sake of ease, he pulled off his pyjama top before placing him into the bath.

Ted jolted upright and sucked in the air.

"It's okay," Simon said, again checking the temperature of the water before trying to look Ted in the eyes.

Ted turned to him, but there didn't seem to be any recognition. Was it possible Ted didn't know who he was? Was it possible that it wasn't Ted at all? Had he been trying to return to the water, to the subterranean world?

"Dad?" Ted reached a hand out to touch him.

Immediately Simon felt worms of guilt wriggling in his stomach. How could he doubt this boy, this weak boy who'd been through a nightmare scenario was really his son? He peered into the water, already become entirely black with the filth from Ted's body. "You okay?" he asked.

Ted took a second. He was staring into the corners of the room. "I think so," he said. "What happened?"

"You were outside. I had to stop you from jumping into the river."

Ted looked blankly at Simon. "Why would I do that?" he asked. His chest heaved and he started to sob.

"Hey, it's okay. It's okay. You're safe now." Simon leant over the bath and hugged his son.

What's happening to me, Dad?"

"We'll find out," Simon said. "We'll find out."

After a moment, Ted broke the embrace. "This water's disgusting," he said, looking down.

"I'll get you a towel." He fetched one from the airing cupboard, helped Ted out of the bath and wrapped him in the towel. While Ted dried himself again, he updated Hodder, who confirmed it was best to bring Ted in tomorrow, as planned, and when he hung up, he tried to call Megan again.

34: MEGAN

The second call stopped Megan from entering the bedroom. She quickly switched off her phone and looked in at the sleeping, old man. He hadn't stirred. But maybe this was a bad idea.

Breaking into Ted Hatcher's house had been so easy that she didn't think she could even call it breaking in—nothing had been broken. Once certain the kids were asleep, she'd crept out of the house. She'd dressed entirely in black to make herself harder to see and tried to avoid passing under any streetlights en route to Poplar Avenue.

As she'd passed through the park, she'd seen some kids still out. Didn't their parents care about them at all? They were gathered under the trees at the far end of the park, too far away to be able to identify which meant they wouldn't be able to identify her either. She heard the laugh of a young girl and swore it was that awful Lauren that Lola used to be friends with. Thankfully she'd been able to quash that particular friendship.

Poplar Avenue had returned to a normal volume of vehicles. The press had either retired for the night or were camped out at the hospital. There was no way Julius was going to be released any time soon, so they might have been tipped off that the hospital was a better place to wait for a story. Both of the Wright's cars were out, so both parents were no doubt at the hospital. Had Alesha ever left?

She didn't have time to ponder Julius's situation; she'd reached Hatcher's house. In the moonlight, it didn't look particularly menacing. The detail of the decay was lost in the low light of the night, and the little bungalow looked almost charming. The weeds were still an ugly mess, but they'd grown tall in the recent hot weather which meant she'd be in cover as she crept around to the back of the house.

As she passed his Land Rover, she peered through the windows, seeing only neglect, not the tools of abduction she'd expected to find. She continued around the side of the house. She'd only intended to look in. She wanted to spy into his rooms to see if there was anything untoward. Were there any trinkets from the boys he'd abducted? Was there rope, tape, or anything he could use to hold them? But the first room she looked in was his bedroom. The curtain was open just a crack, and what she saw disgusted her. On either side of the bed were boxes and boxes of clutter. She could see his chest rising beneath the bedding, but it was clear he lived like an animal in there. He was a hoarder, and things were piled up everywhere. She continued around the bungalow. Next was the kitchen. The sink was piled with plates, some dirty, some having been washed, but not looking particularly hygienic. It was at this point her phone rang for the first time. She'd cupped her hand over her jacket pocket to reduce the noise and let it go to voicemail. She did not dare pull it from her pocket where it would be heard by neighbours who might have their windows open. Once it had finished ringing, she withdrew it and placed it on silent. It had been Simon who had called, no doubt wondering where she was when he got home. She'd tell him she'd gone for a walk. It would be mostly true.

At the side of the house, a door led into the kitchen. Even as she tried the handle, Megan didn't intend to go inside, but the door had opened so quickly, and silently too, that she felt compelled to enter.

The stink of the kitchen brought bile racing into her mouth. She swallowed it back down and grimaced at the acidic taste. A bin in the corner overflowed onto the floor. Hatcher's diet seemed to consist largely of canned fish, with some cans sitting open on the sides, and others spilling from the bin. Stacks of local newspapers covered the table. Megan speculated that he could have been tracking the stories, monitoring the latest news, keeping an eye on the press to see if they were close to catching him.

Megan sneaked into the hall narrowed by boxes lining either side. She peered into a couple: women's clothes, possibly his mother's. She came to another door and quickly plotted the route she'd taken outside the house. No, this wasn't his bedroom. She pushed the door ajar and peered in— not his bedroom, but a bedroom, nonetheless. The lump in the bedding indicated it was occupied. Was he holding someone here right now? Megan stared at the bed, looking for a sign of movement. Should she go over and rescue whoever he held captive? What if it was an associate of his? A silent accomplice that remained in hiding? What if she woke someone and they attacked her?

Looking at the size of the lump within the bedding it didn't look like a large person. Movement was limited or non-existent, so they were in a deep sleep, perhaps even drugged. Creeping up to them would do no harm.

This room was absent of the clutter that blighted the rest of the house Megan noted as she stepped on the plush carpet. This room was practically taken from a show home. She kept her eyes on the bed. Why wasn't it moving? Even in deep sleep, you'd expect movement... Then she remembered the scandal, the way that he'd kept his mother in bed for weeks after her death. She couldn't still be there, could she? He couldn't have got the body back, not after what had happened? Megan couldn't help but sniff at the air, expecting the smell of death, but instead, she picked up the smell of lavender, tainted somewhat by the tuna smell from the kitchen.

She moved toward the head of the bed and gasped when he saw the face resting on the pillow. The sheer white colour of it immediately put the idea of a skeleton into her mind, but this had the smooth curves of a mannequin. Megan pulled back the covers to see that the rigid plastic body was dressed in an old-fashioned nightgown. Had he dressed it like his mother?

Megan backed out of the room. She needed to see what the crazy, old man kept by his bed. But it was while she stood outside the room, having pushed the door ajar to look in that her phone rang again. Thankfully it was on silent, so it just buzzed as it vibrated away, and she was able to pull it out and switch off the phone.

Why had Simon called twice? Was it something urgent? What if something had happened while she'd left the kids alone? That was twice she'd gone out and left Ted in one day. She was almost asking, no, begging for him to be taken away from her again. She looked around. What was she doing trespassing in this old man's house? Yes, it was disgusting, but she'd seen nothing to indicate he was a child catcher. She had to get out of there.

When she turned to retrace her steps, she caught a box with her knee, causing a waft of stale air to hit her. She pulled back one of the flaps and reached in, her hand quickly finding warmth, moisture. Even in the dark, she could tell the box was full of mud. Why would anyone do that? As her disgust with him built again, she remembered her duty toward her children. Hatcher could wait. She left by the side door that led into the kitchen, pulled the door closed, and stayed close to the weeds until she was back on the pavement.

There was no need to hide anymore. She was just out taking a late-night walk, nothing wrong with that. Once clear of Poplar Avenue, and already picking up her pace in her eagerness to get home, she pulled out her phone, switched it on, and called Simon back.

35: TED

Emptiness washed over Ted as he rode in the back of the car to the hospital. Mum and Dad weren't speaking, and the radio was at such a low volume the babble of the local morning show's DJs was barely audible and more of an annoyance that an accompaniment to their journey. Ted had felt the best way to get over missing seven months was to pretend they didn't happen, to accept the time was lost, and try to get back to normal. Last night's episode (and what kind of word was that to explain it, anyway?) made it obvious that there would be no forgetting it and moving forward. There was still something wrong with him which would mean issues would be ongoing, he'd be in and out of hospital, and now and then he'd black out and lose control of his body. Perhaps he'd throw himself in the river and drown and it would all be done with. He looked at his parents. Mum gazed out of the window, her face pale and drained. Sitting behind Dad, he couldn't see much of him other than the way his fingers gripped the gearstick. They were red where he clung on too tightly, too full of tension. If he slipped into the water and disappeared forever, at least they wouldn't have to worry anymore.

With both of his parents, Doctor Hodder and the specialist, Doctor Donaldson, in the cramped consultation room, the temperature rapidly rose. Ted could feel himself drying out. Pain needled his sides (his kidneys, he wondered?) and his mouth was a desert.

Doctor Hodder took Ted to another room, measured him, took his blood pressure, and took a swab from the inside of his mouth which felt like a fingernail scraping against sandpaper.

"Can I take your blood?" she asked.

Ted nodded.

"Have you had any problems having blood taken in the past?"

Ted shrugged. "No, never." They were a normal part of Ted's life.

"Okay. Hold out your left arm for me."

Doctor Hodder ran a finger up his arm, tracing a vein. "Quite dark, your veins. Have they always been like that?"

"I don't know." Ted looked at the vein on his left arm, and then the one on his right. The one on the left definitely looked darker.

As the needle pierced the skin, the smell of mud and stale water wafted into the room. Ted gagged.

"Missed it." Doctor Hodder wiped the trickle of blood with a piece of cotton wool, but it wasn't red, it was black. She looked at it and her brow formed a wrinkle. She placed it in a test tube and then fetched a fresh needle. "Sorry about that."

This time the needle hit the spot. Ted watched it fill with blood, this time of the right colour. Maybe he'd imagined what he'd seen before.

Together, they re-entered the consultancy room. Mum and Dad held hands, and Doctor Donaldson had a stern look on his face, like a headmaster delivering a particularly serious message during an assembly.

"Welcome back, Ted," Donaldson said. He pointed to the empty seat which Ted sat in.

"We are still at a loss as to exactly what happened to you since November, but there are clues which I'm going to talk to you about now."

Ted nodded.

"When you first came to us you were seriously malnourished, and it's good to see you've regained a little weight, but not as much as we would have liked. Do you have much of an appetite?"

"No. When I eat, I get full quickly. I've been drinking a lot."

"Yes, that's another indicator. First, it seems that you were on an incredibly restricted diet which has resulted in shrinkage of the stomach. If you try to eat a healthy portion size, this will again expand to a normal level. I've given your mother some information on a balanced diet."

Ted glanced at the stack of leaflets on Mum's lap.

"I understand you've been feeling tired, suffering headaches, and you've felt like you're going to blackout?"

Ted nodded.

"All of these are symptoms of iron-deficiency anaemia. It's a lack of healthy red blood cells. Do you know what the red blood cells do?"

Ted was sure this had been covered in science, but it wasn't his strongest subject. He shook his head.

"The red blood cells carry oxygen to the body's tissues and to the lungs and get rid of carbon dioxide. If they're not doing what they should, it would explain why you feel sluggish. I've prescribed some iron tablets which will help to resolve this, but it also may indicate something about what you went through."

Ted leant forward. Could it be that he was about to find out where he'd been?

"Your desire to drink the river water, the habit you've formed of eating mud, can all be explained by this condition."

What was this? He hadn't been eating mud. Where had they got this idea?

"The river water here is high in iron, so your body sought it out to try to replenish your depleted stocks. Similarly, soil can be high in iron. It's logical to suggest that your diet over that time could have consisted of a similarly-constituted soil, and water containing similar chemicals."

Dad leant forward. "He was fed on mud and river water?"

"Mr Wallace, don't get me wrong, Ted would not have survived on such a diet, but I believe that what he was eating was perhaps supplemented by this. I would imagine fish caught by the river, perhaps baked in a layer of mud—a primitive practice carried out in this region, I believe."

Dad leant forward, placing an elbow on the desk and resting his head in the palm of his hand. "Do you suspect he was held underground? By something living in an underground river?"

"That sounds rather like something from the realm of fantasy. I'm not about to suggest he was kidnapped by subterraneous beings." Doctor Donaldson smirked.

Ted looked across at Dad, hoping to see a glimmer of a smile, hoping he was making some kind of weird joke rather than making such an outlandish suggestion. Instead, he sat up straight and adjusted his top.

"Now, Ted," Doctor Donaldson had bent down to look him in the eye. "If you're okay with this, we want to send this information to the police as it might help with their investigations. Is that okay with you?"

Ted nodded.

Doctor Hodder placed a form on the desk and took a pen from his pocket to place beside it. "Ted if you could sign this, and Mum, Dad, we need one of you to countersign."

"What is it?" Megan asked.

"An information release form covering Ted's medical records and what we've spoken about today."

Ted took the pen and scribbled his signature on the form.

Mum picked up the sheet of paper and read it through before adding her signature.

"Now, Ted," said Doctor Hodder, handing him a notebook, "to help us track your recovery, we're going to ask you to record a few things for us."

Ted nodded. He opened the book and saw that it was a typical exercise book: simple lined pages with a margin.

"We want you to record what you eat, and also if you get any strange cravings for anything. I know it sounds weird, but if you feel like eating a mouthful of mud, write it down."

"Okay," Ted said.

"And in the back, write down anything you think might be important in terms of the last seven months. If you remember something but can't place the memory, write it down. If you have a dream that you think is relevant, write it down. If you get a sense of déjà vu about something, write it down. Over time, it might be that there's some commonality that will lead to a clue. Is that all okay?"

"That's fine."

"Okay," Donaldson nodded at Hodder, and she nodded back. "Do any of you have any further questions?"

Ted looked from one parent to the other. They seemed poised to say something, but both sat with their mouths hanging open. "When can I go back to school?"

"That's a good question," said Hodder. "It's important to get back to a routine as soon as possible, but the anaemia is still something of a concern. We'd suggest a phased return, so maybe mornings first of all, building up so that you're in for full days by the end of the school year. How does that sound?"

Ted nodded. "Sounds good."

"Well if there's nothing else," Donaldson said, "thank you for your time this morning. We'll send a follow-up appointment out to you for around ten days."

As they made their way out of the hospital, Ted smiled. At least there was a reason for all that had happened so far, no matter how weird it was. He gripped his notebook tightly, hoping that when he filled it out it would provide more answers.

36: LOLA

It had been a day marked by pointed fingers and whispers. Lola was used to the school rumour mill and had heard plenty of stuff about Ted while he was missing, but this time they were very definitely talking about her.

She stopped Jas in the corridor as they came out of science for lunch. "Jas, what are people saying about me?"

"At least I know why you didn't want to come round after school yesterday," Jas said, taking a step back from Lola.

Lola sighed. "I just needed a break from studying and homework. It was nothing personal. Now tell me, what have people been saying?"

"Slut!" came a shout from the other end of the corridor, followed by a load of giggling and the sound of feet trampling in the corridor as they fled.

"Why are people saying that?" Lola turned toward the sound before returning her gaze to Jas.

"So, it's not true?" Jas raised her eyebrows.

"When are any of the rumours ever true?"

Jas stared at the floor as she answered: "Okay, Lola, what I heard is that you shagged Mitchell against a tree in the park."

Lola shook her head and her jaw hung open. She took a second before answering. "That's ridiculous. Who'd you hear that from?"

"Lola, literally everyone's talking about it."

"But who started it?"

"How long have you known me, Lola? Since when have I been at the centre of the social circle? I was the last one to hear it. Why don't you ask your new best friend?" Jas stared over Lola's shoulder.

Lola turned to see Lauren walking toward her.

"There's the most talked about girl in school!" Lauren grinned.

Jas rolled her eyes. "You're still welcome to come over to do homework," she said, but left without waiting for a response, not waiting to get tangled up in Lauren and Lola's conversation.

"You don't need to hang out with Jas no more. Your reputation has just gone through the roof!" Lauren beamed.

Lola's mouth fell open. "People are calling me a slut and pointing and laughing at me."

"Yes, and they finally know who you are!"

Lola frowned. "Did you start this?"

"Me?" Lauren pointed at herself. "No. I heard some year nine girls talking about it. I just pointed out who you were."

"Who started it then?"

"I dunno."

"Have you seen Mitchell today?"

"Why? You going back for round two?" Lauren laughed, her mouth open so wide her gum almost fell out.

Lola glared at her.

"Relax, babe. I know you've not really done anything with Mitchell... yet."

Lola shook her head and held out her hands. She didn't know what to say or do.

"Look, I don't reckon Mitchell's in today. I'll see if I can find Tyler and ask him, okay?"

"Do you think he started it?"

"He might have done. Not deliberately, but if he told someone what we were talking about... you know how these things spread."

"Well can you start telling people it's not true?"

"You don't wanna do that."

"Why not?" Lola put a hand to her forehead.

"That only makes it look truer. Ride it out. If you play it right your popularity will hit the roof."

From the corner of her eye, Lola saw more girls pointing at her.

"I'm not sure I want that kind of popularity."

"Okay, catch me outside in about ten. I'll tell you what I've found out."

Lola continued down the corridor toward the toilets. One of Larry's dipshit mates stood outside the boys' toilets, which she had to pass to get to the girls'. Lola considered turning her back but a glance over her shoulder revealed a group of silly year 9 girls who no doubt would have come up with some immature name for her, so she decided to stride past.

Had she not been distracted by the girls, she might have noticed the boy outside the toilets signalling. When the hand wrapped around her neck, she was utterly unprepared, and all of the air went out of her. She felt her feet scrabbling beneath her as she was pulled into the boys' toilets.

Larry pushed her against the wall, forcing her to take in a gulp of air, tasting the vile aroma of the boys' toilet—ancient piss and bodily odour.

"I thought this would be a good spot for some slut fishing, and I caught me a big one!"

Larry's stupid mates laughed. The shorter one loitered in the doorway, no doubt keeping an eye out. The other tucked into a sandwich. How could anyone eat in there?

"I hear you're sick of taking your brother's space dick now and you're taking a bit of Mitchell's black dick."

Lola tried to draw in a breath, but with Larry's hand around her throat, she could only take in the tiniest gasp.

When he adjusted his grip on her, Lola had time to draw a breath, but he pushed hard again, forcing a slew of drool to run out of her mouth and onto his hand.

"Did you just spit on me?"

Lola couldn't move. She could feel the pressure building in her head. Larry's mate stopped eating the sandwich and stared at her, a look of concern growing on his face.

Lola stamped on Larry's foot. It wasn't hard, but it was enough to distract him, enough for him to loosen his grip and she was able to drop her shoulder to release her rucksack, giving her enough room to squirm out. She pushed past the guard by the door and fell into the corridor holding her throat.

The gang of year nine girls came out of the toilet as she was lying in the corridor.

"What's she doing down there?" one of them said with a look of disgust on her face.

Larry emerged from the toilets. He mocked zipping up his trousers. "My big, old cock was a bit too much of a mouthful for her, but she did insist on sucking us all off."

The girls laughed, and Larry and his friends stepped over her and started to walk away. "This isn't over," Larry said, looking back at her and blowing a kiss.

Lola got up. Her rucksack was still in the toilets. A boy was walking by, one she'd been at primary with, (one she'd briefly held hands with). "Jimmy," she said, "I don't suppose you could get my rucksack from the boys' toilets?"

"What's it doing in there?"

"Just some boys messing around," she said. Why couldn't she tell the truth? Why was she the one who felt ashamed?

Jimmy went into the toilets but returned empty-handed.

"Wasn't it in there?" Lola couldn't remember any of the boys carrying it out with them.

"It was, but..." Jimmy looked down the corridor in case anyone was listening. "Someone shoved it in the urinal. I'm not touching that. Sorry."

"That's okay."

"Do you want me to tell someone?"

"No," said Lola. "Thanks anyway." And when Jimmy had disappeared around the corner, she returned to the toilets, holding her breath, and plucked her rucksack from where it sat, soaking in the pooling urine of a blocked urinal.

37: SIMON

The waterproof box had come free with the GoPro he'd bought some years before, back when he hoped adventure holidays with the kids—mountain biking, snorkelling, hiking—would become a thing. The GoPro had been out of the box a few times but never used in anger. The waterproof box, however, had never been touched. It was still in its packaging at the back of his wardrobe with other ill-considered purchases and unwanted gifts.

As soon as they'd got home, Megan had called the school to discuss Ted's return. The Head of Year was able to get cover for her lesson, so Megan and Ted had gone almost immediately to the school, leaving Simon to consider what had been discussed. He couldn't get Grant's ideas about demons out of his head. Yes, that part was ridiculous, but the bit about subterraneous creatures seemed to have some weight considering what Donaldson had said. While he'd destroyed Grant's card, the number was still on his phone. Maybe if he could pull him away from the precipice of religious fanaticism, he might get some sense from him.

Grant answered on the first ring. "Mr Wallace. What have you seen?"

"I'm not interested in talking about my son as the pawn of some kind of demonic creatures; that's off the table before we begin, okay?"

"Okay, Mr Wallace. I'm listening. Talk."

Simon put one hand on his brow. He couldn't believe he was talking to this man again. "There's evidence to suggest that Ted was kept underground—fed on mud and river water."

"As expected."

Simon moved the phone away from his ear and placed it on the table, on loudspeaker. He didn't want this man's voice so close to him.

"You talked about creatures under the ground..."

"Mr Wallace, when I spoke of demons, you have to think about where this term comes from."

"I don't want to talk about demons."

"We can call them what you like, but let me put this into perspective for you... where do demons come from?"

"Hell?"

"And, biblically, geographically, where is Hell?"

"Beneath us."

"And are you a religious man?"

Simon thought for a moment. He'd been brought up in a Christian household. He'd been christened. He'd married in a church, but no, he didn't believe that there was a God out there, not after the hand his family had been dealt. "No."

"So, you would argue that what's in the bible can be perceived as a collection of stories."

"Okay."

"Now these stories have elements of truth in them, but like any story, they get blown up, exaggerated over time."

"I guess."

"Consider Heaven. Now, what would make people think that goodness was above them? People like parallels. They like to explain what they don't understand."

Simon nodded. "If there was something below..."

"Exactly. There is evidence of these subterraneous creatures going right back throughout our history."

"But how do we know they're bad?"

"If they're not up to no good, why are they hiding?"

"If I accept that these creatures exist, and that they took Ted, what makes you think he's no longer himself?"

"Watch him. See how he acts and you tell me."

Simon cradled his head with both hands. The words kept coming out, but he couldn't stop them. "I think he was trying to go back. Last night, I caught him by the river."

"Now I have to say, Mr Wallace, the geographical features, the access points to the subterranean world, are not my specialism, but I have colleagues who can talk to you about that, but if you find anything suspicious, don't interfere. Speak to us. Let us resolve it."

"I'm trying to find evidence. I've got a camera. I'm going to set it up in the river."

"Okay, Mr Wallace. Let me know what you find."

"I will."

"And thanks for calling back."

Simon terminated the call and pushed the phone away as if it was somehow tainted, as if it had done something sinful.

Next stop was the shed. He found a spool of garden wire and attached it to the camera box. He turned on the camera and its light, enclosed it in the box, and lowered it into the river, wrapping the end of the wire around the gatepost. He'd fish the box out later to see what it uncovered. He had to go to work.

38: TED

Mum had dropped Ted back at the house and left again saying she had somewhere she needed to go. The return to school meeting had been a partial success: yes, he was allowed to go back in for the mornings and his time at school would gradually increase, but he was being placed back in year 9. He could understand why; he'd missed huge chunks of the GCSE course, and he didn't have the stamina to do extra catch-up work. It would mean no longer being in classes with his friends, (who hadn't even bothered to try to get in touch with him since he came back) and a little bit of repetition at the start of the next school year. It meant that the next few weeks at school would be for no more than getting into a routine again, so he wouldn't have to stress too much about that.

He entered the house and called out, "Hey!" There was no answer. Dad would have been at work, and maybe Lola was around her friend's house, or secretly smoking somewhere. He walked through to the kitchen and glanced down at the GoPro box on the table. He couldn't think of any reason why that would be out. Ted left the kitchen again. He didn't want to look out of the window toward the river; he didn't know what kind of effect it would have on him. He tried to tell himself that his actions from the previous night were driven by his iron deficiency, a deficiency that the tablets would resolve, so looking out of the window would be no problem... but he didn't want to risk it.

On his way to his bedroom, when he passed the bottom of the stairs, he heard a brushing sound. He listened for a moment and thought he heard a sniffle too. "Lola!" he called. "You up there?"

"No!" came a shout back. It was definitely Lola.

The brushing sound continued as he made his way upstairs. He was out of breath by the time he reached the top, and he had to take a moment to stabilise before moving along the hall. "What are you doing?" he asked.

Ted pushed the bathroom door open. Lola had laid out items from her rucksack on the floor and had placed others, including some of her books, in the bath. She stood over the sink, scrubbing soap into her rucksack with a nailbrush.

"Bottle leaked?" Ted asked, leaning over Lola for a closer look.

The gentle sobbing gave way to an all-out roar as Lola turned around and wrapped her arms around Ted. He hugged her back until the crying eased to the occasional sob.

"What happened?"

Lola told him about Larry, about how she'd escaped, and what she'd found when she recovered her rucksack.

Ted looked at her neck. "You've got bruises, Lola. You've got to tell someone."

"I told you."

"No, an adult."

"They won't believe me. Larry's a liar, and everyone just believes him."

"Well, I'm going to be back at school tomorrow. I'll sort it out."

"He says he's going to get you, too, when you go back."

"I'd like to see him try. Come on, it'll be okay." He started to collect and dry off Lola's things. He'd been looking forward to returning to school, but only because he'd forgotten about some of its less pleasant features. But everything would be okay if he prepared himself. He couldn't let anything happen to him or his sister again.

39: MEGAN

Poplar Avenue hadn't yet returned to its sleepy street status with a few cars awaiting movement outside the Wright household, but it was much quieter. Megan was able to pull up outside the Hatcher house. She tried to spy into the windows. She'd not made it into the front room, and she wondered what he might be hiding in there.

She could just go up to his door. Pretend she was on some other business. That wouldn't hurt. That wouldn't be suspicious.

She got out of the car and walked slowly along the path. The window on the left was his mother's bedroom, and on the right, the front room. Thin net curtains hung in the window, revealing only shapes on the other side, but a lot of shapes. No doubt the room was similarly cluttered to what she'd seen the previous evening.

She knocked on the door and peered through the frosted glass into the hall. Again, she could only make out the shape of tall structures within but knew they were boxes, piled high. She waited a moment and then knocked again. She didn't want him to answer now. She wanted to be able to look like it was a legitimate house call, and back away with it unanswered, but as she was about to turn away, the door opened.

Hatcher gazed up at her from his stooped position, seemingly unable to straighten his back to meet her at eye level. Yes...?" he said.

"Mr Hatcher, I'm from a voluntary group," Megan began. She was aware of a car door opening nearby and she could feel eyes on her. Paranoia, surely. "We help those who may be struggling in their homes."

"Who called you?"

"We don't record that information," Megan said. "Perhaps a neighbour, or a friend that was concerned for you."

"I don't want any help."

"Mrs Wallace?" the man who had got out of the car called out to her.

Megan looked over her shoulder at the approaching man and then turned quickly back to Hatcher. "If this is an inconvenient time, I can return tomorrow, say 4 o'clock?"

Mr Hatcher nodded and pushed the door closed. Megan turned to the man who swiftly approached her.

"Mrs Wallace, isn't it?" he repeated. He held his phone out toward her.

"You are?"

He offered a hand for shaking. "I'm from the Daily News."

Megan left the hand unshaken.

"Can I ask you a few questions?"

"No, I have to go." Megan walked toward her car.

"How do you feel having your son back home?"

"It's great, thank you," Megan said as she unlocked her car and climbed in. She quickly locked the doors behind her. Yes, it's great having Ted home, so why did she spend every minute away from him, looking for answers?

40: SIMON

Simon cycled through the pictures on the old digital camera, stopping to look at photographs with close-ups of the children. Crazy golf at the Pirate's Cove, Great Yarmouth, three or four years ago, Ted with a massive smile on his face; he'd not seen that smile since Ted's return. Another photo, same day: Ted and Lola making sandcastles. Ted had thicker arms and legs. There was more to it than malnourishment alone. Now his limbs seemed slightly too long, an inferior copy. He kept scrolling: a photograph of Lola with her hair in bunches. She never wore it that way now, always wearing it down, disguising her hearing aid. Yes, she looked different, too. She'd lost some weight from her face, shedding puppy fat as she approached her teens. She was still the same underneath. Hearing movement downstairs, Simon switched off the recently-charged camera, and placed it in a drawer.

It had been Megan he'd heard moving. It was a long time since they were home together on a weeknight, what with him doing so many late shifts. She was loitering in the hall, peering into Ted's bedroom. Simon was eager to know what she'd seen, whether she too sought clues that would reveal something hidden inside him. He crept down the stairs.

Megan heard his approach and met him at the bottom step. "Go look at them two," she said, nodding toward Ted's bedroom.

Simon tiptoed over, feeling strange acting so cautiously in his own home, and looked into Ted's room. Inside, he sat on the bed, with Lola tucked up beside him. They were bathed in the light of the television screen. Simon craned his head in for enough to see Katniss Everdeen sprinting across a plain. He fixed his expression on Ted and Lola again. It might have been the reflection of the television, but Lola looked paler than usual. Ted was staring at the screen transfixed by the action.

Simon left the two of them to their movie and found Megan in the kitchen. "Shall we start on dinner?" he asked. Offering to work on it together would give them the chance to talk. He could find out how she felt about Ted.

"Sure. Could you get the chicken and the peppers out of the fridge?"

As Simon opened the fridge, Megan gathered the two chopping boards, some seasoning, and some baking paper.

Simon bent down and peered into the fridge. "I don't remember Ted being that much of a fan of The Hunger Games."

"No, but Lola is."

Simon spotted the chicken and placed the pack on top of the fridge. "But it's not like him to sit and watch something she likes."

"It's nice for them to do something together." Megan leaned over and grabbed the chicken. "I was starting to worry that things were awkward between them, but they seem better today."

No, Megan hadn't realised this wasn't Ted's kind of manoeuvre. He was more likely to manipulate Lola into watching Star Wars again. He grabbed the two peppers from the vegetable crisper.

"Can you chop them into strips?" Megan said, passing him the green chopping board.

Normally it was his job to tend to the meat while she prepared veg. But how long had it been since they'd cooked together? Back before Ted went missing?

"So," Simon said as he chopped a pepper in half, thinking that it was time to change tact, "how do you think Ted's getting on?"

Megan rubbed smoked paprika into the chicken and then placed the baking sheet on top of it. "He seems... okay."

There was definitely a pause before she said that. Surely, she too had her suspicions?

Megan grabbed the rolling pin and whacked it down on top of the baking-paper-covered chicken breasts. She raised it again and gave it another hefty thump.

"Woah!" Simon said, he stepped over to Megan and rubbed her back. "What did those poor chickens ever do to you?"

She shrugged off his touch. "I'm just tenderising them." She hit them again, gentler this time.

Simon returned to slicing the peppers, carefully cutting out the seeds. He noticed Megan's blows increasing in ferocity again. "So, what's bothering you?"

Megan glanced at him before fixing her attention on the rolling pin again. "I'm worried about him going back to school tomorrow. I'm not sure he's ready." She hit the chicken breasts again.

No, that wasn't it. He could tell when she was fobbing him off. "Is that all it is?"

Megan uncovered the chicken breasts which had been almost entirely flattened onto the chopping board. She picked up the knife and started to slice it. "Can you get the oil?"

He took the vegetable oil from the cupboard (the same cupboard that the new bottle of old Navy resided in) and poured a little into the pan before turning on the heat. "Come on, Megan. You know you can't distract me with menial chores. What's really bothering you?"

Megan shoved the food away from her and leaned against the counter.

Simon could hear her groaning.

She turned toward him; her face had reddened. "I'm still so angry, Simon. You'd think having him back here would make it all okay, but when I look at him..."

Simon knew. When she looked at him, she felt that it was like he wasn't back at all.

The oil in the pan started to hiss and spit.

Megan picked up the knife and pointed at him with it. "Someone has to pay for what they did. They stole seven months of his life—seven months of all of our lives. I just wanna..."

Simon stared at Megan's fingers: they were turning white where she gripped the knife handle so hard and her nails were digging into her palms. She made a stabbing motion and then placed the knife down.

Smoke poured from the pan. Simon stepped past it, to Megan, and took her in his arms. He held on to her, felt the hardness in her body soften until the vulgar trill of the smoke alarm brought their attention back to the kitchen.

Megan grabbed a tea towel and started to waft the smoke away from the smoke detector while Simon moved the pan from the heat.

The noise brought Lola and Ted from the bedroom.

"Should have known Dad was cooking," Lola said with a cheeky grin.

"That was your Mum's fault," Simon called over the piercing alarm. He looked over to Ted who was just staring up at it until the noise ceased.

"How are you doing, Ted? Enjoying the movie?"

"Yeah," he said, his face showing no emotion, but his tone suggesting enthusiasm, "it's brilliant."

"Panics over," Megan said. "You two go back to your film and we'll call you when dinner's ready."

Lola turned away first, "Try not to burn it again, Dad!" she called out and ran away, the kind of thing she would have done when she was younger, making cheeky comments hoping he'd give chase. But Simon didn't follow her. Instead, he watched Ted as he trudged back into his room.

41: TED

Ted looked at himself in the mirror. His school uniform hung on him loosely, the arms of his jumper sagging massively, and there was so much room in his shirt that he could fit another of himself in there. He kicked out a leg. The material of the trousers seemed to flap around for an eternity before it made contact with his skin. But it didn't matter. Being in the school uniform was a normal thing to do. He'd also slept better, not haunted by the dreams of reaching arms. Maybe the pills had started to have the desired effect of restoring the balance to his body.

He left his room and went into the kitchen where Dad hunted through the fridge. Mum had already left for work; she had woken Ted an hour earlier to start him getting ready for school and had asked him half a dozen times if he wanted to go back.

"Hey," called Dad. "I was just making sandwiches. You still like ham?"

What a stupid question that was. "Yes," he replied. Why would his tastes suddenly change? He might not be able to eat as much, but he still liked all of the same things. Dad had become odd since he'd been away. He looked older and he never seemed to relax. The way his head was forever moving, focusing on one thing, then another, turning toward every little noise, was animalistic, or perhaps like a fly always buzzing from one thing to the next.

"You want some toast? Marmite?" He loitered over the toaster holding two slices of bread.

"I'll have some toast. Just one slice, though."

"You want Marmite on it?"

Ted had never liked Marmite. Even the description of it sounded vile. Yeast extract. What even was that? "Just butter, please."

Lola came downstairs a few minutes later. Dad made her some toast, and she happily applied a thick layer of Marmite to her own. The gloopy, thick blackness of it froze Ted for a moment. He couldn't help but gaze into the jar, fixed on where the knife had left a claw of the substance sticking up from the rest as if it had gained sentience and was pulling itself out from the black mass toward him. Before he could drift too far into his dark fantasy, the smell of the stuff hit him. Gagging brought him back to the real world.

Lola saw his reaction to the Marmite, smiled, and edged her tainted knife toward him.

Ted held a hand out, deliberately dramatic and mocking warding off a great evil. But then the smell hit him again...

Lola laughed, but Ted's stomach was turning over. There was a knock at the door, and Ted dashed from his seat, eager to be away from the foul stench.

He looked over his shoulder for his dad. He was standing over the sink. Had he not heard the door?

Ted headed into the hall and opened the door. The first thing Ted noticed about the man standing on the porch was the gaping hole where his right eye used to be, a smooth concave layer of skin suggesting there had never been an eye in the socket. His other eye was present, though watery, the colour of the iris and pupil dulled, as if viewed through tracing paper. Beneath the eyes the cheekbones stood out, the skin thin and white, the bone almost showing through, and loose skin hung on the rest of his face and neck as if draped on the cheekbones. He reached forward with a bony finger and his brow furrowed. "Home," he said in a hoarse voice.

Ted stared at him, not knowing what to do, not knowing what to say.

"My house?" the old man said, turning to look behind him before facing Ted again. "My farm?"

When he spoke, a stench came out of his mouth like the river. Ted looked at his clothes and realised they were soaking wet. He'd been so transfixed on the man's face, that he hadn't noticed he was dripping. Already, a pool had formed beneath his feet. He was wearing a pair of green overalls that had darkened to an olive colour as result of their sodden condition. He wore nothing else, so tufts of white chest hair reached out around the neck, and he had no shoes on. Ted stood, mouth agape. He didn't know what this man wanted, or what he was doing there, though there was something strangely familiar about him. It was as if he had known him in another life. Ted wanted to invite him in, to talk to him, to find out what he wanted, what he knew, but the words wouldn't come.

"Can I help you?"

Ted turned to see Dad approaching, wiping his hands on a tea towel.

"My house," the old man said again.

A string of drool hung from the old man's lower lip, stretching unbroken toward the floor.

"Lola, Ted," Dad called, half turning his head, but always keeping one eye on their visitor, "Hadn't you better go if you're going to make it for the bus?"

The old man leant against the door frame, his fingers gripping it as if it was the only thing keeping him in this world.

"Go out the back," Dad called.

Even though it was a little early, Ted and Lola followed orders and left the house. By the time they reached the front of the house they could see Dad on the phone and the old man had slumped into a sitting position, facing the streets, his head slowly drifting from side to side as if he was looking upon the world for the first time.

"Who was that?" Lola asked.

"I don't know, but I think I know him."

Lola chuckled. "Know him? Know him how? He looked like he was eighty. Didn't know you hung around with many eighty-year-olds."

Ted looked back again. "I mean, from before. When I was... away."

"Shouldn't we go back to find out who he is? What he wants?"

Ted gazed down to the end of the road, imagining the path that led to the bus stop. He was so close to moving on with his life. He didn't want to turn around now. "No," he said. "It's fine. I'll get Dad to tell me about it later. It's probably nothing."

Ted came to a stop at the end of the road.

"Changed your mind?" Lola asked.

"No, but before we get too close... are you okay after yesterday?"

Lola looked at her rucksack—now clean and dry. "Yeah," she said. "I can handle it. Plus, I've got my big brother back in school to look after me now."

They continued on their way, and a few minutes later they were at the bus stop. People Ted would once have considered friends greeted him, but there was a distance between them. He stood on the periphery of a group he'd known since primary school, wanting to join their conversation, but they were talking about things he didn't understand, referring to memes he'd not seen, imitating dances he had no awareness of the origin or the purpose of. Was this all their friendship ever was? A pointless regurgitation of what they'd played or seen online? And if it was so pointless, so worthless, why did he feel so desperate to catch up and become a part of it again? He thought getting back to normal would just be a matter of getting back into the old routine, but there was more to it than that. The social hierarchy was a fragile structure, and it didn't take much of a wobble to topple from your place. Ted had had more than a wobble though. He'd been sucked from the structure altogether and was only now learning that as soon as you stepped away, your space would either be filled, or the circle would close, leaving you on the outside, and it wasn't easy to slot back in.

He looked over to Lola. Her position had changed, too. She was chatting to Lauren, someone he hadn't seen her with since she started at Fenland Village Academy. She looked over her shoulder and made eye contact with him. She smiled.

Ted smiled, too, but in his head, he was drifting back home, back to the doorstep, thinking about the visitor and desperately trying to force his memory to reveal his connection to the old man.

A couple of his old friends were performing an elaborate handshake. What was more important, figuring out what was going on there, or figuring out his connection to an old man in his eighties with a missing eye? The very fact he struggled to decide told him he was still a long way from being normal again.

42: LOLA

Mitchell hadn't been at the bus stop that morning, so she was surprised to see him coming toward her in the canteen at break time.

Part of her was glad he hadn't been there. She didn't want a confrontation with him about the rumours about them in front of her brother, especially after he'd aired her on social media last night. She didn't want Ted to think she could have done that, and she didn't want it to get back to her parents. She wasn't even thinking about having sex, but she knew if Mum heard the rumours, she'd want to talk to her about it and no way was she ready for that.

With Mitchell striding across the canteen, Lola knew it would get people gossiping again. She could hear the whispers; she could feel their eyes upon her.

"He is here," she mouthed to Lauren.

"Yeah, he came into my science classroom about halfway through—said he'd been at the doctor's."

He looked at Lola, with a massive smile on his face.

Lola turned away and caught the looks on the faces of others in the canteen, their heads thrown back in cackles. She heard someone wolf-whistle and she wanted to fall between the cracks in the floorboards and disappear forever.

Mitchell continued toward her. He lapped up the attention from the crowd, feeding on their noise. While she'd been called a slag, he was basking in the adoration being thrown at him. He was ever so close now. Lola wasn't ready for the humiliation. She couldn't take everyone staring. She looked around, trying to see if Ted was watching, but there was no sign of him. She tried to spy a safe place, and her eyes fell on the door. It was a pretty clear path. She could run. Or walk calmly out: running would attract too much attention. But when she went to move, Lauren locked her arm around hers. "Wait," she said, and then it was too late to do anything.

Mitchell was so close, and he was staring at her, and she was caught in the tractor beam of his eyes.

He kissed her on the forehead and then leapt onto the table they sat around. His foot caught the edge of a tray, causing the contents to lift off it for a second, and all fall stably back into place other than a carton of chocolate milk which sloshed onto its side. Its owner picked it up, leaving only the slightest dribble on the table.

The crowd in the canteen cheered and laughed at Mitchell's antics, and the senior teacher on duty, Mr Butcher had to switch his attention from a muffin he was stuffing into his face to the increased level of noise. "Mitchell Rose, get off that table at once." He started to march across the room.

"Okay, quiet, people," called Mitchell as he looked over his shoulder at Butcher and realised he only had a few seconds.

For a second, Lola thought Mitchell was going to start singing, that he was going to serenade her with a song in front of all those people. God, it would be so embarrassing, but would it really be that bad? But then he started to speak, not sing, and what he said was a whole lot better.

"Quit talking shit about this girl." He pointed down to Lola. "I've not had sex with her. She's not a slag. And if I hear anyone say different, they'll have me to answer to."

Butcher had arrived at the periphery of the table.

The crowd waited in anticipation.

"If I have to ask you one more time to get off that table, there will be serious consequences, young man."

"It's cool," Mitchell said, hopping down to the floor. "I'm done."

Butcher stood over Mitchell, staring at him and speaking much too loudly with no control over the muffin-loaded spittle that flew from his mouth. "I can assure you it is very much not cool. You'll be in detention for this. Today, lunch time, and after school too."

"It had to be said," Mitchell said.

"This is not up for discussion."

"It's fine. I'm happy to take the punishment. But if this school actually did something about bullying instead of turning a blind eye to all the name-calling and other shady shit that goes on, I wouldn't have had to get up there in the first place."

"Okay, Principal's office. Right now." Butcher placed one hand on Mitchell's shoulder encouraging him to turn away toward the exit, toward the Principal's office.

"Get your meat hands off me," Mitchell said, shrugging off Butcher's touch and marching for the office unaccompanied. Butcher quickly followed, still spouting nonsense about conduct.

Lauren gawked at Lola. "Bloody hell," she said. "I've never seen nothing like it. I bet you bloody well do want to have sex with him now, don't you?"

"No!" said Lola. No, she wasn't ready for anything like that, but she certainly felt something more for him than she had before.

The canteen was a wall of noise again, excited chatter, not about Lola or what Mitchell had said, but about what he'd done. That was sure to keep the attention off her for a bit. Lola gazed around the room, glad that eyes were no longer on her until she saw a pair that were: Larry's. He drew his thumb across his throat as he continued to stare at her, stripping her of her elation and placing her back in his grip, unable to get her breath. She looked away, but the damage had already been done.

43: TED

"So, how was your day?"

Could Dad have thought of a blander question? Ted had found him waiting in reception at the start of lunch. Part of him wanted to stay on for the rest of the school day: he only had one more lesson to get through, after all, but he could also do with putting the whole morning behind him and lying down for a bit. Moving around the school had been exhausting. He'd seen Larry harassing some year 7 kids in the corridor, but otherwise, the morning had been dull. Having been put back into year 9, he was in no classes with anyone he was close to in any way. Everyone knew who he was, and he recognised many of them. His story interested some, but when the answer to every question about the last seven months was, "I don't know," people soon lost interest. Teachers had obviously been given a specific approach to take. Welcoming, clear with tasks, checking in to see if he was okay, but absolutely no questions about the missing months.

"It was fine," Ted replied. He filled Dad in on some of the classes and tried to sound positive as they walked out of the school grounds to where the car was parked.

"What happened with that man?" Ted asked once they were in the car.

"I called the police."

Ted stared at Dad. "Why, what did he do?"

"No, it wasn't like that. He seemed lost and confused. I called them so they could help him, not to have him arrested."

"Oh, good. So, who was he?"

"He couldn't give me a name. From what I could gather..." Dad paused for a moment as he waited for a break in the traffic to pull out of the school car park. He looked both ways before turning left and continuing. "From what I gathered, he used to live in the area. He claimed he used to own the land—before it was our housing estate."

"Could he have done?"

"I don't know. I remember it before they build the houses. But I'm pretty sure the farmer was an old man back when he sold the land. I'm sure he wouldn't still be around today."

"But could it be?"

"I think that must have been nearly twenty years ago, and as I said, he was an old guy then."

"What if he hadn't aged since?"

Dad took his eyes off the road and glared at Ted. "What do you mean?"

"I don't know. Nothing. So, what did the police do?"

"Talked to him for a bit and then took him away."

Ted gasped. "Arrested him?"

"No, they were kind. I think they suspect he'd wandered off from one of the homes. They were going to make some calls."

"I hope he's going to be okay." Again, the feeling he had some connection to the old man hit him. He'd smelled like the river. It was the same smell that had haunted Ted until he started to take the iron pills. Had he too had the same cravings? And if so, was it because he'd been in the same place, a captive, fed on river water and mud? And what about his missing eye? Had they taken that just like they'd taken Julius's arm? Is that what they did? And if so, what had they taken from him?

Dad took a corner too sharply, and Ted felt like he was on a boat, his head taking a second to catch up with the movement of his body. His stomach rolled over, and he wanted nothing more than to go home.

"You still thinking about that poor, old guy? It's not for you to worry about. Your mum's going to be late home. Do you want to come with me to the supermarket and we'll get stuff to make dinner?"

It was the last thing Ted wanted, but it was also such a normal thing to do. "Sure," he said. It was a much healthier option than trying to rack his brain to discover the connection between himself and the old man.

44: MEGAN

Megan felt bad for lying. She'd lied to Simon about working late. She'd lied to her manager about having to take Ted to an appointment. The only person she didn't feel bad lying to was that child-touching bastard Ted Hatcher.

She knocked on his door again. She knew he was in; she'd seen him scurry away from the hall through the frosted glass beside the door when she'd first knocked. She knew persistence in this manner would eventually yield results. He wouldn't be able to bear the sound and eventually, he'd let her in. At heart, he was a coward. Why else would he prey on children? He wouldn't do that for much longer. Ever since she'd got a close look at his ageing face the other day, when she'd called at his door, she'd fantasised about how she could injure him. She may have already done so had it not been for that irritating reporter. She looked behind her once more to check she wasn't going to be similarly disturbed. No. Good. She knocked again, picturing herself wielding a shovel, waiting for Hatcher to open and smacking him on the top of the head with it. She pictured his balding pate like a boiled egg cracked with a spoon. And when he fell to the ground, she could dig the blade of the shovel into his neck, slice through it cleanly. She felt the corners of her mouth turn up into a smile.

Seconds later, Hatcher opened the door. He only stuck his head through. It was so ripe for an attack: an upward thrust into the windpipe with a screwdriver leaving him gasping for breath, choking on nothing but his blood. No, she had to do this properly. What was the point if she ended up locked behind bars away from her children anyway?

"Good afternoon, Mr Hatcher!" Megan hated the feigned enthusiasm in her voice. How could she bear to be pleasant to such a heinous individual?

"What do you want?" Hatcher said.

Even the feebleness of his voice revolted her. No wonder Ted had blocked out all memories if he'd had to listen to that.

"Do you remember, Mr Hatcher, I called by the other day about giving you some help around the house?"

A hand emerged. He gripped onto the doorframe—an act of defiance, clinging on to make a weak barrier.

The appearance of his fingernails, thick with a layer of grim at the tips, grime which could have come from the mud of the riverbank, made it almost impossible to keep up the charade. "Now Mr Hatcher, we've been looking carefully at your records and the last assessment suggested you were still capable of looking after yourself unaided, but if you don't prove cooperative, we may need to rethink that decision."

Hatcher stepped away from the door and let Megan inside. She quickly closed the door behind her. Still, the smell of fish saturated the bungalow. She could sit him on a chair and force-feed him cans of tuna until either his stomach exploded, or he choked on a rogue fish bone.

"Who are you?"

Megan pulled out her council ID card. She'd already doctored it to show a fake name and department.

"What do you want?"

"As I said previously, you fall under our jurisdiction, and we have a duty of care toward you. We received reports that you were struggling to live by yourself, and given your previous issues..."

Hatcher pointed at himself. "I am coping by myself. I'm fine here."

Megan made an obvious point of staring at the boxes in the hall that so significantly narrowed the space, and Hatcher hung his head low.

"Can we go through to the living room? We'll talk there."

Reluctantly, Hatcher led the way through. Megan glanced into some of the boxes she passed but saw nothing significant inside, nothing incriminating, only seashells, costume jewellery, and curling paper.

The living room was also free of any suspect materials. On a low mahogany coffee table were a collection of coupons clipped from magazines, unopened letters, and a spiral-bound book of word searches with a large crease across the front cover. Maybe calling at his door the previous day had resulted in him hiding everything. No matter. If she could get him talking, he'd give something away. He didn't seem too smart.

Two Edwardian-style armchairs flanked the coffee table. Megan took a seat in the one nearest the door. There would be no easy way out for him.

Megan took a clipboard from her bag and removed the lid from a biro. "So, have you always lived in the area?"

Hatcher sat down and shifted uncomfortably in the chair. Clearly, that was not his usual seat. Megan could tell that when he did his crosswords he would have been sitting where she was. Maybe he was now sitting in his mother's chair. Maybe that would make him feel awkward, would make him feel guilty. Good. That would work in her favour.

Hatcher scratched his head. "Yes."

Megan tried not to be disturbed by the flakes of skin drifting from the top of the old man's head. "And what about in this house? For how long have you lived here?"

"We had it when it were new."

"And 'We' is?"

"Me and my mother." Hatcher smiled and gazed at a photograph of a prim-looking woman on the fireplace. "She bought it with her savings. Had me move in with her."

"Have you always lived with your mother?"

"Yes. Mostly."

"What do you mean, mostly?"

"Well, she hasn't been here the last few years… and…"

"And what Mr Hatcher?"

"There was some time when I was away, but I came back to mother after."

Time away? Living or working elsewhere seemed unlikely. Prison? An asylum? There would be information on the database. She wasn't supposed to access just anyone's records at work, but as the IT guys that monitored security had been laid off, it wouldn't be a problem.

"And how do you get on with neighbours? Is it a friendly street?"

Hatcher gripped the handles of the armchair. "There's some nice folk about, but, some of the children…"

"Have a problem with children, do you?" Megan leant toward him. She dropped the inflexion from her voice and returned it to its normal, deeper level.

Hatcher noticed and leant back. In reciprocation, his voice became higher. "They say… things."

"What do they say?"

Hatcher's eyes narrowed. "Call me names."

"What do they call you?"

"Names."

Megan rose from her chair and took a step toward Hatcher. "Do they call you the child catcher?"

Hatcher covered his face. If it were possible to sink back any further into the chair he would have done so.

He looked so pathetic, cowering there. She could grab the cushion from her seat and smother him with it. She didn't think she'd have to overpower him or struggle with it; she was sure he'd acquiesce, let it happen. And why wouldn't he? He deserved it, and he knew it.

"It was you that took those children."

Hatcher's hand dropped from his face, and he looked up at her. "I never took no children."

Megan spoke through gritted teeth: "You took my son."

"I never. I don't know him."

"What about the boy next door," Megan pointed in the direction of the Wright house. "Julius."

Hatcher turned his head to where Megan pointed. "Yes."

"So, you admit it then?"

"Admit what?"

Megan leant down in front of Hatcher, her hand clutching the arm of his chair. "You took the boys. You cut off that poor lad's arm."

"I never."

"You said 'yes'."

"I said 'yes' I know him, that's all I meant." Hatcher stared into Megan's eyes. "Please leave me now. I can cope on my own. I just need to be left on my own."

"I'm not going until you tell me what you did to my boy." Megan looked around the room for a weapon. By the fireplace, which hadn't been used in many years, there was an empty brass coal scuttle, and beside it a poker. That would do. It may not have been red-hot, but she was still sure that she could insert it somewhere that could do damage. She stepped across the room and grabbed it. The weight of it surprised her. The handle was chunky, and made of brass, and the shaft a good half-metre long, blunt at the end though. It would take some effort to force it through flesh. Bludgeoning was an option, though.

Hatcher's arms moved to cradle the top of his head. "Just go," he said, over and again.

Megan crouched down next to Hatcher and hissed in his ear, "I'll go when you tell me what you did. Maybe I'll do the same to you. Maybe I'll leave you be."

"I did nothing. I don't go nowhere near the river."

Megan sprang up. She hadn't mentioned the river. He knew something. She pointed the poker at him, prodded it into his chest, roughly where she thought his heart should be.

"What's this got to do with the river?"

"I told the people."

"What people?"

"That came before. I told them about those things at the river. They took me away."

"Took you were?"

"To the other place." He turned his head to make eye contact. "Please go now. All this fuss and nonsense will make them come back after me again."

Megan withdrew the poker. Why should she believe he was a victim and not the perpetrator? But now she had doubt; she couldn't harm him if she had doubt. She wanted justice, but she couldn't take it until he confessed. She could push further, but…

She glanced out of the window and saw that the traffic was building on the street. She heard a car horn beep, and when she looked out of the window, through the net curtain, not wanting to lift it, not wanting to be seen inside that house, she realised it was Alesha driving home, and she was pretty sure that the figure sitting beside her was Julius.

The press would swarm the street any minute. They'd encroach on Hatcher's yard looking for a better angle for a shot. They'd camp out all night if they had to in order to get what they wanted. That meant Megan had to leave, but not without giving one last warning. "Listen, I don't know what happened to you in the past, but if there's even a hint of you having done anything wrong, I'll be back. You got that?"

Hatcher nodded and looked away from her.

Megan left the living room, passed through the hall and into the kitchen. She could leave through the side door and push through the hedge at the back. That would get her away from the scene. She could come back for the car later.

"Miss," called Hatcher from the living room.

Megan chose to ignore it, and heard only his question as she opened the door to leave: "Did I pass the assessment?"

45: SIMON

When they got back from the supermarket, Ted was so tired he could barely walk. He shuffled across the hall, his feet not lifting more than a couple of centimetres from the carpet, his head nodding forward.

"Why don't you lie down?" Simon said.

Ted didn't respond; he lumbered to his bedroom and closed the door.

Simon stared at the door for a moment to make sure Ted wasn't coming out and went into the back garden, out to the riverbank and fished his camera out of the water. The box had sunk a little into the bed of the river, and thick, black mud clung to the edges. No matter, it would be going back into the water shortly. Simon quickly switched off the camera, removed the micro-SD card, replaced it with another and set the camera recording again. It was returned to the water and sped back into the kitchen. He stood by Ted's door for a moment and listened. Nothing. He was either asleep or relaxing.

Simon tiptoed up the stairs and grabbed his tablet from beside his bed. He put in the SD card and played the video. He watched the image darken as the camera had sunk. At first, the image showed only a cloud as the camera box disturbed the mud at the riverbed. When this settled, there was little to see. The camera's dull light illuminated only a few feet in which he could see nothing but a few aquatic plants drifting into view. Simon watched for a few seconds before he realised he couldn't possibly sit and watch the whole thing. He sped up the footage, making the plants come into view more frequently. Realising it would still take hours, he sped it up again and again until the plants moved in a blur. He spotted a flash of something come into shot and hit pause. He viewed the footage in reverse, at speed until he saw the flash again, and then hit play at normal speed. Minutes passed, and there was nothing. He started to doubt whether he'd seen anything at all until it appeared, slowly coming toward the camera and moving around it to the left: a fish and nothing more. Simon thought there must be a better way, software that could highlight the bits in which something happened, but if there was, he didn't know about it. He could spend so long trying to find suitable software that he could watch the whole thing (at high speed) instead. He increased the speed and kept the tablet in front of him as he tried to one-handedly put away the shopping. Another flash. He saw it again in reverse, slowed down the footage and watched it back in real-time. Probably another fish, but the image has suggested a little more colour. The fish around Wiseham were far from colourful. It only entered the edge of the footage at first, something light blue, material. It moved along revealing a stripe of red and, seconds later, as it continued to pass, he saw something flesh-coloured, and then... fingers? Before he could be sure, they were caught in the river's pull and were gone, out of shot. He rewound it and watched it back. Yes, what entered the shot could definitely have been an arm, complete with hand. He had to report it. He picked up his phone and saw a message from Grant. *Police picked up another missing. The floodgates are opening.*

He'd call Heimlich first and then give Grant a call, tell him all about his morning visitor.

Simon wanted to keep his findings from Ted, so agreed to meet Heimlich at the station. The only available space was a small interview room, grey, with no natural light. The plastic chairs dug into Simon's back as he pulled up the video to show Heimlich. Heimlich wanted details. Where had the camera been placed and at what time first of all so that they could accurately calculate when the arm (if that's what it was, Simon was sure, but Heimlich refused to acknowledge that) passed the camera. He told Simon he would get diving crews out to investigate further, but he had one more question for Simon: "What were you doing putting a camera into the water?"

Simon didn't know what to say. Should he be honest? He was hoping to find evidence of subterranean passages? That he hoped to catch a glimpse of the creatures that lived beneath the Earth's surface, creatures which had been commonly misconstrued as demons? Would they ever let him leave the place if he said that? "You heard about Ted's episode the other day?" he said, choosing to go for the simple answer, the one that wasn't quite a lie.

"We did."

"It made me think there might be something in the water he needed, something he was drawn to. I thought the camera might pick up what it was."

"Is that all?" asked Heimlich.

"That's all," replied Simon. He was ready to leave the police station, after all, he'd arranged to meet with Grant, and he didn't want to keep him waiting.

46: TED

Ted woke when he heard the front door open. He'd drifted off to sleep still in his school uniform, and he must have gone under pretty deep as his mouth tasted like a bog.

He crept out of his room to catch Lola at the bottom of the stairs. Her hair looked wet, and when she turned around, she had an enormous grin on her face.

"You look happy," Ted said.

"Yeah," Lola replied. She put her hand on the bannister in anticipation of climbing the stairs.

"Better day than yesterday, then, I guess?" He touched his chest with both hands and put his thumbs out to the sides, British Sign Language for 'how are you?'

Lola nodded.

"Why's your hair wet?"

Lola thought for a moment and raised her hands to head height and brought them down again wiggling her fingers, symbolising rain.

Ted smiled. Falling back into signing with Lola showed they still had a connection. It was something so simple, something unnecessary given the way Lola's hearing had developed and the success of the operations, but it was something which felt very much theirs. "Hey, when you're done up there can you come back to my room? There's something I need help with."

Lola gave him the thumbs up and then thundered up the stairs making more noise than her tiny body seemed capable of.

While waiting for Lola, Ted booted up his laptop. True, they could probably do this on their phones, but since his phone had been in the hands of the police, it seemed slow and buggy. He'd probably missed some upgrades in his downtime, either that or the police had put secret spying software on his phone that slowed everything down. Did they do that? Could they? Were they allowed to?

He'd started searching by the time Lola returned. She'd changed out of her school uniform into the kind of scruffy clothes she liked to wear around the house since he came back: leggings that were baggy at the knee and loose-fitting hoodies.

"So, what do you need?" Lola said.

"Do you wanna help me find out more about that man that came to the door this morning?"

"Sure," Lola said, perching on the end of the bed next to Ted.

Ted typed *one-eyed man Wiseham* into google. All that turned up was a book and an album called One-Eyed Man and a picture of a Victorian gentleman with an eye patch and the slogan *In the country of the blind, the one-eyed man is king.* Wasn't it supposed to be Kingdom, he wondered and as he was about to type that, Lola gave him the eye.

"You're not searching for the right things." Lola reached across and pressed the delete key.

"Okay, little Miss Google Champion, what do I need to search for?"

"Well, I don't know, because I didn't hear him. Tell me what he said, and we'll work it out from there."

"I didn't think about what he said. He was standing there dripping wet, and he only had one eye. Dad spoke to him for longer."

Lola sighed. "Well, you don't know what he said to Dad, so that doesn't help."

"Ha!" Ted said waving his finger mockingly in Lola's face. "It just so happens that I do. Dad told me."

Lola batted away the finger. "What, then?"

"He seemed confused. Said he used to live around here. He even claimed he owned the land these houses were built on."

Lola reached toward the keyboard.

Ted shifted his body to block her. "I don't want your grubby hands on the keys. Tell me what to search for."

Lola grinned. "Look up old maps."

"Dad didn't seem to think it could be him. Reckons the man who owned the land would be dead by now."

As Ted had yet to start typing, Lola reached across again, only for Ted to swat her hands away. "See if you can find a site that has old maps of the area. Go back to before this house was built."

"Why?"

"If you can find the name of the farm, you can find the name of the man."

Ted started to type. "Are you sure someone didn't take you away too? Give you a new brain when you were gone?"

Lola punched Ted on the arm. "Fists of iron too."

Ted rubbed his arm and gave Lola a sideways glance, feigning injury but surprised by the strength of her punch. No doubt his puny arms would bruise from the blow. He deleted what was in the search bar. "Stop messing about, anyway. Tell me what to type."

"Try Cambridgeshire maps 1990; that should be old enough."

Ted followed orders. He clicked on one of the images. He could see Wiseham on there, in the upper left-hand corner close to the twin villages of Greater and Little Mosswick, but it was too great a scale to show the detail they needed.

"That's no good," Lola said.

"Well, that's what you told me to look for."

"Try typing Wiseham map 1980."

"Why 1980?"

Lola rolled her eyes. "Because that's old."

"Okay." Ted typed and hit enter. Several maps of Wiseham came up, many with the level of detail needed.

Lola reached across and pointed at the screen. "That one."

Ted clicked in. It was titled 'Wiseham in 1920'. He looked at Lola and grinned. "Too old."

"No, it might be okay. If there's a farm in the right place, it won't have changed its name."

Little of the village they knew existed on the map. It consisted of but a few streets and far more farms than Ted realised used to be there.

"Whereabouts are we?"

Lola scanned the map and shrugged. "Hang on," she said and leaned over him, moving too quickly to be brushed aside again. She launched a new window, hit a few keys, and used the keyboard shortcuts to switch between the two browser windows, comparing a modern google map centred on their home, and with the 1920 map in the other window.

"We're there." Lola pointed to a bit of land by the river. Beside it were some buildings and the name. "Norfolk Farm," Ted said. "Why's it called Norfolk Farm when it's in Cambridgeshire?"

"Dunno. Google Norfolk Farm, Wiseham."

Ted saluted. "Okay, your majesty, as you command."

Lola smiled at him. "Look, you're the one who asked for my help."

"I know. I appreciate it. Also... I like hanging out with you."

"Thanks," Lola smiled again, and then screwed up her face as she commanded him: "Now get on with your work."

Ted searched for the term, and the first thing that came up was a news story from the local paper about the development of Fenmore. Ted started to scroll down to look at other results.

"Go back," Lola said. "Check the first one."

Ted clicked on the link. He scrolled quickly to the bottom to check its length and then hit control-F.

"What are you doing?" asked Lola.

"Ah, so there are some things the search master doesn't know." He typed Norfolk Farm into the find box, and the only occurrence of the words was highlighted toward the bottom of the article. Ted read the line aloud: "The failure of the local community mirrors the controversial events of 20 years prior, when the ancient buildings of Norfolk Farm were torn down to develop the area now known as Riverview Terrace."

The phrase 'the controversial events of 20 years prior' was hyperlinked. Ted clicked on it.

The headline was irrelevant, but the sub-header caught his eye *Residents rage over Riverview outcome in absence of the farm's owner.*

Ted skimmed through the article. He could sense Lola reading over his shoulder. A couple of paragraphs down, he found what he was looking for. "Possession of the farm had been taken by the bank when repayments on a loan taken on the property were not made in the absence of the farm's owner and life-long resident Arthur Norfolk, who disappeared three years ago."

"So that's the name, Arthur Norfolk. Look him up," Lola said.

"That's what I was doing."

Lola furrowed her brow. "Well, you need to be told."

Ted rolled his eyes. His sides hurt from suppressing laughter. He copied the name and pasted it into the search bar.

James Arthur had at some point played a concert in Norfolk. Ted wasn't sure who he was. There were a number of butchers called Arthur operating in Norfolk. There were Arthur Norfolk Battersby Trust retirement properties.

"Try putting it in quotes," Lola said.

Ted went one better, typing "Arthur Norfolk missing".

With the image, he felt like he'd hit the jackpot. That was him, the man that had stood at his doorstep that morning. The only difference was that, back then, he had both eyes. The image came from a newspaper archive from the late '90s. How could he still look so similar? Yes, he'd looked thinner in the face and a little less bulky, but the facial features didn't show twenty years of wear, and the hair was the same cut and length. How was that possible?

He skimmed through the news story. The circumstances in which he disappeared were very similar to Ted's own. There was no trace of him. He'd lived alone on the farm so there was no clear date of his disappearance. Ted checked another article, found rumours of him running away due to debts which were refuted by friends in the same article who said he wasn't the sort of man to do that. And if he'd really run off, what would bring him back today?

Ted returned to the search results and scrolled down further.

Lola leant forward and stroked his arm. "You okay?"

He could feel where he was going to bruise when Lola brushed past the spot. He turned to Lola. "Yeah, I'm fine. It's all so similar, but that's not a bad thing. Not if it helps me get to the bottom of this."

There were many news stories from the time Arthur went missing. Ted selected the fifth page of results, trying to find something different, and it was in scrolling through that he stumbled across a link titled *'East Anglia's Missing Epidemic'*. It was an ugly and ill-formatted blog that hadn't been updated in some time. Some of the images sat outside frames and text went outside of boxes and became almost unreadable without being highlighted. It told the stories of a number of people in the region who had disappeared with little trace of them. Some had text in red at the bottom–UPDATE. A couple had this information. Some to the south of the map, not far from Ipswich, were marked as BODY FOUND–MURDERED. Another, just south of Cambridge was marked RUNAWAY–CONFIRMED ALIVE. The remaining dots on the map numbered six, and Wiseham seemed to be at their very centre. He clicked on the circle closest to the middle and it linked to one of the accounts of the missing higher up the page, a man both Lola and Ted had spent the best parts of their lives trying not to cross: Ted Hatcher, and the update information: RETURNED IN MYSTERIOUS CIRCUMSTANCES. Beside the article was a picture of Hatcher, several years old but still containing the same features: the lank and greasy hair, but more of it, as it had yet to start its pacey retreat from his forehead, the beady eyes, the strange, upturned nose.

Ted heard the key in the door which compelled him to slam the laptop shut. Whatever he'd discovered about Hatcher, he was not yet ready to venture any further.

47: MEGAN

"Ted, are you home?" Megan's heart raced. She'd had to take a meandering route back from Hatcher's house and had dashed from cover to cover, in bus stops and under trees to avoid the falling rain.

Ted emerged from the bedroom. Lola poked her head out a moment later. It was so good to see the two of them together. If anything was going to make them feel like a normal family again, it was the in-jokes and closeness between Lola and Ted. And of course, this state wouldn't be allowed to thrive. One of their petty squabbles would have to occur and ruin the tranquillity. It was odd that she desired this, the one thing she used to fear.

"What is it?" Ted said. He looked at Lola and rolled up his sleeves.

"I heard that Julius is coming home, isn't that great news?"

Ted nodded.

Something in his eyes suggested not only a lack of enthusiasm about this news but something else too: concern? "Are you okay?" she asked, scrutinising his face for more tell-tale signs of anxiety.

"Did Dad tell you about the man who came here this morning?" Ted said.

"What man?" She spotted the mark on his arm. "Did he try to hurt you? What's that?"

Lola was trying to slink away in the background. Megan didn't think she liked being part of the conversations about the missing situation, but if she was going to be a mature member of the family, it was time to get used to it.

"Lola punched me." He looked over his shoulder at Lola.

Megan was never going to reprimand her daughter for doing something that she would have so typically done in the past. It was such a normal thing to do. "Tell me about this man. And where's your father?"

"Dad? Isn't he at work?"

"No, he's off shift for a few days. Tell me what happened."

Megan listened intently as Ted told the story of the one-eyed man, dripping wet, and his theory that it was Arthur Norfolk. That was all before Megan's time in the village. She'd not heard the name before, but she immediately felt angry with the man. How dare he come knocking on the door and disturb her family? She was glad the police had taken him away. And it was while she thought of the police, that one of their number knocked on the door. Megan dashed to open it.

Heimlich stood on the porch, back hunched against the rain. "May I come in?"

Megan nodded, and as he stepped inside, she noticed that there was a small convoy of vehicles with him.

"I take it Mr Wallace has brought you up to date with the situation?" Heimlich asked.

Mr Wallace had very much not brought her up to date with the situation. She glared at Heimlich.

"Okay, let me fill you in. As result of something Mr Wallace discovered in the river this afternoon, we need to carry out further investigative work. Mr Wallace assured me it would be okay for us to access the river and your back garden by the side of the house. I assume that's also fine with you?"

"What did he find?" Megan was irritated to have to ask, but as Simon had let her down, she had little choice.

"It's confidential, Madam," Heimlich said, glancing at the kids.

"Can you two go to your rooms for a moment? I need to talk to the inspector about something."

Ted and Lola scooted off, Lola heading upstairs and Ted to his room.

Heimlich waited for a moment for quiet. "Listen, I'm only telling you this because your husband was supposed to have briefed you already. This afternoon he showed me a video recording of something that looked like a severed arm drifting along the bed of the river."

"A what?" Megan had heard him, but there were so many questions that came with the statement. One of them was what her husband had been playing at and why he hadn't told her, but then she thought about the arm and who she'd seen earlier that day.

"Wait, Julius's arm?"

"We can't confirm that, Mrs Wallace." He leaned in closer to her. "But we've got a kid with a missing arm and an arm with a missing kid... what do you think?"

Heimlich stepped back and looked Megan in the eye. She stared at him. Not only was that a deeply insensitive thing to say, but it was also awfully unprofessional. Where did he get off making jokes like that? But Megan had seen it in her line of work when she had colleagues who had to deal with difficult members of the public in horrendous situations, they'd blurt out something improper. Perhaps it was another coping strategy: dehumanise the victim, make it easier to deal with. Whether this was an example of that, or if Heimlich was just an utter prick, Megan didn't much care. She wanted him gone.

"Use the side of the house," she said. "Come and go whenever you need. Only tell me if it's something that directly affects my family."

Heimlich nodded. He opened his mouth to say something more, but Megan had already opened the door, so he remained silent.

She gave him a second to move out of earshot on the other side of the door and then took out her phone. She was glad it went to voicemail. She wasn't sure she'd be able to get anything coherent out. "Simon," she said when invited to leave a message, "get home now."

48: SIMON

Back in The Boar, Simon struggled to remember the last time he'd been to a pub twice in a week. Maybe eight years ago in the build-up to Lola's last operation. He never saw it as a problem. When things got tough, a bit of booze was a way to smooth the sharp edges. At that moment, he felt like things were getting snagged on them all the time. It wasn't like he was going straight for the top shelf and necking the shorts. No, he'd treated himself to a pint. He needed it. He couldn't get that image of the arm out of his head. It wasn't so much the arm as the hand and the bloated fingers. They were only on the screen for a second, but they'd be in his memory for a lifetime. He'd taken a stool by the bar. He'd not located Grant within the pub, so assumed he'd arrived first, which gave him control of location. Here, the lighting was better. Here he had witnesses and people in earshot that would hopefully stop Grant from turning the crazy up to eleven. Because that's what he was. Simon just needed to hear enough of it to realise. His family were in a situation which didn't make a whole lot of sense, so of course the crazy demon story could be applied to their situation. Due to a lack of any actual evidence, if someone had told him that mermaids had lured Ted from the bedroom and then he'd flown off on the back of a Pegasus he'd have just as much reason to accept that as a possibility.

It was twenty minutes past their scheduled meeting time when Grant walked in, breathless and soaking wet. Yes, the rain had been coming down hard from time to time all day, (typical British summer) but Grant also looked like he'd sweated hard.

"You're here," he said, taking the seat next to Simon.

"Yep, I'm here." The state he was in gave him even less credibility.

"You saw my earlier text, about the latest demon." Grant leaned toward him.

Simon held his hands up both to maintain his body space and halt Grant's enthusiasm. "Can we not call them demons?"

"Okay, okay," said Grant. "What would you suggest?"

"Returnees?"

"Hmmm. Problematic as it suggests that those that arrive are the same as those that left."

"Is that what you're arguing? That they're not?"

Grant shook his head with enough ferocity to shake a little of the excess water from his head. "It may be the same vessel, but something inside is very different."

"Look, we took Ted back to the doctor. They said that a lot of how he was behaving was due to vitamin deficiency–because of what he was fed while away."

"Yes, because the diet he would have been put on would have made him ripe as a host."

Simon rubbed his forehead. "I don't know what I'm doing here."

"The right thing." Grant's eyes widened.

"So, this other returnee, is it the guy who turned up at my house this morning?"

"Ah, so they're seeking each other out. We believe he is a gentleman who disappeared from a farm close to your house, but here's the thing: he disappeared 23 years ago."

"He was an old guy."

"He was old when he went missing. Somehow these de... these creatures from the subterraneous domain put his body in some kind of stasis. Now they need to use it. Why would that be? Why are they using your son? Why is your son unharmed when the others, these 'returnees' as you call them, have all lost something?"

Simon sighed. He wanted to dismiss it, but despite everything, there was some semblance of rationality and logic to it. "What is it you want?"

"For now, we keep each other informed. Tell me what happens with your son, and I'll tell you what's going on elsewhere. Let me examine your boy."

"I can keep you informed about his life, but only so you can see how normal it is. I'm not going to let you touch him." Simon touched his pocket as he felt his phone inside vibrate.

"There's another man in your village of interest."

Simon faced Grant and raised an eyebrow.

"Ted Hatcher. Heard of him?"

Simon nodded. He had nothing to say about the man. He'd always been the village weirdo.

"He was missing for two years. Came back and has barely been able to function since."

Simon nodded. As a youngster, he'd not been aware of Ted Hatcher, but when he returned to live with his parents again, after failing his second year at university due to spending more time in the bars than the lecture theatre, Simon became aware of the rumours about him, that there was something wrong with him. It was several years later, after Simon had married Megan and lost his parents, that the whole community became aware of Ted Hatcher and the stories about his mother's corpse.

"This isn't common knowledge, but I've seen his medical records. They say part of his brain simply isn't there. They've done scans and all sorts, but the guy doesn't have any scars that suggest surgery. Those things took away a part of his brain so they could control him. I've seen him. I've observed him. I reckon they made a mistake with him. Tried to turn him into a vessel but ruined the craft in the process. What kind of man doesn't report the death of his mother?"

Simon glanced at Grant. He seemed the sort to do that and a lot worse. "Look," he said. "I came to see you today about something I saw in the river."

"Go on."

"An arm. A human arm. Reckon it belonged to that Wright boy."

Grant nodded. "Something's changing. The way I see it we've got one of two situations. One, their power is slipping. Something has upset their home and they can't hold on to those they've taken anymore and they're slipping away. Two, they've given up on their home because they know an invasion is imminent."

"What do you mean invasion?"

"What's the old saying about there being no more room in Hell? Forget Hell. There is no Hell. Never has been. But there is this subterranean world, and they recruit, and they grow and they've got so many now that they're ready to come topside and fight to be the dominant species."

"The police are investigating the river now," Simon said. He could stick with Grant's branch of the conversation, but it was at that moment he realised what he was really doing talking to him. He didn't want to be persuaded by any of Grant's crazy theories. He just liked to hear them because it made him feel normal by comparison.

"Promise me you'll keep me in the loop," Grant said, hopping down from his bar stool. "Things are manic, and I've got to run—more investigations to follow up."

"Will do," Simon said. When he was gone, he pulled out his phone. He listened to the voicemail and realised he had to leave urgently but not before signalling the barman and ordering a rum to chase the pint down.

49: LOLA

Ever since she was dismissed by her mother, Lola had been messaging Mitchell. She had to use her tablet as the phone still wasn't switching on, and she didn't know what to do about it. They had one of those conversations which went everywhere and nowhere. Lola was giving Mitchell periodic updates on the activity she could see from her bedroom window, but it was little more than accounts of men in wetsuits bobbing in and out of the water, playing with equipment she didn't understand. They talked about Lauren. Mitchell proclaimed her the biggest bullshitter in the year, but if you could get past that, a decent person. He talked about Julius and what he meant to him. He had told her about the guilt he felt when Julius had gone missing, that he was supposed to meet him up that day, how they'd spend some time messing about near the railway tracks, and part of him had believed that Julius had gone alone and somehow been hit by the train and completely obliterated by it, disintegrated into non-existence. In turn, Lola had told him about how she got on with Ted, how they seemed to be getting closer now, closer than they were before he went away, how secondary school life had got in the way of that. He'd told her why he'd got on top of that table, that it wasn't right that people had been talking about her when it wasn't true. He told her what had happened in the principal's office, how Butcher had tried to explain the situation, but the head could only see that Mitchell had followed the instructions, so the after-school detention sanction would stick, but not the suspension Butcher pushed for. Lola was glad of that.

After all of the meandering messages, the wandering, indirect conversation, Mitchell finally got to the point. *Any chance you can pop out for a bit?*

Yeah, typed Lola. *Where do you want to meet?*

The place I surprised you the other day?

K. Give me 10 minutes.

Lola shuffled back on her bed and took a few deep breaths. Why did he want to meet in person? It could only be one thing. She wondered if she should change, but no, she didn't have time, and it would only make Mum suspicious. Make-up was out for the same reason. She'd go as she was.

Before she left her room, she invented a reason for leaving the house. On the way downstairs, she called out, "Mum, I've just got to pop out."

"Okay," Mum called back.

No interrogation. She'd invented the excuse of popping to Jas's house for a book for no reason.

The rain had stopped falling, and the sun threatened to push through the clouds, so the walk to the meeting place had been a pleasant one. As she approached the passage, she saw Mitchell was already present, looking down Poplar Avenue. He had no idea she was behind him. If she wanted to, if she really wanted to, it would be an opportunity for revenge for him jumping her the other day. But, no, that would be cruel. She decided to go for the opposite shoulder tap instead, making him turn the wrong way.

"Hey, Lo," he said when his eyes eventually caught up with her.

It was the first time she'd been called that. She kind of liked it.

"Look down the street," he said. "What's the Child Catcher doing?"

Was this why he'd called her there? She looked down the road and saw he had a pile of bin bags stacked up outside his house. There must have been at least six.

"What do you think he's got in there?" Mitchell asked.

Lola shrugged.

"You think it's dead bodies?"

"Listen, I can't be out long." If Mum wondered where she was and decided to call, she'd be in trouble for not answering. Then she'd have to reveal that her phone was broken, and she didn't want a lecture about money. Why did her parents think she wanted to know when they had financial difficulties? She did her best not to ask for anything and turned down things she was offered that she thought she could do without.

"Okay," Mitchell said. He grabbed one of her hands. "Lola, will you go with me?"

"Go where?" As soon as she said it, she felt stupid. Her understanding of the question had come a second too late. "Yes, I mean."

"Phew!" Mitchell said. He drew the back of his hand across his forehead. "Listen, I know all of the shit Lauren goes on about—sex and all that—but I'm gonna be honest with you, I've never done that. I just like you, and I want to hang out with you. I want you to be my girlfriend. We'll see where things go from there, okay?"

Lola smiled and nodded. "Yeah, that's cool. That's what I want, too."

"Did you mean that you couldn't be out long?"

"Yeah, sorry."

"Can I walk you home?"

"I'd like that."

Mitchell took hold of Lola's hand and slowly, enjoying the sun on their faces, they wandered back to Riverview Terrace.

50: MEGAN

She'd been fuming through dinner, a dinner which, if Ted was to be believed, Simon had planned to cook and prepare. Instead, he'd cleared off and left her in the dark about body parts floating down the river. Ted had stuck to his part. He'd helped prepare dinner until tiredness again got the better of him. He did look like some weight was coming back into his face though, so that was a plus.

When Simon had arrived home, he'd come into the kitchen and said, "I was gonna do that."

Megan waited until the kids had left the table after a strange and awkward dinner in which Megan had refused to speak to Simon, and in return, Simon avoided saying anything to rile her, Ted had been close to nodding off at the table, and Lola had been grinning away and staring into space. Thankfully, as soon as the meal was over, Ted stumbled off to his room, almost certainly going straight to sleep, and Lola, who couldn't stop giggling as she tucked in her chair, seemed desperate to get back to her room.

Simon had pulled his phone out before the kids had even left the table and stared at the screen.

Megan went over to the kitchen window and looked out. There were still a few people out there, but their activity had significantly reduced.

"So, when exactly were you planning on telling me about the body parts in the river?" Megan turned to face Simon, her arms folded across her chest.

"Sorry, love, I couldn't." He continued staring at the screen.

"Can you at least look at me when I'm talking to you?"

Simon put his phone on the table. "My first call was to Heimlich, and then I had to go to the station."

"You could have tried to call me before heading to the station, or when you left. You could have sent me a message."

Simon sighed. "It all got a bit hectic."

Megan glared at Simon. "It got a bit hectic? How do you think I felt hearing it from Heimlich? Hearing that my husband had been secretly recording something and found a bloody arm in the river."

"Secretly recording something?"

"Well, you hadn't told me about it. What exactly were you trying to capture with that camera?"

Simon rolled his eyes. "When Ted went back to the water, he had this hunger in his eyes. He was so desperate, frantic, almost inhuman."

"You were there at the hospital. You know what caused that. Don't you trust the doctors?"

Simon glanced at his phone again, and then ran his fingers back through his hair. "Don't you think it's strange? He was gone so long, and then he comes back and won't say a thing about where he's been?"

"He doesn't remember. What, don't you believe him?"

"Well, it's convenient, isn't it?"

Megan threw her hands into the air. "Convenient? Convenient, Simon? I'm going out of my head, here. I thought having Ted back would help, but not knowing what happened to him is driving me insane. You don't know the things I want to do. You don't know what I'd do if I ever got my hands on who did this to him."

Simon thumped the table. "You know why I don't know? You stopped talking to me when Ted went missing. Remember that? I wanted to talk about our strategy for finding him, and you went and signed up for a training course in bloody Croydon. I was arranging search parties and you were covering sick members of staff and doing home visits."

Megan leant on the table. "Don't turn this on me. Where did you go after you left the police station? How did Heimlich get here with a team of divers before you managed to make it back here?"

"I... went to the pub."

"The pub?" Megan leant forward further still and sniffed. There was a hint of alcohol on his breath.

"I had to meet someone."

"Who?"

"It doesn't matter."

Megan stood up. "It does matter. I don't like being left in the dark. I don't like having the police turn up giving me information that you should have told me."

"I've said I'm sorry. That arm, it freaked me out. I had to speak to someone about it. You understand, right?"

Megan sighed. "Yes… but… couldn't you have talked to me?"

Simon opened his mouth to speak, and closed it again, before deciding he would speak. "That's the problem though, isn't it?"

"What is?"

"As I said, we stopped talking when Ted went missing. We did things our own way…"

"I guess I thought things would go back to how they were before now that he's back."

Simon stared at Megan, wide-eyed. "Is he though?"

Megan bent down again to make direct eye contact with him. "Back? Ted? You tell me, you just had dinner with him."

"But he's not as he was before. It's not like it was before."

"I think we both made the mistake of expecting our lives to reset and to go back to how it was."

Simon's head turned and his gaze drifted toward Ted's room. He was clearly thinking about his son. "Maybe things haven't gone back to normal as Ted's not…"

"Ted's not what, Simon? Of course he's going to be a little bit messed up. He's got to come to terms with this, and that's going to be difficult. We've got to stop pretending things will go back to normal without a bit of input on our part. We're the adults; we have to make the effort to fix it. Agreed?"

Simon nodded.

Megan wasn't entirely sure he was on board. But that was part of the problem. Where once she could read him easily, could tell his thoughts by his expression, these days it was as if it were made of plastic, fixed and rigid, giving nothing away.

She watched him pick up his phone and stare at the blank screen.

Megan opened her mouth to speak again. She wanted to say something about his drinking. She didn't want him to go back to how he was before. She didn't want him to lose control again. But she also knew from experience that his reaction to raising the issue would be to go and pour himself a drink and raise the glass. No, there would have to be a better time. Things would calm down just as soon as she got to the truth.

51: TED

Ted had been too tired after dinner to do much more digging. He returned to the website and read the information on Hatcher, the man they all called the child catcher. If anything, it was that which was of most concern to Ted. This man might have suffered the same fate he had, and now Hatcher was mocked by all the kids and could barely function in life. Was this the same fate in store for him? Would he find himself unable to communicate clearly with people, leading to them calling him a freak and ostracising him from society?

He started to doubt the authenticity of the site. The 'about' page was unprofessional waffle, which immediately shifted it from investigative journalism to fiction in Ted's head. Yes, he knew the area and he knew some of the history, but it was all speculation with no grounding in any kind of reality. What's more, the page hadn't been updated in a couple of years. He was thankful there was no mention of him on there, and it probably meant that the creator had lost interest in tracking missing people and had moved on to some other unsavoury activity.

Ted jerked awake and had to react quickly to catch his laptop as it went sliding off his lap. He'd dropped off for long enough for the computer to go to sleep, but not so long that it was dark outside. And with it still being light, Ted wished for some fresh air. He made his way out of his bedroom and into the living where Mum and Dad were sitting on different sofas, Mum reading, Dad on his phone.

"Is it okay if I pop out for a bit?" Ted said.

"Where to?" Dad asked.

"Just for a walk."

Mum looked up from her book. "I don't think you should go on your own." She folded the corner of her page and placed the book on the arm of the sofa.

"Don't worry, love," Dad said. "I'll go. I don't mind accompanying Ted on his journey."

Something passed in the air between them during a brief conversation, most of which Ted felt was going over his head. They were good at talking in riddles or a secret code when they needed to be. At its conclusion, Mum picked up her book again, and Dad went into the hall and pulled on his shoes.

"Where are we heading then, Ted? Not by the river?"

"No," said Ted, smiling.

"Good. I don't want to be grabbing you to stop you jumping in again."

Together, they left the house. As soon as they reached the end of Riverview Terrace, Ted knew where he wanted to go: the vicarage. The building had been on his mind and he couldn't figure out why. Dad happily followed him as he made his way along the few streets that would take him there, all the time peppering him with tedious questions about things he liked and disliked. Despite Ted using the word "still" for most of his responses, Dad didn't get the message that none of his tastes had changed.

Ted stopped when they reached the vicarage and looked up at the building. The earlier rain meant the gargoyles were still busy, dribbling water out of their mouths and onto the ground, saturating the vegetation at the perimeter of the building.

"You never used to be interested in architecture," Dad said.

"I'm not... there's just... something about this building."

"What do you mean 'something'?" Dad placed a hand on Ted's shoulder and looked him in the eye.

"I don't know." Ted gazed up at the gargoyles again. The sun had begun to set somewhere behind the building, so they were mere silhouettes. "It's like there's a memory there from when I was away."

"You think you might have been here?" Dad nodded toward the building.

"No, I don't know. My head feels funny when I look at it—like there's something there, but it's somehow blocked."

Dad moved away from Ted and over to the door to the vicarage. He pounded on it, waited for a moment, and then pounded again.

"Dad, don't."

"It's okay son. If the vicar's there, if you can get a look inside, it might spark something else." Dad pounded again, but no one came. He moved over to one of the windows and tried to look inside, but the blinds blocked his view.

"I don't think it would help, Dad," Ted said, feeling needles of pain coming up from his chest, travelling up his spinal column, and spiking into his brain. They always came when he tried to remember.

Dad shook his head. "Yeah," he said re-joining Ted. "Fair enough. We should probably get you home and ready for school tomorrow anyway."

52: SIMON

Simon wasn't the biggest fan of Wiseham's vicar, and he had a healthy mistrust of religious figures on the whole, but the man didn't strike him as being capable of kidnapping a child and holding him against his will. He was an overly pious man and rather humble: he never thought himself as worthy of a building as grand as the vicarage and as such hosted a number of different gatherings there on a regular basis, but when Ted suggested the vicarage might be of importance, he had a strong desire to get inside the building to find out more.

His walk back home with Ted had been quiet. The boy had begun to shuffle his feet and needed warning of curbs and low-hanging branches. When he wasn't watching for hazards, his mind wandered to his last conversation with Grant. All of the demon stuff was surely nonsense, but now there was a religious link. What if the vicar wasn't as holy as he appeared? What if behind the façade he was a gatekeeper to the subterranean world of demons?

When they reached home, Simon unlocked the door to let Ted in and told him he'd be in shortly. He pulled the door closed, took a few steps away, to the other side of his car, pulled out his phone, called Grant, and reported the event.

"I'm sorry to tell you," Grant said, his voice distorted and clipping slightly, "that the behaviour you've seen is typical of hosts."

Simon sighed.

"It's what they do," Grant continued. "Build a mistrust of the religious authority in a community so the institution is easier to tear down, less of a barrier to their plan of dominion."

Simon shook his head. He had no idea why he was doing this. "So, what do we do?"

"Keep me in the loop. I've got to get in touch with the others, let them know that they're moving ahead with their plans."

"Okay."

"Simon, you could be a real asset in the war that's to come." Grant ended the call.

Simon put his phone into his pocket and as he turned toward the door, it opened.

"What are you doing out there?" Megan asked.

"Coming in now."

"You better not have been planning to slope off back to the pub." Megan glared at him.

Simon shook his head. He hadn't been planning on it, but now it sounded like a mighty good idea. He'd never get away with it though. It would cause too much grief. A couple of swigs of the bottle of Old Navy would have to do, as long as there was some left.

53: TED

By the next morning, the idea of school had quickly lost its lustre. His return had stopped being a talking point after only one day. No one acknowledged him at the bus stop as he stood on the periphery of the same circle of former friends again. Even Lola was distant, standing with a boy called Mitchell who Ted was now in the same year group as.

The school day too was boring, and it hit Ted, at some point through the third period, after a break spent alone that this dullness was almost comforting. People might have talked about him behind his back. There might have been announcements in tutor time before his return to inform pupils that they shouldn't raise the subject of his missing months. Altogether, it meant he could go back to school, be anonymous, and get on with life. It was the most normal he'd felt since his return, other than the obsession with obtaining normality, but perhaps that too would drift away in time.

Ted felt so anonymous that he didn't for a second suspect that the shout of, "Hey," was directed at him as he made his way through the corridors from science to design technology.

It wasn't until Larry was right in front of him, breathing his hot and sour breath in his face that he realised he was being addressed at all. "Space Dick, I'm talking to you."

His stomach felt suddenly hot, like boiling water was sloshing around inside him. Then Larry grabbed him and slung him into the toilets.

"We don't want your sort around here," he said and thumped Ted in the stomach.

Heat exploded inside. He retched, thought he was going to vomit, and what came up would surely be molten lava. Despite the pain, he couldn't help but wonder about Larry's choice of phrase. "You lot...?" he said, a whisper all he could manage.

"Fucking anal probe," Larry said between gritted teeth that did little to hold back a tide of saliva.

Was that an answer? An insult? Did he even know? Ted had never been beaten up before, and he was frustrated to find his mind racing but his body incapable of moving his arms to block the next blow that hit him in the stomach. This time the contents did rise, burning in his throat before a black mess dribbled out of his mouth, falling onto the floor and onto Larry's feet.

"What the fuck is that? Is that alien blood?"

How stupid was this guy? Ted's mouth filled with the taste of mud, but the burning had ceased. He looked down at the floor, expecting Larry to leap out in agony at any second, his feet dissolving in the molten vomit, but, other than causing revulsion, his blackened stomach contents had no effect.

Larry grabbed him, balled up his jumper in his fists and slung him across the room.

Ted had no control; he felt himself turn and stumble back. The floor was wet, his feet had nothing to hold on to, and he was going down, twisting and spinning as he did so. His shoulder clipped the edge of the urinal and exploded in pain. He cried out, but then there was another pain, digging in his gut. His vision blurred and it was like someone switched on an amp inside his head. He couldn't make out the garbled insults coming from Larry through the electric buzz in his head as he kicked him in the stomach again and again and again until the pain was all he had. The last kick came not to the gut, but to the underside of the jaw causing a double burst of pain, first when the foot connected with the jaw, second when the jaw clamped down on his teeth. Perhaps it was the splatter of blood that he coughed out that stopped Larry's attack. Perhaps he'd exhausted himself. Perhaps his rage had dissipated, and he had realised the error of his ways (Ted doubted this last one).

"If I catch you in the corridor tomorrow, an anal probe will be the last of your worries."

Ted wanted to move, but every effort caused agony. His heart thumped in his ribcage like a rhinoceros trapped in a box, and any second Ted was expecting its horn to erupt through his chest. At least then the agony might subside. At least then he might be able to draw in a breath again without feeling like it could be his last, for with every breath, he drew in blood from his lacerated tongue. He swallowed again and tasted only the copper tang of blood. He had to raise his head a little—if only to stop the blood from running straight down his throat.

His head hurt, his neck, less so. He could angle it without feeling like he was going to be sick. From there he could draw in air (not fresh air, not in a school toilet), and let the blood run out onto the floor. Any other movement would have to wait.

But not for long.

"You okay?"

Ted tried to focus on the source of the voice. It was him! Pee Kid! Jimmy Will Wilson! The poor kid must have been in year 8 now, Lola's year. He'd hadn't half got some grief after a private email got out. Ted's class were in maths. Mr Levin hadn't frozen his screen, and while his pupils were supposed to be silently working through some algebraic equations, Levin scrolled through his emails. He didn't know that everyone in the class could see the confidential information being broadcast through the projector onto the screen. In fact, it was the presence of the word CONFIDENTIAL in the subject header that sparked interest.

Someone in the class had called out, told him his board wasn't frozen, but if anything, this made matters worse. Only certain details had been skimmed. The kid's name had been presented as Jimmy (Will) Wilson, as he was often called Will. The school had received a letter from his mother stating that he had a weak bladder for which they had sought medical attention and asking if Jimmy could be allowed to use the toilet whenever he desired.

Ted was suddenly very thankful for that kid's weak bladder.

Jimmy helped Ted into a sitting position. He got Ted's water bottle out of his bag for him and took the lid off so Ted could have a drink. Only the first couple of gulps tasted entirely of blood.

"You want me to get a teacher?" Jimmy asked.

"No," said Ted. He hurt, but it wasn't so bad. He didn't want the attention, all of the office staff looking him over. He was supposed to be going home in a bit anyway.

"I really need the loo," Jimmy said.

Why did he need permission? "Go on then."

Jimmy went into one of the stalls. Ted was thankful since he was propped up at urinal height. He could feel the wetness from the floor seeping into his trousers. He was almost thankful for a sensation that wasn't pain. It motivated him to stand. Leaning on one arm was painful, but the other was okay, and his legs were fine. He had to lean forward slightly. When he was straight, his gut ached. His shoulder, where he'd crashed into the urinal was painful, but he could move it. If anything, he'd been lucky. Maybe Larry had a lousy technique–a poor student in every feasible field of study. Ted chuckled to himself, but it hurt to do so.

He looked himself over in the mirror. He looked dishevelled, no worse. His jumper hung even looser where it had been pulled out of shape and his hair was all over the place, but no one would immediately know what he'd been through.

He heard a flush. A second latter Jimmy was beside him, washing his hands in a sink. "Are you okay?" he asked.

"I'll be fine," Ted said. "I'd appreciate it if you didn't mention this to anyone?"

Jimmy nodded. If anyone was going to value discretion, it was him. He dried his hands and left.

Ted checked his watch. Period 4 would be over in half an hour, then he could go home. He decided to wait it out in a cubicle.

54: SIMON

Ted even walked differently. He stooped like a geriatric, rather than swaggering with teenage bravado. Every time one of these thoughts hit Simon, he felt guilty. He shouldn't be spending his time looking for proof that his son was carrying some kind of demon on his back. Or maybe that's what he should be doing? Maybe it was wrong to turn a blind eye to this kind of thing. What if his vigilance here could stop an invasion from these subterranean creatures?

He turned on the radio and turned it up, hoping to drown out the discordant voices. What better way to do that than some cheery pop? Ted reached the car just at the point in the song where the rapper started mumbling something misogynistic. Was this the kind of crap they were listening to these days? Ted used to have decent music taste. Lola had always been into pop pap.

"Your morning okay?" Simon asked as Ted climbed into the car. There was something awkward about his movements. Even the way he sat down was strange.

"Yep," Ted answered.

He hadn't said much, but his voice was off. Simon reversed out of the parking space. He angled the mirror to better see Ted.

"So, what lessons did you have today?"

Ted listed them in a voice that wasn't his own. Since when had he had a lisp?

When they reached the stop sign, Simon turned to look at his son. Ted grimaced as he shifted in his seat, struggling to get comfortable. He opened his mouth and moved his tongue around awkwardly.

"Are you sure you're alright?"

Ted sniffled, and, a couple of seconds later, he burst into tears.

"Hang on a sec..." Simon said as if that would somehow stem the tide of woe. He pulled into the road, and then almost immediately turned right into the forecourt of a petrol station.

"What's up?" Simon said. He turned toward Ted. His tongue looked swollen. His jumper also appeared baggy and stretched. "Has someone had a go at you?"

Ted shook his head. It took a moment for him to get control of his breathing, but eventually, he could talk. "I slipped on the toilet floor," Ted said. "Hit my shoulder on a urinal and bit my tongue when I hit the ground."

"Oof," Simon said, looking on in concern. "And you're sure that's all it was? No one else involved?"

Ted shook his head.

"Stick your tongue out."

Ted did so. The way he shaped his face made it clear it wasn't a comfortable experience.

The tongue was dark and had swollen to look like a cheap supermarket steak. There were clear serrations on both sides. Ted's teeth bore a red tidemark. It would heal, but it would be painful for a while.

"Looks nasty. Caught it on both sides."

Ted closed his mouth and nodded.

"I'll take a look at your shoulder when we get home. Anything else?"

"That's it," Ted said.

"While I've stopped you want me to get you something that might be easier to eat? Soup? Ice cream?"

Ted screwed up his face. The poor bugger had probably swallowed so much blood that he didn't have much of an appetite. Again, the voices niggled at Simon. He was reminded of the things he'd thought about his son and guilt washed over him, telling him what an awful father he was, bringing bitter bile burning up his throat. More than ever, he could do with a drink to take the taste away.

When they pulled up at the house, Simon urged Ted to stay seated. He then rushed around the car to get the door for him, watching him struggle out of the car. Once both of Ted's feet met the drive, Simon dashed ahead to unlock the door so Ted could go straight in.

"Get your top off and let me take a look at your shoulder."

Ted winced as he struggled to pull up his jumper and polo shirt.

A bruise the shape of Australia (and only fractionally smaller) had spread across Ted's shoulder, already a vicious purple.

"Looks nasty. How's it feel?"

"Sore."

Ted looked pale. Paler than usual.

"You feeling okay?"

"I think I might be sick."

Simon went ahead and opened the toilet door.

Ted only just made it down onto one knee before he launched a torrent of black stuff into the loo.

Whatever gushed out of his son's mouth, it wasn't vomit. There was a red hint, but mostly it was black and sludgy.

Ted heaved again, and another torrent of filth sloshed into the toilet bowl. There was less of it, but it was redder. It didn't have the smell of vomit but held the scent of blood, and a hint of the river on a hot day.

"I'm calling your doctor," Simon said.

"Don't," Ted said. He spat into the toilet.

"You're vomiting blood, Ted."

"It's only where I swallowed so much after I bit my tongue."

"That may be, but it's best checked."

He left Ted in the bathroom and dialled Hodder's number. Simon answered her questions as best he could but agreed that it was best to bring Ted in to be checked over.

"Okay, get in the car."

"Dad, I'm fine." He looked far from fine. He could barely talk because of his swollen tongue and a dribble of vomit/blood/god knows what remained on his chin.

"If that's the case, we won't be there long."

He told Ted to get in the car again and called Megan to let her know. He wouldn't make the same mistake again.

55: MEGAN

Megan had completed sixty-five per cent of an online training course for a new system when the phone rang. She told Simon she'd meet him at the hospital and quickly called her manager to explain the situation. Her manager had been understanding throughout everything, though she did couch her empathetic demeanour with the news that another round of redundancies was to follow in the final quarter of the year and attendance would be one of the factors they'd look at. That was months away. In the past, she'd had plans for her career, ideas about what stage she'd like to be at and when. Now, six months into the future was utterly incomprehensible. Day by day she'd been trying to cope by taking on extra work to keep her mind busy while Ted was missing, and Ted's return gave her only more to think about. Without her work, all she had was the worry, the needling fear that would bring horrific images of worst-case scenarios, always capable of adding another layer of misery to her thoughts. Simon had been brief on the phone. Ted had fallen over in the school toilets and was throwing up blood. There didn't seem to be any link between the two events. Why would falling over in the toilets make him do that? Had he collapsed in the toilets because of another factor, and it was that factor which caused him to cough up blood? Had someone found him there, unconscious? Why had this condition that caused him to cough up blood not been detected at his recent check-up?

She was on the wrong side of town for the hospital, but it was still before the end of the school day, so traffic wouldn't be too much of a problem. It would just allow her to build Ted's status to critical in her head.

With Ted back in a hospital bed again, it felt like they'd made no progress since he'd been found. He still didn't know what had happened. She still didn't know who to blame, and they'd gone full circle and returned where they were when they found him.

Doctor Hodder met Megan in the corridor with Simon following behind her.

"Is he okay?" Megan asked.

"Yes, he'll be fine," Hodder said.

"Why's he vomiting blood, then?"

"We have checked for internal injuries, and there are none. The blood he vomited was simply bringing up what he'd ingested as result of his injured tongue."

"Which he did when he fell down?"

"I'm not sure Ted is being completely honest."

"What do you mean?"

"He claims he fell, and that looks like the cause of the bruising on his shoulder, but the bruising on his arms, on his stomach, on his chin, look to me like the result of an assault."

Megan wanted to run into the room and hug her son, and once she was sure he was okay, she'd interrogate him, find out who'd hurt him, and pay them back.

"Can I ask one thing, Doctor?" Simon said.

"Sure, go ahead."

"When Ted vomited, it came out black. Why would that be?"

"It would only be what he'd eaten, partially digested and the amount of blood he'd ingested."

"But that doesn't explain why it'd be black."

"I'm afraid I can't say. There are no abnormalities showing in his gut whatsoever."

"Okay, can I see him?" Megan asked.

"Yes, in one moment. There is some good news. The iron tablets are clearly starting to have an effect. The white blood cell count is on the increase. We have no reason to keep him in, so you can go home when you're ready."

"And what about his heart?" Megan asked.

"Obviously, and kind of strenuous activity is a huge risk, especially with the need for further exploratory surgery, but we've been monitoring it since he came in, and it has remained stable."

Megan nodded and exhaled slowly, feeling the comforted smile spread across her face. "Do we need to wait for discharge forms or anything?"

"No, we consider this a check-up for an out-patient, given Ted's peculiar circumstances. Genuinely, if there's ever anything you need or you're concerned about, get in touch as you did today." Hodder smiled, hugged her clipboard to herself, and left.

Megan went into the room with Ted. He stared blankly at the wall. Megan took hold of one of his hands. "So, are you going to tell us what really happened?"

"Like I said to Dad, I slipped and fell. Hit my shoulder on the urinal and bit through my tongue."

Megan rubbed Ted's hand. "Your doctor doesn't think that sounds right. You've got bruising on your stomach and arms. How did that get there?"

Ted continued to stare off into space. "I don't know."

"Someone attacked you, didn't they? Come on, Teddy, you can tell us."

"I must have bruised them when I hit the floor."

Simon leant in, resting a hand on the metal frame of the bed. "You know that's not true. Is someone picking on you?"

Ted raised his voice and turned to his dad. "No! Can't you just leave it?"

Simon reciprocated. "No, I can't leave it. Someone put you in hospital. We can't let them get away with it."

"You're the one who brought me here, Dad." Ted sat up. "I told you I was only sick because I swallowed too much blood."

Simon turned to Megan, anger burning in his eyes. "You talk to him."

Megan spoke in a low, calm voice. "If you want it sorted out, give me a name. It'll be done. I swear to you."

Ted's brow wrinkled in concern. "Honestly, it was just someone messing around. If it turns into something serious, I'll tell you. I promise."

Megan nodded her head. "Okay." That would have to do for now. Hopefully, Ted was being honest. Hopefully, it really was nothing because if she found out different, she'd do everything she could do to make the life of the person who hurt her son full of so much pain, and despair. God, she wanted a name, she wanted to inflict pain on someone. She imagined a faceless bully. She imagined sliding something into his skin, something barbed, and leaving him to struggle to pull it out. She imagined pulling at his fingernails and toenails with a pair of pliers, and when they'd been extracted, starting on the teeth. She imagined hammering every single bone in the hand and felt a pang of disappointment that she had no face to visualise the pain on and no name to inflict it on.

56: LOLA

Arriving home to find it deserted was like a flashback to Ted's missing days. Where were they? At least Lola had her key. She went straight in and checked her messages on her tablet. It was so frustrating being without a phone. It didn't take long for Lola to realise that if no one was home, no one would miss her if she was out. She messaged Mitchell: *Wanna meet up?*

Sure. Usual place?

Again, she caught Mitchell staring down Poplar Avenue, but this time he seemed more nervous, kept looking back over his shoulder. That's how he spotted Lola before she got to him.

"What's the child catcher up to now?" Lola said, looking down the road past Mitchell. There were about a dozen bin bags piled up outside his house alongside several boxes.

"It's not that house; it's Julius's."

"What's going on?" Lola asked.

"I was waiting here for you, when I heard a car door slam, and Julius's dad went speeding off."

Lola turned her attention to the Wright household. An upstairs light flicked on and then off again. "Did you see that?"

"Yeah, it's been doing that from time to time."

"What for?"

Before Mitchell could respond, a different light flashed on and off again.

"Has it been doing that?" Lola asked. "Different lights?"

"Yeah, it's just, random, like someone's running around the house turning lights on and off for no reason."

"Should we go check on them? Make sure everything's okay?"

"Let's move closer, see if we can figure it out."

Mitchell moved first, crouching down. It was ridiculous as so many houses overlooked them, but Lola followed suit. She recognised the yellow car parked close to Julius's house, but couldn't be sure where she'd seen it before. Mitchell sped over to it and peered over its boot. Lola looked into the car window. The black roof, the part that could be folded back on hot days, had faded to grey in places and flecks of mould decorated it all over. There was a duvet and a pillow on the back seat and in the footwell the remains of a supermarket meal deal. She looked in the front. On the seat was a leather pouch, totally out of keeping with the rest of the car's contents—it looked like it was worth something. From Julius's house, where a single light now flickered through the downstairs window, came a shout. Mitchell sprang toward the house, remaining low until he was under a window.

Lola was about to follow when she heard a door close. She turned toward Hatcher's house, where the sound had originated and saw a skinny man coming out of the door. He had tiny round glasses like someone out of a history lesson, and his thin hair looked ready to escape from the top of his head and blow away. The look on his face was one of panic. He moved quickly, not quite breaking into a run, but certainly in a hurry—the quickstep of the reserved gentleman, though he looked pretty far removed from the realms of gentlemen. It was pretty clear to Lola where he was heading: toward the car she squatted beside. She looked over her shoulder for a place to go. She wasn't doing anything wrong, but her body, wracked by panic, refused to move. She'd played games on the streets before, and many had involved hiding and running around. She could run off and it would look like nothing more than a child's game, but there was something about the man's face that told her she didn't want to be spotted by him. If he was getting into the driver's side, then there was no reason why he'd pass her, no reason why he should spot her. The only problem would be when he went to pull off... but she could run then, once he was in the car. If she waited until he started the engine, he wouldn't hear anything either.

Lola crouched down and didn't look up until she heard the car door open. She knew she should have kept down, but she couldn't help it. She always had to look toward the source of the noise. Her hearing difficulty had made that a habit when looking at someone helped to work out what they were saying. She was hardly a trained lip reader, but she'd developed some skills through practice. But when she looked up, she realised he wasn't getting in to drive away; he was getting in to grab the leather pouch. How did he not see her? Clearly, his eyes were focused only on the pouch. It flapped open as he pulled it toward him, showing a flash of silver, making it seem even more out of place there.

He closed the door.

"Hey," he called. "What are you doing?"

Lola peeked, but could only tell that the man had turned to face the Wright house. Surely, he was looking at Mitchell, wondering what he was doing crouched beside someone's window.

Lola stood up and walked around the car, calling out "Here, kitty."

She moved onto the pavement and feigned surprise at seeing the man standing over her. He had an unpleasant odour, as if he'd been sat around burning incense, but with a sour flavour. "Excuse me," Lola said, looking up at him, smiling, willing her dimples to show her extreme innocence, "have you seen our cat?"

He looked down at her. Her attempted sweetness had no effect on the bitter look on his face. "No," he said. He looked back at Mitchell.

"Any luck over there?" called Lola.

Mitchell started to trot back toward them.

"No sign of the cat?" Lola said, staring at Mitchell, hoping to force her thoughts into his brain.

"The cat?" he said, momentarily looking confused. "No, it wasn't there."

"I guess we'll have to keep looking." Lola turned away and called the cat again. She crouched down and peered under the car. Mitchell quickly imitated her calls. She moved toward Hatcher's house, a place she'd spent every living moment trying to avoid and looked into the thick growth of weeds in the border. "Here, kitty," she called again, and then paused. She stood behind the Land Rover, peering through both sets of windows toward the Wright house.

Mitchell looked over his shoulder. "What are you doing?" he whispered.

Lola checked too. The man was loitering by the car. As he turned to look their way, Lola spun back round to face Hatcher's house.

"He looks dodgy."

They heard another shout, again coming from the Wright house.

Lola put every ounce of effort into not turning around. "Here kitty," she said again, louder. "There you are!" She stared into the weeds. "He's stuck." She turned to Mitchell and spoke loudly, clearly. "Can you knock on Mr Hatcher's door and let him know what we're doing?"

"Are you crazy?" Mitchell said between clenched teeth, as if it would stop the sound from carrying.

Lola lowered her voice too. "The man came out of his house. Just knock, see if he answers."

Mitchell approached the door.

Lola could see his chest heaving as he prepared himself; then he banged on the door three times in rapid succession.

"Leave me alone," came a cry from the other side of the door.

Lola turned as she heard an engine start and saw it cough smoke from its exhaust. The yellow convertible moved to the end of the road, turned around, and drove off, leaving a trail of smoke carrying a hint of blue in the air behind it.

With that, Lola and Mitchell hurried from Hatcher's garden.

"Who was that?"

"I don't know, but there was something wrong with him."

Another shout came from the Wright household.

"What's going on over there?" Lola asked.

"I don't know," Mitchell said. "I heard something, not words, just a noise, the same noise again and again, and his mum, she shouted back at him. 'It's ungodly,' I heard her say, but then I think she was crying."

"Should we go over?"

Mitchell shrugged. "I dunno. When I went to the hospital, Julius was like that, just shouting out."

"Do you think she's okay?"

Mitchell smiled nervously. "I should check, shouldn't I?"

Lola nodded. They both walked slowly toward the Wright household, listening for more shouts.

Once on the doorstep, Mitchell rang the doorbell.

After what felt like a couple of minutes, but may have only been thirty seconds, Mitchell looked at Lola. Everything was quiet. They'd made a mutual decision to walk away rather than ring again, but as they turned, the door opened.

Mrs Wright gazed at them with bloated and strained eyes, her brow furrowed. "Ah. Mitchell," she said, trying to sound welcoming, but the words sounded heavy and she struggled with their weight. She kept hold of the door with one hand, in the other she held a book.

"Hi, Mrs Wright. We just wanted to know how Julius was getting on."

Mrs Wright sighed. "It's so kind of you to think of Julius."

Mitchell tried to peer round her. "Is he... doing okay?"

Mrs Wright couldn't stop her head from shaking, her body betraying the sentiment she hoped to share. "It's been a tiring day," she said. "But we're holding on to hope." She turned the book in her hand and looked down at it. It was a tattered bible.

"Thank you for stopping by," Mrs Wright said, stepping back and edging the door toward a closed position, politely indicating that the conversation was over.

"That's okay, Mrs Wright," Mitchell said. "Tell Julius we stopped by."

Mrs Wright nodded. "You're a good boy, Mitchell," she said before closing the door.

Another shout came, meaningless noise from a nearby room, and again the lights flashed on and off.

Lola and Mitchell looked at one another and, desperate for something to hold, took each other's hands.

57: TED

Ted's gut felt like a furnace. He hadn't mentioned it to Doctor Hodder, not when she'd betrayed him and told his parents about the likely cause of his injuries. His stomach had been checked, and there was nothing medically wrong with it, so the feeling, the fire in his belly, was something else. They'd also told him his heart rate was normal, but to him, it sounded anything but that. With his hand on his chest, he could feel it skipping. Maybe it was his acute attention to the rhythm that made the seconds grow longer, made him doubt his heart would start to beat again after it had missed one.

He lay on his bed, The Cure's *Disintegration* album playing in the background, while he poked at different bruises on his skin. They were all of a similar shape, little purple eggs. The worst of them started yellow at its edges before turning to brown and then onto the deepest, darkest purple at the centre. Prodding this one made his stomach boil. He even shut off his music momentarily, stopping 'Prayers for Rain' midway through its long intro to listen, sure he'd be able to hear something bubbling away. But no. There was a rumble of hunger—he'd not had lunch and had turned down a snack when he got home both out of a desire for solitude and to get away from Mum and Dad. A storm seemed to be brewing between the two of them. The air was charged, and it was only a matter of time before there was thunder. It never used to be like that. He started the music again and prodded away, feeling the burn, almost enjoying it. He imagined stirring up the cauldron of his gut, letting something brew all night, something which he'd spew over Larry. He pictured him on fire, screaming. As Robert Smith's vocal kicked in, he thought that Larry would be the one praying for rain. Imagining his scream brought comfort. The grease in Larry's hair would light up like an oil spill in the middle of an ocean, thick black smoke billowing from the top of his head which Ted would breathe in, consume and it wouldn't make him choke, no, it would give him greater strength, allow him to breathe out fire, burn the flesh from his bones, the little fat on his body sizzling and popping.

Ted poked at his wounds again. They didn't even hurt that much. That was Larry doing his worse, when he caught him by surprise. He had a bit of height on Ted and the experience of aggression, but little more. He'd heard him huff and puff after he'd slung him across the toilet. Ted remembered the pain of striking his shoulder on the urinal. But it wasn't Larry's strength that had done that. Ted's legs had only gone because of the water on the floor. It was his momentum that made him hit it with such force. And yes, there was blood, but only because his tongue had caught between his teeth. If he had any real strength, Ted would be sitting there with his jaw wired up. He poked at his teeth with his tongue and then tried to give them a wiggle with his fingers. If anything, they were more firmly held in place than when he'd first awoken from his seven-month missing period, when Hodder had spoken of shrinkage of the gums as part of his malnutrition. He'd put on weight since then; she'd confirmed that while at the hospital. He didn't have much strength, but he never did so. That was something he could build over the coming weeks, but in the meantime, he'd have to shock Larry with sharp words and anything else he could find to stand up for himself. Larry was a bully, and like all bullies, he preyed on the weak. Ted had to show him he wasn't weak. Larry wasn't a big player in the scheme of things. He wasn't even on the periphery of the circle of popular kids. He was one of the outsiders, but neither the cool loner nor the counterculture type others secretly longed to be. He had a couple of cronies who were weaker than he was. He reckoned if he stood up to Larry, even just verbally, he'd back off pretty quickly. But then he remembered the image of him aflame. Did he want him to back off, or did he want to destroy him?

There was a soft knock at the door, and then Lola poked her head in. "Hey," she said.

Ted beckoned her in.

"You okay?" she asked.

"Bit bruised, but yeah, fine. Worst thing was swallowing blood." He'd not spoken much since leaving the hospital; he was too angry with Dad for taking him in, and Mum for continually probing him for information. Now when he spoke, he realised his swollen tongue was affecting his speech, making him phlegmy and giving him a slight lisp. Good luck having stern words with someone when all the words sounded like they were being delivered by a marshmallow.

"Was it..." Lola looked back to the door, "Lanky Larry."

"Yeah." Acknowledging it aloud made Ted feel weak and angry too. This dick had been hassling his sister, and now he was getting it, too. That wasn't on. He had to be stopped.

"Do you want me to ask Mitchell to have a word with him?"

"Mitchell?" Ted looked at his sister. Was she old enough to have a boyfriend? One in year 9? "Are you... a thing?"

Lola smiled bashfully. "I guess."

Ted grinned. "Lola's got a boyfriend!"

Lola raised a finger to her lips and shushed Ted. "Mum and Dad will hear."

Ted grimaced. "Maybe I could do with directing their attention to you."

Lola's eyes grew. "Don't!"

Ted smiled. "Nah, I wouldn't."

"So, did you want me to ask Mitchell to do something about Larry?"

"Nah, I can handle it. I heard something about Mitchell getting a bollocking for standing on the tables in the canteen. You know anything about that?"

Lola looked sheepishly to the floor.

"Was that because of you?"

"Kinda..."

"How much other stuff have I missed?"

"Listen, have you seen a yellow car with a black roof around recently?"

Ted pondered for a moment. He wasn't great with car types, but he was sure he'd seen something like that one morning when stuck at home. "I reckon it was parked out here the other day. Why?"

Lola told him about the strange goings-on on Poplar Avenue and then left him by himself. The more he wanted things to get back to normal, the crazier the world became. Perhaps the tension in the air wasn't just between Mum and Dad. Perhaps it was bigger than that, for he felt more than ever that the storm was coming. He started his own prayers for rain, hoping it would wash away all that was wrong and would finally allow things to go back to normal.

58: MEGAN

Simon's glass had filled while Megan was out of the room. Either he was regurgitating rum, or he was disguising his drinking. That was dangerous. That was more than just the one to settle the nerves. Did she want to call him out on it though? She'd agreed that finding an arm floating down the river was a cause for concern. Having to take your son to the hospital because he's vomiting blood is also distressing. Was she wrong for making a big deal of his drinking? They'd all had it tough and all needed a way to cope, but Megan worried that the booze had a hold on Simon, especially if he was topping up his drink in secret.

"What did the school say?" Simon asked without looking up from his drink.

"No answer. Wasn't expecting one at this hour. I've sent an email to the Head of Year and the principal, and I'll follow it up with another call tomorrow."

She watched him swirl the glass around, listened to the tinkle of the ice cubes as they collided with each other. He took a sip and exhaled with a satisfied "Ah!" Was it really so bad?

"Do you think we should keep him home tomorrow?" Megan asked.

"You know how eager he is to get back into a normal routine. Do we want to disturb that after only just sending him back?"

If the routine involved daily beatings, then yes, Megan was very keen to disturb that. "Maybe he should only go in for lessons one and two. You could pick him up at break?"

"If anything, he needs to be there longer."

"I don't want anything happening to him."

Simon drained the rest of his glass. "Something happened to him when he was right under our roof, Megan. We can't protect him every second." He stood up.

"Where are you going?"

"To get another drink."

"Don't you think you've maybe had enough?" The words were out there before she had time to censor herself.

"You know what, I don't think I've had enough. I think maybe you should have a drink, too. Maybe that'd get the stick out of your arse."

He left. Yes, she felt uptight, but drinking wouldn't change that. That would make her less effective when she had to be vigilant. She had to find out what the threats were and eliminate them.

Simon returned with two glasses. "There you go. Drink." He held a glass out toward Megan.

She didn't want it. She'd never been a regular drinker: A few glasses of wine with dinner sometimes, the odd night out on the cocktails, but in the months leading up to Ted's disappearance a glass or two in the evenings had become more common. She'd always felt a little uneasy about those rosy-cheeked colleagues who constantly told her they were looking forward to getting home so they could sink a glass of red. It smacked of dependency. But with the latest wave of cuts and having to decide on who'd to cut with the redundancy knife, the draw of the bottle had increased. At first, it was having one bottle (white, not red, so it was different) in the fridge so she could have a glass if she fancied. She'd only buy one bottle for the week, and when it was gone, it was gone. But when one Wednesday found the bottle already empty, she'd increased that to two bottles a week. How many glasses had she drunk on the night Ted disappeared? She genuinely couldn't remember. It was more than one: enough to be over the drink-drive limit, enough to impair her judgement. If she didn't have her wits about her, she would have missed something that might otherwise have woken her—the sound of footsteps on the landing or the stairs, a window opening, movement in the garden. But she'd had a drink and while she was sleeping with her senses deadened, something had swooped in and snatched her boy.

"I don't want it," she said. The look of the amber liquid and its strong scent made her stomach clench. If she let herself have a drop, she wouldn't have the strength to fight them off if they came back. She wouldn't have the awareness, the mental sharpness, to figure out who was responsible and put a stop to them forever.

She looked away.

"Fine," said Simon. He drained the glass he'd held out for her, and then the one he'd poured for himself.

She knew he was drinking too much, but there was no telling him. He wasn't blaming himself for what had happened in the same way she did. He'd been working that night, and he'd been off the booze since the kids were young. Until Ted disappeared. Then he liked an Old Navy in the evening while he cycled through social media looking at responses to his messages and clues within the rest of the dross. She thought it would end once Ted was back, but now each day brought with it a new challenge, and there was more drinking than ever.

He burped.

The smell of sausages and rum floated toward her, surrounded her, made her feel vile.

Simon headed back out of the room.

"Don't you think you've had enough?" Megan followed him to the door.

"I'm going out."

"You're not driving."

He turned to look at her, his brow furrowed in annoyance. "Course not. Getting picked up."

"Who by?"

"A friend."

He squeezed his feet into his shoes without lacing them and left, pulling the door closed with force behind him. Megan wanted to think he hadn't slammed it, just used more force than necessary because of the alcohol. She returned to the living room and looked out of the window, watching Simon struggle into the passenger seat of a yellow Saab convertible. She was certain she'd seen that car around recently, but couldn't figure out where. She caught sight of the driver and shuddered. No, there was something strange about Simon's new pal, and she didn't like it one bit.

59: LOLA

Every time Ted turned round from his seat near the front of the bus to look over his shoulder at them, Lola stopped talking.

"Did he ask you to ask me to do something?" Mitchell said.

"No, he says he's got it sorted."

Mitchell shrugged. "If he doesn't want me to do anything, I don't want to step in and make it worse."

Ted looked over again, so Lola stared casually out of the window, turning back to Mitchell seconds later. "I'm not saying you should do anything. Go up to him, see what he's saying, and if he plans to do anything."

"Okay. I'll see if I can get wind of his plans. Put him off if he's up to anything."

When they arrived at school, Ted got off the bus before Lola. He was standing by the door, waiting for her. "What are you up to?" he asked.

"Nothing," Lola said, walking away from the bus.

Ted followed. "I know you. You kept gawping at me. What were you talking about?" He was smiling, inquisitive rather than probing, but Lola didn't like the slight edge to his voice. Maybe it was because he was trying to disguise his lisp.

"I told him what happened–your side of the story."

"Good, because I'm okay." As he said 'okay,' he put his thumb up.

"Be careful."

"Don't worry. If anything happens, I've got it covered." He tapped his pocket and walked off. Tapping his pocket? What did that mean? They'd only used that before to confirm that had things. Got your ticket? Tap the pocket to confirm you were carrying it. What was Ted carrying that meant he was going to be okay? She turned to look for Mitchell, wanted to tell him she was worried about Ted, thought he was perhaps going to do something stupid, but he was gone. He'd already be on the prowl for Larry. Lola knew where he liked to hang out first thing in the morning: the side entrance between the science rooms and the design technology rooms—the one closest to his favourite toilet hangout. It was a popular smoking spot for those that didn't care if they got caught as teacher patrols were regular. Those that were sad enough to think getting caught and having their cigarettes confiscated would boost their status were sadly mistaken. Maybe a loser like Larry would never be popular, no matter what he did. It had to drive him crazy, being so desperate for attention, but to most people he was an annoyance, rather than one to be respected or feared—someone to be avoided, not admired.

Lola hurried along the corridors and out the side entrance. One of Larry's cronies, Eagle-face, came into view, no doubt playing the role of lookout. Mitchell had beaten her there and stood close to Larry who pointed a finger but stopped millimetres short of placing a finger on him.

"Look who it is," said the short kid with the acne problem.

Larry leant back to glance past Mitchell. "Hey, look, it's your girlfriend."

"That's right," Mitchell said, stepping forward to close the gap between himself and Mitchell again. "Don't you forget that. You mess with her, or you mess with her brother, you've got me to answer to."

"As if a shit stain like you's gonna worry me." Larry poked Mitchell in the chest. "You, your slut girlfriend, and her space-dick brother are a waste of fucking space."

Mitchell kept his arms down by his sides, but Lola could see his fingers start to curl up in case fists were required. "The point stands. Mess with us, and you'll regret it."

Larry jutted out his chin. "You'll be the one to regret it when I end you."

The cronies giggled until Mitchell glared at them.

"You end me? Mate, you couldn't end a sentence," Mitchell said, shaking his head in disdain.

"Come on," Lola said. "He's not worth it."

Mitchell turned away.

"Go on then, do what your little slut commands."

Mitchell spun round and darted his head toward Larry who stumbled backwards, caught one of the uneven paving slabs, and had to take a step back to right himself. Mitchell laughed, caught up with Lola and went back into the school just as a teacher was coming down the corridor. Any second, they'd be out there to check for smokers. Lola hoped Larry had sparked up again.

"Those guys are such dicks," Mitchell said.

"Thanks for saying something. You didn't have to."

"I'll tell you, it would be a pleasure to batter them." Mitchell balled his right hand into a fist.

"You can't. You'll get in trouble."

He smiled at Lola. "I'm more sensible than to do it here."

"So, are they planning anything?"

"They talk shit all the time. 'Anal probe's gonna get it,' stuff like that."

Lola shook her head. "I think Ted's gonna do something stupid."

"Like what?"

"I dunno. He said he'd be ready for them. Tapped his pocket. What's that mean?"

"Not a clue. We'll keep an eye on him at break, make sure nothing happens."

"That'd be good. Thanks."

"No problem, babe. For you, anything."

He gave her a hug as the teacher that had earlier been walking down the corridor emerged from the side door, stuffing a packet of cigarettes into his pocket. "Okay, put her down. Off to registration, you two."

Lola and Mitchell quickly made arrangements to meet later and went their separate ways.

60: SIMON

Simon woke with his mouth tasting like an ashtray and the discomfort of a remote control jabbing into his back. The light shining in through the crack in the curtains revealed what he'd already sensed from the pain in his back, neck and shoulders: he'd slept on the sofa last night. Exactly why he'd done so, he wasn't sure. Had it been his choice? He'd had a few rums before he left the house, and then Grant had picked him up. They ended up back at The Boar. He remembered cadging a cigarette from someone even though he'd not smoked since he was a teenager. Grant had talked to him about something of great importance. He'd kept telling him to go easy on the booze. Had he pulled a knife on him? He scratched his head. Surely, he was misremembering.

The door edged open. "Ah, I thought I heard you stir." Megan poked her head through the door.

Simon tried to detect an edge of annoyance in her voice. Nothing obvious. He hadn't been kicked out of bed. With the taste in his mouth, anything could have happened, but he was certain that if he'd vomited anywhere, Megan would have made him aware of where he had to go clean up.

All he managed was a grunt in agreement though he tried to make it as pleasant as a grunt could be.

"I told the kids you weren't feeling well," Megan edged in and came and sat on the single armchair opposite him.

"Thanks," Simon said. His throat was dry. There was a pain in his head, mostly focused above the right eye, but it wasn't too bad.

"Sorry I gave you a hard time about drinking yesterday."

Simon tried to respond, but his throat was too dry.

"Tea?" Megan asked.

"Coffee," Simon replied, knowing she'd make it as he liked on mornings like this: strong, black and two sugars, like she did back in the days that hangovers were a common occurrence.

Megan left, and Simon focussed on the pain above his eye. He massaged the area, just above the eyebrow, thinking about how his skin never used to feel so loose, so pliable. In doing this action he got the idea that something important was going down today. This was the kind of feeling he got when he almost missed an appointment at work, and suddenly realised when he was back in the office doing something menial. But no, it wasn't work; he was off shift until Monday. It couldn't be anything family-based, as Megan would have been on that. He checked his watch. She was at home at almost ten on a weekday. Maybe.

"How come you're at home?" he called.

There was no response. She probably couldn't hear over the sound of the boiling kettle.

He got up. His legs felt fine. A touch of pins and needles made the first couple of steps problematic, but, after stamping some life into his right foot, it was okay. His neck, back and shoulders cracked as he straightened up, but he was able to walk quicker after that. In the kitchen he found Megan standing at the back door, looking out at the garden and beyond. He stood in the doorway. It was a warm morning, and almost immediately he could feel the heat and his dirty clothes sticking to him.

"What are you doing home this morning?"

Megan looked round. "Working from home for a bit. Network upgrade in the office, so no point going in."

Simon looked down the river to where Megan had been looking. "What are they up to today?"

Since starting their investigations at the bottom of their garden, the police divers had spread in both directions along the river. Now, their attention focussed on the source end as a number of vehicles were parked close to where the work continued on the development of infrastructure for Fenmore.

"Would have thought they'd be looking the other way," Megan said. "Where the arm would have drifted to."

"Perhaps they're looking where it came from," Simon said, trying to look out past Megan to the Fenmore site. It was a hazy morning, the railway bridge that crossed the river barely visible. His sight settled on the police van at Fenmore. Something definitely seemed to be up with the site. Work had started with haste, and everyone in the community was commenting on how quickly the new roads went in, how quickly some of the structures were built, but then it stopped. There were rumours about the developer's bankruptcy and legal wrangles over new contracts, but Simon wasn't sure how much truth there was in it.

The kettle reached its boiling crescendo and clicked off. He wandered back into the kitchen. Megan had already placed sugar and coffee in his cup, and a teabag in hers. Feeling the need to prove himself capable of completing minor tasks, he poured boiling water into both cups.

As Simon headed for the fridge to get milk for Megan's tea, his phone buzzed. Probably a low battery warning: he'd not put it on charge overnight as was his usual practice, and it didn't last long without its nightly charge. He checked it anyway, a habit from the days when he was awaiting news about Ted.

It was a text message from Grant: *It's beginning. Where are you?*

What was beginning? Flashes from last night: ordering straight rum from the bar, Grant holding his hand up, refusing drinks, Grant putting his hands on top of his head, fingers pointing upwards, making ridiculous demon horns, the knife.

Simon dropped the milk. The plastic lid cracked as it hit the tile floor and milk seeped out. He picked up the plastic bottle and placed it on the side, and then grabbed a dishcloth from the sink and mopped up the spill. Why had Grant pulled a knife? What was beginning?

He thought back again. He'd placed the knife on the table. It was less of a knife, more of a dagger: polished silver that even managed to gleam in the gloom of The Boar with jewels in the handle, a green emerald coloured one (surely not real) a ruby red one, and a purple jewel. He remembered

Grant telling him how the dagger had been treated in water. Simon had queried whether it was holy water, but Grant had insisted there was nothing biblical about the scenario. What was he planning?

Simon's phone trilled again, a phone call this time. As soon as he saw the caller ID he knew where he needed to be. He glanced outside to check that Megan was still captivated by the police activity by the river and headed for the front door.

61: MEGAN

When Megan's phone rang, it had the effect of pulling her out of her trance. She looked at the caller ID, saw it was Alesha Wright and accepted the call. The sound coming from the other end was like nothing she'd ever heard before. It was a grief-filled wail, a sound coming from the pit of the stomach loaded with despair and anguish.

"Alesha," Megan said, only half sure that it was her.

From the other end, there was an attempt to make words, but it broke down into a visceral sob.

Simon knew her better than she did. He'd worked with her on missing person appeals and they'd formed a friendship. She'd see if he could get some sense from her. Returning to the kitchen, she first noticed the damp patch on the tiles, then the coffee and half-made tea on the side. With one ear to the phone, she called Simon's name. No response. She went into the hall, noted the shoes he'd left in the middle of the doorway, the ones she's placed to one side to stop the kids tripping over earlier, were gone.

"Alesha," she called down the phone. "I'm coming over. I'll be there as soon as I can."

She was right that Alesha was closer to Simon. It didn't make sense that she'd called her and not him. Unless she'd called him first, and in seeing her number, he'd already headed out to see her. But why would Simon not say?

She put on her shoes, grabbed her keys and headed out. Simon's car was still where he'd left it. He had a thing about driving in the village. He'd take the shortcuts and be at Alesha's in less than five minutes. Driving meant Megan would have to stick to the road, but there was a chance she could get there before him.

She got into the car and reversed out of the drive and sped through the village. There a little guilt about breaking the speed limit given how much she'd complained when others had done so, but this felt necessary—a life-or-death situation. She kept hearing Alesha's wail and hoped she wouldn't be too late, but as she turned onto Main Street she cursed: temporary traffic lights brought her to a stop.

Five minutes later, when she pulled onto Poplar Avenue, she saw the yellow Saab that had picked Simon up the previous night. She caught sight of someone going round the back of the house: Simon, it had to be. She pulled up across the Wright's drive and headed for the side door.

She could hear the wailing before she entered the house. There was an ebb and flow to its pitch, as if the sound was as natural as breathing, but there was nothing natural about it. That was despair multiplied. That was anguish squared.

It became louder when she pushed the door open and entered the kitchen, but it was overpowered by the sense of smell. The metallic stench of blood coupled with Alesha's cries struck Megan like a physical blow to the gut. Part of her wanted to turn and run rather than face something which was already making her gut turn inside out. She was still moving, impulsively, toward the sound, toward the smell, but she slowed when she heard voices.

"What have you done?" Simon's voice.

"Can't you see it?" A voice she didn't know.

All of this was masked by the continuing wail of Alesha Wright. Whatever had been done, Megan had to see. She hurried into the living room.

Initially, Megan didn't see the body. All she saw was a cavernous opening in a mass of scarlet. Her vision centred on the point in the boy's centre, and only after did she understand there was an arm, legs, and a head too, all equally lifeless. The arm had slashes on where he'd tried to defend himself, and Julius's lifeless face bore a gash that went from cheek to chin. But it was his stomach that had taken the brunt of the attack, carved open so nothing more remained.

"He's free now," said the man Megan didn't know. Insanity burned in his eyes as he spoke through gritted teeth.

Simon moved over to Alesha and placed his arms around her, trying to comfort her, but there was no change. Her hands were linked at her chest and wet with blood. The fingers were stained red, almost as if she'd bathed them inside her son's open gut. The phone she held in one hand was almost entirely camouflaged. A silver dagger with jewels in the hilt lay on the table, stained with blood, marking it as the murder weapon.

"Can you see what's inside him?" said the man.

Simon leaned forward.

Megan couldn't bear to look at the body, but she watched a transformation come over her husband's face. Initially, he shared her look of horror and revulsion, but it was almost as if he were looking upon the Holy Grail when he glanced into the bloody abyss.

"Oh my God, Grant, you were right."

"This has nothing to do with God." The man, Grant, continued to survey the scene, a perverse grin on his face. "Take the dagger. We need to move on. There's another on this street."

Simon reached out and grabbed the blade from the coffee table while Alesha continued to look on in horror at what she'd done.

"Simon, don't," Megan called, incredulous that her husband could grab the murder weapon, that he could go along with a madman's plan.

Simon looked at her blankly, then turned to Grant.

"The cause is bigger than all of us. We can't let anyone stand in our way," Grant said.

Megan moved in front of the door. "I'm not letting anyone go. Simon, call the police."

Simon shook his head. "I can't do that."

Megan pointed at Julius's mutilated corpse. "This is madness. This is murder. That boy's dead."

"I know you can't see it yet, love, but that's no boy. He was carrying a demon." Simon stepped toward her. "Now let us pass."

"I'm calling the police." Megan pulled her phone from her pocket.

"Stop her, Simon," Grant said, his voice forceful, commanding—unexpected from such an unassuming weasel of a man.

Megan looked her husband in the eye. He may have been holding a dangerous weapon, but there was no way he'd hurt her, of that she was sure.

He stepped back.

Megan looked at her phone screen in order to place an emergency call, and before she knew what was happening the weight of Simon's shoulder knocked her to the floor. He continued past her and Grant followed him out, evading Megan's desperate lunge for his foot.

She scrambled up and dialled the emergency services as she ran. She knew exactly where Simon and Grant were going.

62: TED

Throughout his English lesson, Ted had felt stabbing pains in his stomach, and every time they'd flared his heart fluttered. They weren't like the pain he's experienced when kicked in the gut or the boiling sensation he got from poking at his bruises. This was an entirely different sensation, almost like tiny pinpricks against his skin. He found himself reaching into his polo shirt to feel his stomach to check for blood. As unlikely as it seemed that he'd be allowed, when it became almost too much to bear around halfway through a lesson on Robert Frost's poem, 'Out, Out', he put up his hand and asked to be excused. It was school policy to not let pupils use the toilets unless there was an emergency, but Ted was released without question. Maybe a discreet email about him had passed among the staff. The English classrooms were in the tower block. He had to go down the stairs and through humanities to get to the toilets (the ones between science and design technology were probably a little closer, but he was avoiding them). As he passed a geography classroom, he caught sight of Larry at the back of the class, leaning back on his chair and fiddling with what looked like an elastic band. Ted continued, hoping he'd not been spotted. But what was he going to do, run out of the class and attack him in the corridor? Not likely. Even if he did, Ted thought he'd be alright. Ted had security.

In the toilets he went into one of the cubicles. The pains had been coming less frequently, but still freaked him out. He pulled his jumper and polo-shirt up and tried to look at his stomach. In the awful light of the toilets, he could see nothing abnormal. The bruises remained in all their purple, blotchy glory, but no evidence of a new injury. He ran his fingers over the spots where he'd felt most pain and checked them for blood. Nothing. It was like some kind of phantom pain, without cause or explanation.

As he tucked his polo shirt in, the main door crept open.

"Where are you hiding, Space Dick?"

Larry! Damn. He must have seen him pass the classroom. Another pain shot through his gut, this time sending tingling electric pulses up his left arm.

There was a bang on the cubicle door. "What are you doing in there? Making a call to the mother ship?"

Ted remained silent, hoping he'd eventually go away.

"Or maybe you're giving yourself an anal probe. Come out, you sick fuck."

Ted reached into his pocket, pulling the paring knife from its sheath. He looked at the short blade. Surely it couldn't do too much damage. He only had it as a warning, anyway. If Larry forced his way in, he'd show him the knife, and he'd back off. He hadn't planned to bring it. All of his fantasies had been about breathing hot fire onto Larry's face, burning him to a crisp, but then he'd seen the knife on the worktop in the kitchen, sitting there, away from the other knives as if it had been left out for this very purpose.

"If I have to force my way in, I'm going to snap off every one of your fingers and shove them up your arse."

The door thumped against the frame. He could see it bowing top and bottom, either side of the lock which held firm.

"I'm giving you to the count of three."

Ted held the knife in one hand and shifted his stance so he was as far back as possible, either leg straddling the toilet bowl, his lower back pushed against the cistern.

"One."

Ted saw the thin plywood holding the latch start to buckle.

"Two."

There was an audible splintering as it twisted further. Ted changed his grip on the knife, using both hands to hold the handle.

"Three."

The constant push on the door ceased, and with a barge, the door flew open, swinging a foot from Ted's face and swirling a gust of toilet stink toward him. Larry's momentum took him into the cubicle, crashing into Ted and knocking him into an awkward seated position on the toilet. Larry had fallen to the side. Ted scrambled up and out of the cubicle, awkwardly twisting on one ankle as he stood on Larry's calf. He knew he only had a moment to show him the knife, to warn him what he'd get if he didn't leave him alone, but he wasn't holding the knife anymore. Had he dropped it when Larry crashed in? If so, he was done for. But he was nearer the door now with Larry on the floor. He could run. But something was wrong. Why wasn't Larry getting up? Why wasn't he hurling abuse at him?

He didn't know how long he spent looking at Larry's prone body. Over the sound of his heavy breathing, over the erratic beat of his heart, he could hear Larry wheezing. A pool of liquid grew around the body. The dim light of the toilets at first made it hard to tell what it was. Had he pissed himself? If he could share that story, then Larry would be the laughing stock. All of his power (what little he had) would dissolve in an instant. But no, it was too high up the body to be piss and it looked too dark, more like blood. And that's when he realised what happened to his weapon. Larry had crashed through the door and into him, but not before he met the knife.

Ted's heart rate rushed, rapid uneven palpitations that made him want to vomit, and his left arm felt too heavy to hold up, like a deadweight he had no control over. He leaned over the body, part of him still afraid it was some kind of ruse, that Larry would grab his leg if he got too close and what had he threatened to do? Tear off all of his fingers and shove them up his arse? But when Ted saw Larry's face, he knew he wouldn't shove anything anywhere in a hurry. He was pale and blood pooled around his head. The handle of the knife was visible in Larry's neck, blood ebbing out around it.

There was still a slight wheezing sound. He wasn't dead yet, but it could only be a matter of time if nothing changed.

But what could Ted do? He couldn't get help; people would know what he'd done. Even if he tried to explain the accident, the evidence was stacked against him. He'd deliberately brought a knife into school. The school knew he'd been beaten up by another pupil the previous day. Two plus two would equal murder if Larry died. But leaving him would be worse. Then he would have deliberately left him to die.

He had an idea. He left the toilets and headed toward the exit, toward the fire alarm. All he had to do was break that, and they'd have to evacuate the school, get everyone out to the emergency meeting point on the field. They always checked the toilets were clear when they did a drill. With his elbow, he smashed the small 'break glass' panel, and seconds later the alarm sounded.

A fire drill always resulted in panic. He started to move out of the building as the first classes emerged from their classrooms. He merged into the crowd of pupils heading for the field. The route was well defined: years 7, 8, and 9 to the left of the tennis courts and around them, past the modern foreign languages block and onto the field. When he got to the corner, he slipped the other way, squeezing between the building and the bushes until he was heading for the front of the school. But they locked the gate to stop people from sneaking out. He couldn't very well go over it; he didn't have the strength to lift his own weight, especially with pins and needles in his left arm. But his small size did allow him another way out. He went back to the trees. The conifers were thick and planted close together, but at the bottom, there was room to crawl between the trunks. Years of litter had collected there, dropped by pupils and subsequently blown by the wind to where no one ever checked. He crawled over crisp packets and plastic drink bottles, over yoghurt pots and sweet wrappers until he got to the browned conifer needles. He found the gap between two trunks and crawled toward it, having to turn onto his side to wriggle through, the low branches pushing against his body, scratching at him until he forced his way between them. Once on the other side, the sound of the fire alarm was deadened, muffled by the thick conifers. He was free of the chaos, but it wouldn't be long before they realised he was missing. He had time to get home, grab a few things and then he'd disappear again. After all, Wiseham had coped perfectly well without him for seven months. Maybe everything could only go back to normal for everyone else if he permanently removed himself from the area.

63: SIMON

Simon had entered a status of hyper-reality. The pain over his eye had exploded into a feeling of euphoria that pulsed positive waves throughout his brain. When he received Alesha's call, he linked it to Grant's text, and everything came back. Grant had shown him the dagger the previous evening, an ancient relic he'd obtained from some of his contacts on the continent. With that, he'd be able to fell the demons. He'd revealed that he'd been meeting with Alesha, that she too had her reservations about whether the boy that returned was really her son. Simon was to meet with Grant at Alesha's house that morning, after Mr Wright had gone to work, to reveal the presence of the demon.

It had played out as Grant intended with Alesha seeing her son for what he truly was and cutting the demon from him to free him from his curse. While its essence was fading, Simon had arrived in time to see the last remnants of the demon within the poor boy's gut. Megan had arrived too late. God knows what she'd have thought, but she was following them. She'd see the next one.

Grant had told him about the history of Ted Hatcher and all of the inhuman things he'd done since his reintegration with the Earth. He was an early emissary to scope out the landscape to find a fitting time for invasion. He used the persona of a local oddball to get away with his peculiar actions. All of this made sense. Why else had Julius been chosen as a carrier? Hatcher had scoped him out from next door and given the subterranean creatures access to him.

Now the culling had commenced, it was time to take him down. And if Ted had to go next, so be it. Now he knew what he really was. Now he knew it was no longer his son.

Hatcher's side door had been open. The layout was similar to the Wright household, without any of the modern conversions the Wrights had made. Grant had told him what to expect in the house, and that's what he found. The kitchen and the hall were spotless. Grant had told him that once it was piled up with rubbish, something that helped maintain the pretence of lunacy—a weirdo and a hoarder who was a danger to children. Who'd ever suspect him of being a representative of a race that planned to overthrow humanity? But now he was tidying up, no doubt as part of the next stage of the plan. When Grant had visited and found this drastic change in behaviour, he knew, he'd told Simon, that it was time to act.

"Hatcher, we know you're here," Grant called as he poked his head into the bedroom. Simon looked into a second bedroom, a room that was immaculately kept and clearly not the room of an ageing single man.

"We know you're here," repeated Grant, "and we know what you are."

"Leave us alone," came a weak call from the living room.

Grant went in first, and Simon followed. He heard a noise from the kitchen and knew Megan wasn't far behind. Good. She had to see this happen in order to believe. Together, they'd be able to bring their son peace and rid him of the vile demon.

While the rest of his house was free of clutter, Hatcher had barely started on the living room and had left only a path to the armchairs clear.

Simon didn't see Hatcher at first. He'd crouched down between two stacks of boxes on the far wall.

"Time's up!" called Grant, causing Hatcher to raise his head.

There was something revolting in his eyes. They had a glassiness to them as if they weren't real, as if his real vision was fixed on another place, another world. He opened his mouth, but he clearly didn't have full control of his facilities as a trickle of drool ran down his chin.

Grant strode into the room, and Simon followed. He looked at the dagger, still stained with Julius's blood. Their great work had begun, and the dagger would feast many more times before they completed the mission.

Megan arrived at the door and looked in. "Stop this," she called.

Hatcher's head turned toward her. "Miss, I've started doing what you said. Call them off."

A look of confusion came over Megan's face.

Grant was the only one who kept moving. He struck Hatcher in the stomach, forcing him to double over. Grant grabbed Hatcher's hands and dragged him out of his junk-constructed nook.

"Simon, we don't have much time," Grant said, moving to stand behind Hatcher, holding his arms up, exposing his belly. "Act now. Take the dagger, go in at the top of the gut, and draw it down. It's the only way to get the demon out."

Simon edged forward. He wanted to be sure he was doing the right thing. It wasn't a man before him, not anymore. Something had taken possession of the body and had let it go to ruin. The colour of the skin was yellowing, the hair wiry and brittle. No life resided in those watery eyes. He stepped into position and lifted the knife.

The old man's lip quivered. From its centre, more drool ran. He was disgusting. He wasn't human. Simon moved to bring the dagger down, but a flash of bronze made him pause. He saw Megan strike Grant with the poker, opening up the skin on his cheek and causing him to release Hatcher. The poker flew from Megan's grasp, but that didn't stop her from turning round to face Simon. She reached up and grabbed the dagger by the blade.

Simon saw blood appear on her palm as the blade dug in and he let go. He couldn't shed his wife's blood. She was human. That would be murder. But she had the dagger now and she was running away. With one hand, as she left the living room, she pulled on a pile of boxes, forcing them to topple in the doorway.

"Get her," cried Grant, steadying himself against the wall with one hand and holding his wounded cheek with the other.

Simon took off. He looked back to see Grant push Hatcher to the ground, and as he headed out of the front door, he heard a sickening crunch.

64: MEGAN

Pain exploded across Megan's right palm as she grabbed the dagger. Was Simon about to murder Hatcher? Hadn't she fantasised about killing the same man only days earlier, broken into his house with the intention of doing so? But... this was different. This was madness. This seemed to be some kind of ritualistic killing.

Simon had let go of the dagger. He'd looked into her eyes, and he'd let go. Whatever madness had taken over him, surely it was only momentary. If he'd truly gone insane in his bloodlust he would have sliced through her fingers and gone on to butcher Hatcher.

Grant called the shots. Was this the guy he'd been talking to? She wished she'd struck him harder with the poker. As she fled the room, she pulled a stack of boxes across the doorway behind her. However sure she was there was some element of humanity in her husband, he was certain to give chase. She turned for the front door and reached straight for the chain. Had she not visited previously that would have caught her out, cost her valuable seconds. She slammed the door shut behind her but never heard it catch. Simon must have been close. She'd parked across the Wright's drive, not far away. She had no idea if she was quicker than Simon; she only knew she had to be. Adrenaline pumped through her, firing up her legs to make longer leaps. She got to the car, pulled the door open and swung in, slamming the door closed behind her. She'd kept ahead of Simon, but not by much; he was at the front of the car and coming round to the door. She hit the lock button as he pulled on the handle. He slammed on the window as she threw the bloody dagger into the passenger seat and dug in her pockets for the keys.

The car started first time; she shifted into gear and pulled off. It was almost impossible to grip the steering wheel with her right hand. The pain was like a blowtorch being run across the centre of her palm continuously, and with the bleeding not slowing, the steering wheel became slippery. Once in second gear, she was able to steer with her left to the end of the road. Simon followed, but he'd give up once she hit Downham Road and increased her speed.

A little way along Downham Road, she turned onto Beech Way and pulled over, and, always with one eye on the rear-view mirror in case Simon appeared, she hunted for something with which she could stem the tide of blood. She had a black cardigan on the back seat. That would do. She tore off a sleeve and wrapped it around the palm of the hand. Immediately the pressure on the wound made it feel better—less like a searing, burning hacksaw constantly being drawn against the wound and more like it had hot coals shoved inside it: still agony, but a whole lot more bearable.

Megan started to think about where she needed to go next. She could go home, but Simon would look for her there. Sirens blared and she watched a police car speed down Downham Road, blue lights flashing. Surely it was responding to her call from Poplar Avenue. Maybe they'd catch up with Simon and that psycho, Grant. She'd called in about the Wright house though. That's where they'd go. They'd discover that poor boy's butchered body at the hands of his mother who no doubt still stood there captivated by the devastation inflicted by her own hand. They had no murder weapon, though. Megan had that. She could turn it in at the station later or give Heimlich a call.

Looking out the back window, she saw the yellow Saab go by. It had to be Grant's car. But where were they heading? If Grant and Simon had gone after Julius because they thought he had a demon inside him, and Hatcher for the same reason, there was only one other target: Ted. He'd be at school. She hoped he'd be safe there, but given what had happened the previous day, Megan wasn't so sure. Would they go after Ted, or did they need the dagger? She could ditch it, throw it out of the window, but what if it got back to them first? Was it not safer in her possession, where she could stop them from getting hold of it? She didn't have time to take it to the police station, not if they were after Ted. She had no choice but to head for Fenland Village Academy.

As she pulled onto the A10, there was more activity from the emergency services. The sky around the Fenmore development illuminated in blue, and police cars and an ambulance headed in the other direction, the direction she was to take. She knew it was insane, Simon and Grant couldn't possibly have reached the school already, but she had this horrible fear that the emergency services were heading for the school too, that she was too late. She turned her radio on and hit the button for the local station.

It was almost impossible to pick up the main story. An eyewitness spoke, someone onsite in Fenmore. Something significant was going on there. They talked of an almighty bang and speculated that there had been an explosion. They spoke of houses sinking into the ground. Whatever it was had nothing to do with her current emergency, so she switched the radio off as she turned off the A10 and headed toward the school. Traffic was particularly heavy that way, almost gridlocked on the normally quiet country roads. She had to pull over onto the verge to let another police car by. While sitting in the queue she could see a few cars ahead. None of them looked like Grant's Saab. She had to tell herself that whatever the emergency was, her husband couldn't possibly have had anything to do with it, but the longer she sat there, the longer her mind started to drift to the awful possibilities. What if the bully that went for Ted yesterday struck again and this time did something much worse? What if something had happened to Lola?

No, she couldn't sit there and wait her turn to reach the school. It wasn't far away, less than half a mile. There was a cul-de-sac a little further up to the right. She pulled out of the flow of traffic, driving on the wrong side of the road hoping nothing would come the other way for a moment and pulled into the side road. She checked the rudimentary bandage around her hand and prepared to run for the school. What else could she do?

65: TED

Ted dusted himself off. He squeezed his arms across his chest, trying to get the pain within to recede. His heartbeat pounded in his ears and he could feel the irregular beat pulsing through every muscle and squeezing at his brain. But he couldn't let that stop him. He didn't know the village well enough to know where he was, but he had a rough idea of the way out having spent so much time travelling there on the bus. The biggest danger would be trekking down the A10 in full view of so many cars. He figured most people would mind their own business, but it would only take one busybody to pull over, or for a police car to drive by and then he could be in a world of trouble.

No doubt they would have found Larry by now. Someone would have checked the toilets as they passed by. They had to. It was someone's job, right? And if they found him, there was a chance they could save him. Then it wouldn't be murder; it would just be an accident. He backed into the trees to see if he could hear anything, but the alarm still blared. He dusted more conifer needles from himself and had to pick a particularly sticky sweet wrapper from his knee. He took off his jumper, thinking the white polo shirt was less conspicuous than his school jumper. Anyone could be wearing a white polo shirt; only someone from the school would be wearing a jumper featuring the Fenland Village Academy logo.

He headed for the pavement and took a second to decide which way he'd need to go to get to School Lane. Once there he had to head away from the school. Simple. But at soon as he made for the road, he realised someone stood at the corner. The stranger faced away from him, but from the way he held himself, and the hint of a white beard, he looked like an older person. Maybe the sound of the fire alarm had drawn them from their garden, a nosy neighbour looking for some excitement. With a bit of luck, he wouldn't even suspect Ted was from the school, and if he said something, so what?

Ted continued to walk along the pavement. He tried to move as normally as possible to avoid raising suspicion, but he knew the more he thought about walking normally, the harder it became. He was about two metres from the man when he turned.

He didn't say anything but stared with his one good eye: Arthur Norfolk.

It's time to go back, Ted.

He heard the words in Arthur's voice, though his mouth never moved. Go back? Go back where? Of course, that was what he had in common with Norfolk, the shared missing status. He'd been gone so much longer, so maybe he had knowledge of that other place.

"Go where?" Ted asked, but Arthur failed to acknowledge the question.

From the distance, he heard a siren.

Arthur turned and walked back down the road, in the direction from which Ted had come.

Follow.

Ted heard it loud and clear, though he again got the impression Arthur hadn't spoken it, and, as against his intuition as it was, he couldn't help but do as commanded.

Long before they reached the school, Arthur turned down a narrow passageway flanked by two six-foot fences.

The sound of the siren made Ted glance over his shoulder to see a fire engine pass by—must have been alerted by the fire alarm and no one had told them it was a false alarm. Other factors must have taken precedence—like finding a boy with a knife in his neck in the toilets.

Ted continued to follow Arthur through the passageway to a residential area made up of small bungalows with a car park in the centre. Ted looked around for the street sign: Castle Court. Most of the houses had neighbourhood watch stickers on their windows and no cold-callers signs on their doors. Was this where Arthur lived now? Did he have a relative in one of the bungalows? Had he been given a temporary home? He didn't seem to be heading for any particular building. He moved to the area of grass in front of the car park and stood, seemingly waiting for Ted to reach him.

For a while, Arthur did nothing, and while Ted was aware of the passing of time, he waited, too. Ted wanted to ask Arthur where they were going. He wondered if he thought about the question and tried to project it toward Arthur, he'd be able to pick it up, that he'd send thoughts back the other way, and they could communicate through their minds, but Arthur showed no indication that he'd picked up Ted's question. Were they... alike? Had they been held in the same place? If so, why had Arthur been gone for decades but he for only months?

"Where are we going?" Ted said.

This time, Arthur turned toward him. He pointed in the direction of Wiseham. *Home.*

Ted stared between the houses and across the fields. Was there smoke in the air?

Arthur started to move again, heading not for the road, but for a passage that led into another cul-de-sac. Ted turned to look behind him. Why, he didn't know. To check he wasn't being followed? Glancing back through the passage he saw traffic crawling toward the school which was unusual for that time of day. Had the word got out about what happened? Were parents flocking to the school to pick up their children before they too could be victims of a violent knife attack? As they passed into the passageway one end, the view was cut off. When the passage opened up onto the next street, the view across the fen was clearer. Yes, there was smoke drifting from somewhere but not smoke like Ted expected to see. This was not the thick, black smoke of a fire. It had a pink tinge to it, its edges the colour of candyfloss. And Wiseham wasn't the point of origin. No, it was further south: it was coming from the stalled development at Fenmore.

Arthur continued walking down the road. This would lead them out onto the main road, toward home.

Before they reached the end, Ted saw a familiar car: Mum. What was she doing here?

Ted sped ahead of Arthur (which wasn't a challenge; his pace was slow) and approached Mum's car. She hadn't noticed him. She had a look of panic on her face. She kept looking over her shoulder, back at the road behind her.

"Mum!" Ted called when she opened the door.

She looked over at him, a look of elation spreading over her face. "Ted! What are you doing here? Have you seen your father?"

Words wouldn't come. There was too much to say and it was all blocked within his throat. Instead, he ran over to Mum and let himself fall into her arms.

She hugged him tightly. "Are you okay, Ted? Have you seen your dad?"

Why did she keep asking about Dad? Should he tell her what had happened, what he'd done?

Come.

Ted heard Arthur calling to him and was compelled to follow, but didn't want to leave the warmth of Mum's embrace.

"You're not hurt, are you?" Mum said.

Ted shook his head as he pulled himself away from her. The pain in his chest continued, but it hadn't become worse. He couldn't worry about it now. He looked over her shoulder to where Fenmore continued to smoke.

"Arthur wants me to go with him," Ted said.

Mum looked confused. "Go where?"

Ted pointed to the plume of candyfloss-tinged smoke.

"Who's Arthur?"

Arthur continued, slowly, toward the main road.

"He's like me, Mum. He was taken away, and he wants us to go back."

Ted watched his mother as she turned to Arthur, first of all with a look of anger on her face, before it mutated into one of concern.

"We're not safe here," she said. "Get in the car."

66: LOLA

What seemed to be a regular fire drill soon descended into chaos. Lola had followed her maths class out, trying to engage Lauren in conversation over the bleeps of the alarm, only to be shushed by members of staff who insisted on silence during an evacuation. She lined up with the rest of her form, and her form tutor quickly registered them. Lola glanced across to Lauren's line and smiled. One of the teachers at the front again urged silence, and another told someone to stand still. Lola craned her neck to look at year 9. She could see Mitchell's form, but other pupils obstructed her view of him.

A normal fire drill didn't take long. Once they were registered the principal would tell them they did well, or they needed to be quicker, quieter or more efficient, but today that didn't happen. The alarm still sounded. Maybe there was a genuine fire. She could tell others were thinking the same as heads turned to sneak glances at the school, only for them to be directed back in line by a shout from their form tutor. The caretaker, office staff and senior teachers all had either mobile phones or walkie-talkies to their ears, and the principal stood at the front, ashen-faced.

Several minutes passed in this way. Form tutors stopped shushing those who started quiet conversations as they looked to their leaders for answers. The senior teachers turned away from the pupils when they spoke into the walkie-talkies and some disappeared back toward the school. Surely it wasn't actually on fire? Lola chanced a glance. No smoke. No one told her to face front either.

"Okay, listen," called the principal.

Other members of staff then returned to their shushing duties to allow her to speak unopposed.

"Unfortunately, we can't return to classrooms, yet."

A cheer went up from a number of pupils.

"So, you will need to remain on the field for the time being. The canteen, the toilets, and the classroom areas are currently out of bounds until further notice while we resolve an issue. If there are any problems, please speak to a member of staff."

This had never happened before. The fire drills normally came and went, and they were back in class before the end of the lesson. They'd never been barred from the rest of the school before or left on the field. Pupils drifted away from their form groups as the teachers came together in groups, guarding the routes back to the school buildings. People started to speculate: a gas leak from the science rooms, a wild animal, a madman with a gun. Lauren came over to Lola. "I heard they've called an ambulance."

Lola looked at her friend. "Who told you?"

"Just heard."

Lola scanned the crowd for her brother. She didn't know which form he'd been moved into. Mitchell might have a better idea as he was in year 9. Lola spotted him standing with Tyler and a few others, and headed over, Lauren in tow.

"Hey, Mitch, have you seen Ted?"

Mitchell cast his eyes around the field. "Can't say that I have."

"Help me look for him?"

"Sure, Lo."

They moved from cluster to cluster, keeping an eye out for Ted, Lola growing more frantic as the pool of possibilities shrank.

"There's trouble," Mitchell said, nodding over to where Larry's cronies stood by a tree.

Lola marched over to them, leaving Lauren and Mitchell behind. "What did you do to him?"

The two of them looked spaced out. "What?" said the shorter of the two.

"My brother, have you seen him?"

"Anal probe?" asked Eagle-face. He snorted. "Nah, not today, mate."

"Where's Larry?"

"That was what we were saying, weren't we?"

"Yeah."

Lola sighed and walked away from them. Lanky Larry and Ted both missing, staff acting strangely, and rumours of an ambulance being called? This was not good.

Lola returned to her group.

"Tyler reckons they're closing the school," Lauren said.

"What do you mean?"

"Heard what's her name on the phone to the bus companies." He pointed over to where the office staff stood.

Lola grabbed Mitchell's hand. "We've got to get out of here."

Mitchell looked toward the field's exit where groups of teachers stood looking sorrowfully at the pupils they should have been teaching. He then turned to face the back end of the field. "We can get out that way," he said, pointing to the back corner. "We just have to jump the ditch."

There were teachers patrolling the perimeter of the field.

"They might be a problem," Lola said, pointing to them.

"Leave it to me," Lauren said. She started to walk off and looked back over her shoulder. "Start heading over that way."

"There's gonna be a scrap," Lauren called in her booming voice as she headed over to the opposite side of the field. Heads turned all around the field, and a group started to follow her. Lauren headed toward Larry's cronies and started yelling. By this time, Lola and Mitchell were too far away to understand exactly what was being yelled, but it was clearly having the desired effect as it drew a crowd, and pupils crowding always summoned teachers to break it up.

"Run," called Mitchell grabbing Lola's hand to carry her with him.

Lola's legs pumped like never before. Mitchell had much longer legs than she did, and he was a better runner, but his pull gave her the boost she needed. They made it to the corner in no time at all. Some of the teachers might have spotted them, but if they had, they were too far away to do anything about it. They might have been calling out and telling them to stop, or they might have been completely oblivious to their escape. Either way, it didn't matter. Mitchell leapt across the ditch first, barely slowing his pace, launching from the grass and landing cleanly on the other side. He'd done it before. He knew what he was doing. That wasn't the case for Lola. There were weeds growing up the other side of the ditch: stinging nettles, brambles, wild grass. She'd almost come to a stop and had lost most of her momentum.

"Come on," called Mitchell.

Lola jumped and landed halfway up the bank. She could feel the soil beneath her feet rolling, could feel herself sliding back. It didn't matter that there was only a trickle of water in the bottom. There was also a string of barbed wire. If she got caught in that, the teachers would surely have time to catch up with them. But before she scrabbled back too far, Mitchell grabbed her arm and yanked her up the side.

It was quiet on the road. The school's fire alarm, which had continued to blare the whole time they were out there, was almost inaudible under Lola's heavy breathing.

"Right," Mitchell said. "Where are we going?"

"Let's go to mine," Lola said. "Dad will be there. He'll know what to do."

Mitchell looked both ways down the road to ascertain which was the quickest and then they headed off, too out of breath to run but managing a quick walk.

The sound of sirens came moments later. Were they right to run? Lola's doubt was only momentary. They were being held there like prisoners: no access to food, no access to water, no access to shelter. Whatever was going on, they were in the dark about it, and they'd only find answers from the outside. But as the sound of the sirens neared, she wondered about Ted. What if he was in trouble inside? What if the sirens were especially for him? She couldn't worry about that. She just had to stick to the plan and get Dad to sort it out.

67: MEGAN

Ted sat beside her, and as long as he was beside her, no harm could come to him.

The man in the back remained silent, his eye contact shifting between Ted and the distant smoke from Fenmore. Megan knew she should keep her eyes on the road, but she couldn't help but stare, particularly at where he'd lost an eye. Lost seemed entirely like the wrong word, for it looked like no eye had ever been there. An odd understanding existed between Ted and this strange man, as if they were having a conversation through silence.

As Megan reached the main road, noting the traffic streaming into the village and heading for the school for reasons Ted had not yet explained, she remained unsure where she should go. Part of her was certain Simon and Grant would come for Ted. If they were after people who had been missing, then her other passenger, Arthur, would also be on their list. She thought about the dagger beneath the passenger seat. Did they need that to do whatever it was they were trying to do? Her main priority was to keep Ted (and with him, Arthur) away from harm. Where she'd failed to keep him safe seven months ago, this time, she would succeed. She was willing to put her life on the line to ensure it.

She couldn't stay near the school. While there were plenty of people there, and the emergency services were present (and more still en route), Simon would expect to find Ted there. While she wished to return home in order to be somewhere familiar (she told herself it was to pick up 'supplies' whatever 'supplies' were in this context) what if Simon awaited them? If Simon and Grant had split up, then the most likely ports of call were home and the school, so she needed to take Ted and Arthur away from there.

Ted, under Arthur's silent persuasion, urged her to go to Fenmore. Megan had to admit it had its appeal. When she'd left Wiseham, she was aware of the police presence in Fenmore. She'd heard something on the radio about an event there which might draw the press as well as emergency services. While they'd not be anonymous, surely, they'd be safe. Simon and Grant wouldn't necessarily think to look for them there either, and if they did, they'd have trouble attacking in broad daylight in front of the police and the press. And yet... there was something off about Ted's mood. His companion, Arthur, had an ethereal aura about him, too. Did she really want to take them to this place they sought so strongly? Ted had suggested that Arthur was like him, a returnee, and this place would offer answers. Maybe that was needed more than anything else. If taking Ted to Fenmore would get his memories back, if she could discover where he'd been, then it would be another step in getting things back to normal. Whatever madness had come over her husband could surely be dissipated if he knew the truth. After all, he hadn't been present when Julius had been murdered; he'd not so much as touched Hatcher, regardless of his murderous intent. This guy, Grant, had put him in some kind of trance, making him temporarily insane. Grant led the cult of craziness but how many followers did he have? Maybe his people had something to do with the events at Fenmore and they'd be walking into a trap.

Before she could decide where to go, she'd driven past the first entrance to Wiseham. The smoke continued to rise from above Fenmore. Did she really want to take her son there? It wasn't like any smoke she'd seen before; the hint of pink made her think of a flare, but it was too faint for that purpose. Normally, any sign of smoke was a huge indicator of danger, but this smoke felt different; this smoke seemed to be saying she'd be welcome.

She reached the roundabout. It was about the only part of the Fenmore construction which was complete. It used to be a junction to turn into Wiseham, but the roundabout would allow access to both Wiseham and Fenmore. That's where she turned. As she drove along the road, she pondered whether the village would ever be completed. The foundations were in place on the housing estate on her right, but the road was unfinished. She noticed the quality of the road she drove along drop, from the professionally completed access road down to a track suited for larger vehicles to deliver building supplies, not finished to the aesthetic quality of a village road. The housing estate on the left was closer to completion. All of the buildings looked ready to live in, but Megan had heard that they were almost empty shells: unplastered walls, unfinished ceilings, concrete floors. That's what this man, Arthur seemed like: empty somehow. Julius had been the same, missing key components that made him human. Megan recalled his gore spread across the Wright's living room and grimaced. He'd never get the chance to recover now. She continued into another estate of half-built houses seeing the smoke billowing from somewhere behind them.

From the curve of the road, Megan became aware that this road, as yet unnamed, mirrored Riverview Terrace. She was curving around toward the river. The houses, while modern looking, were of a similar size to those on Riverview. It was like an alien doppelganger of her home street. Was that what Grant and Simon were arguing? That those that returned were different? Empty copies of the originals? She looked across at Ted. His eyes were fixed on the smoke. Yes, he seemed different, but it was the trauma he'd been through that had affected him. The boy beside her was unquestionably her son. And if following this road would reveal who had taken him, she was ready to execute every single one of them. She even had the special ceremonial dagger to do so.

She rounded the corner, approaching what she considered to be her mirror house, where the road was blocked by a pair of police vans. Media vehicles flanked the road. Beyond that, were squad cars and dozens of people and a little further away, the remains of a house. The wall on the left was intact, and parts of the back wall too, but the rest of it had fallen away.

Megan brought the car to a stop and gazed at the building. It looked like what might remain after an earthquake, but the neighbouring houses were unaffected. From within the building, the smoke poured forth. No, this wasn't where Megan needed to be. There was something very wrong with this place. She started a laborious turn in the road, but just as she put the car into reverse, she heard the click of a seatbelt being released. Before she could do anything to stop him, Ted was out of the car.

"Ted," she called, winding down the window.

He moved toward the police blockade.

Megan stopped the car, got out and followed him.

68: SIMON

Grant was utterly losing his shit about the knife, and Simon questioned the sanity of his decision to take him back to his house. Grant had kicked one of the kitchen cabinets so hard that the door had splintered in two, with the top half coming off and spinning momentarily on the tile floor.

"Are you one hundred per cent sure we need that knife?" Simon asked. He needed to understand whether it was the reason he'd been able to see the impression the creature had left inside Julius. Would killing Julius by other means have had the same effect? And if the knife was needed, why had Grant pushed the old guy to the floor and stamped on his head? That wouldn't have released the demon.

"The knife is part of it, yes," Grant said. "And I think you're right. It does help us to see the demons."

"What do you mean, 'think'?"

"I haven't exactly done this before, you know, Simon. I don't encourage mothers to cut open demons every day of the week. This is not my normal job." As Grant spoke, he marched around the room.

"So, what next?"

Grant stopped marching and stared at Simon. "Next? Next? Have you seen the sky? We're too fucking late, man."

Simon had no idea what he was talking about, but he could feel Grant's eyes boring into him.

"Did you not see it?"

Simon shook his head.

Grant marched past him, to the back door and unlocked it. He went back to Simon and grabbed him, pulling him out of the door and positioning him in the garden where he could see down the river to Fenmore.

"Look at the sky and tell me that's not a sign of the end of days?"

Simon looked up as the pinkish glow. It seemed to spread from a single point. "What does it mean?"

"It means we're too late. They've opened the gates and the demons are pouring out. They'll destroy anyone who gets in their path and not rest until they're the dominant species."

"What can we do about it?"

"There are people I can call, fellow believers, but it might take a while to get hold of them."

"Anything I can do in the meantime?"

Grant pointed down the river to the origin of the pink smoke. "Follow the river, not the road. Head down there. Act as scout. Report back on how many, what they're doing, how they attack. Report back anything that you think will help us in this war against those creatures."

Simon gulped. Was this for real?

"In years to come, when they look back on this day, if we're victorious, and if you do your job, then we're more likely to be victorious, it'll be you that they talk about as one of the Christian soldiers."

Simon was pulled out of his reverie by the word 'Christian'. "I thought this wasn't a religious thing?"

Grant threw his hands in the air. "It's an expression. We know the truth, but the church will spin it as a religious war— and in that war, you will be considered a hero."

Simon nodded. He looked at the sky again and imagined the creatures spewing out of a hole in the ground. What he'd seen inside Julius was little more than an impression, but it was a figure that felt familiar to him. Curled inside the boy's body and fading from view it had not looked like he'd imagined a demon would, but more like a gargoyle. If creatures like that were pouring out of the earth, they had to be stopped and if it was his job to scout out the scene, then that's what he'd do.

He headed through the back gate and to the river and set off to face his destiny.

69: LOLA

Seeing the yellow Saab outside her house didn't alarm Lola at first. Yes, she'd seen the car around recently and it was that car the man who'd caught them spying outside Julius's house had driven off in, but it wasn't a car she associated with anything particularly negative. Maybe the guy was visiting a neighbour. Maybe he was working in the area. It didn't matter. What mattered was getting to Dad so she could do something about Ted.

She cursed herself all the way back to the house for not knowing Dad's number, otherwise she could have called him on Mitchell's phone, saving loads of time. At least Mitchell was able to get in touch with his cousin who'd dropped them at the end of the road. The traffic had been crazy with emergency vehicles everywhere. Every siren pained Lola, felt like it was a dagger plunging into her brother's back, and she was powerless.

She got out her key, fumbled with it in the lock for a moment and eventually pushed it home. "Dad," she called from the hall.

No response.

"Dad," she called again, louder this time.

Mitchell followed her in as she stepped inside. "Isn't he home?"

His car was on the drive, so he had to be. "I'll check upstairs in case he's having a nap. Do you mind waiting here a minute?"

Mitchell told her it was no problem and she thundered up the stairs, only aware at the last moment that Mitchell was watching the childish way she climbed stairs at speed, almost on all fours. "Dad," she called again once at the top and then she checked the bedroom. Nope, the bed was made, and everything was neat and tidy. She decided to check the other upstairs rooms just in case. Her bedroom was clear, as was the bathroom. She pushed open the door to Ted's old room. Through the window she could see that the sky had turned to a strange shade of pink, but there was no sign of her father.

From downstairs she heard a muffled thump.

"Mitchell," she called. "You okay down there?"

Nothing.

She half expected him to jump out on her, like he had that time in the passageway, but when she returned to the landing she saw him—flat on his back, eyes closed as if he were fast asleep and being dragged away by someone out of view.

It couldn't have been Dad, could it? She hadn't told him about Mitchell. What if he thought he was an intruder and hit him? But if that was the case, why was he dragging him into the kitchen?

She had to stop her instinct from calling out. Instead, she ducked down on the landing and listened. There was a voice.

"One of them got in here..."

It wasn't Dad. But if he was speaking to someone, was he with him? Was it the driver of the yellow Saab, the man she'd seen the previous day?

"I'll get a knife from the kitchen." The same man spoke again. Get a knife? What was he planning to do?

"Perform the ritual... Yeah, yeah, cut it out. How soon can you get here?"

So, he was talking to someone on the phone. How Lola wished she had her phone, so she could call for help. But if he was talking on the phone, it suggested he was alone. But what was he doing in her house, and what the hell was the ritual he hoped to perform?

If he was by himself, she might be able to lure him away from Mitchell, wake him up, and escape.

First, she had to find out what he was up to. He spoke about a ritual, so he wasn't likely to be wandering around the house. He'd dragged Mitchell into the kitchen which meant he wouldn't be able to see her coming down the stairs. He'd hear her though, unless she was absolutely silent, which was far from her forte.

With each foot on each step, she grimaced, half expecting a creak that would give her away. Even when she heard nothing, she worried that he might have heard something. She might only think she was being quiet as she couldn't hear herself. But she reached the bottom and saw and heard no movement. On the floor was a small syringe, half-pushed-in, but with about a third of the clear liquid remaining. He'd drugged Mitchell!

She crept along the hall and peered into the kitchen. It was the man from the other day. He was on the floor. He had the bucket from beneath the sink between his knees with Mitchell laid out in front of him. His phone rang. He took it from his pocket and answered it.

"Simon, one sec... gonna have to put you on speaker."

Simon? He was talking to her Dad?

He awkwardly prodded at the screen for a few seconds. "Okay, go ahead," he said, laying his phone on the floor.

"Grant, you've got to see it down here," Dad said. "There's a massive sinkhole. It's swallowed up one of the houses." His voice sounded different—almost robotic, liked he'd lost the edge of humour which he normally had. In truth, he'd lost it most of his day-to-day conversation when Ted disappeared, but Lola always heard it when he spoke to her. But this voice, it so far removed from everything she recognised as her dad.

"There's a problem this end," Grant said. "One of them got in. I managed to stop him, but more will come."

"An intruder? Who?"

"Doesn't matter. I'm going to cut it out of him, and then I'll be on my way to you."

"Have you got what you need?"

Grant reached into the bucket. "Blessed and bathed a blade from your kitchen. It'll do the trick." He pulled out the knife.

Lola gasped, but her father spoke at the same time. "You're going to kill him? There?"

She hoped he'd not heard her.

"Don't think of it as a 'him', Simon. It's not anymore. It's merely a vessel for a demon." Grant raised the knife.

"They're here!"

Lola could hear excitement in her father's voice, but it still didn't sound like him. It was a menacing excitement, one laced with a desire to do harm. But the excitement momentarily stalled Grant.

"Who? Who's there?"

"Ted!" Dad said. "Ted's here with Megan, the old man too."

"Then you know what you have to do." He ended the call.

Ted was okay? Relief swept over Lola, almost knocking her off her feet. Perhaps it would have done if not for a counter-emotion of absolute fear hitting her from the other side. What was it Dad had to do to Ted? And what was Grant going to do with that knife? There was no time for clever plotting. There was no time to construct a trap. She just had to go with what she had. And what exactly did she have? What skills did she have at her disposal to deal with this situation? She couldn't exactly jump out in front of him singing, 'Chim Chimney'.

Lola took a deep breath and thought about her training. *Commit to the performance.* No time for a full round of breathing exercises. She stepped out into the kitchen.

"We're here for you, Grant," she said, trying to make her voice sound other-worldly. As far as she could tell from his brief conversation with her father, that was his wacko theory, creatures coming from another world to take over.

Immediately he sprung up and whirled round to face her, grasping the knife, but the look on his face was not one of threat, but one of fear.

"We want you," Lola said, stepping forward. She afforded herself a brief glance at Mitchell. She could see his chest rising, but there was no sign of consciousness.

Grant took another step back, slashing with the knife.

"There are so many of us," Lola said. "We want to take you with us."

Grant had backed up to the sink. He turned to look out of the window.

He'd know Lola was alone in seconds. She reached out with her foot and toppled the bucket over, letting the water splash onto Mitchell, wetting his legs. She hoped it would be enough to rouse him, hoped the dose of whatever drug he'd been given was too weak to keep him out for long, but there was little sign of change. With that kick, Lola had broken character, and she knew it. She was aware of Grant's movement, but until the mug struck her shoulder, she had no idea what he was doing.

He picked up another and hurled it at her.

This one she had to dodge to the left to avoid and it shattered against the wall behind her.

He slashed the knife through the air—he was still a distance from her so she was in no danger from that strike, but it was a clear sign of intent and that the tables had turned.

His irrational fear had given way to a semblance of logic. He was bigger than her, he was stronger than her, and he could beat her. Similarly, as the odds tipped in his favour and he grew in confidence, Lola's slipped away. Yes, she might have momentarily stopped this psycho from killing her boyfriend in some kind of ritual, but what good was that if he plunged a knife into her neck a second later?

She ran.

She could hear him following her which was equal parts good and terrifying: good as it meant that Mitchell was temporarily safe from a stabbing, bad as it meant her chances of one increased.

She left the kitchen and turned her head to the stairs: no way, a dead end. Instead, she went out of the front door, slamming it closed behind her knowing it would take Grant a few more seconds to open it and continue his chase.

Lola hoped she would have slipped round the side of the house before he was outside, before he could see her. She didn't give herself a chance to check; she knew she had to stay focused. Where the police had marched all manner of equipment to the back garden and out to the river, they'd carved the turf up pretty bad. If Lola wasn't paying attention, she was liable to fall, and then he'd definitely win, so Lola continued at a pace that allowed her to leap over the divots and ruts. At the side of the house, she reached out an arm to use it to pivot around the corner and stopped outside the back door. She hurriedly opened it, went inside and slammed it closed before turning the key in the lock. She leapt over Mitchell and headed for the front door, knowing that Grant wouldn't have closed it; what benefit could it have given him?

She could see Grant out of the front door, standing on the drive, his head moving from one side to the other as he looked down the street. Lola hurried for the door. He turned and saw her, but Lola knew she had the advantage. She only had a few steps to take and was already moving at speed and he was at the end of the drive and stationary. She slammed the door, dead-locked it, and then put the chain across too. Seconds later she heard Grant's bulk slam against the door.

If he was desperate to get in, then he would, sooner or later. But that gave Lola time. First, she went to the phone in the hall. She had to warn Mum that Dad was there, and he was after her and Ted. She opened the small drawer on the phone table and pulled out the address book. Mum always left a slip of paper in there with her number on it in case of emergencies ever since she'd first left them with a babysitter.

At first, Lola thought the phone was going to ring off to voicemail, but on the sixth ring the call connected.

"Lola?"

"Mum—watch out. Dad's there."

"Where? What are you talking about?"

There was a thump on the door. She imagined Grant was throwing himself at it.

"Dad's coming after you."

"Okay." Her voice had an assured calm, but she sounded tired. "Where are you? Are you safe?"

"I'm at home. There's a man here. Dad's friend."

There was another thump at the door. Lola thought she heard splintering.

"Stay there," Mum said. "I'm coming for you."

The phone went dead as Mum hung up. Lola was expecting another bang on the door any second, but it didn't come.

Next in her plan, if it could even be called that, was to try to wake Mitchell, but as she went into the kitchen, she saw Grant pass by the window. She ducked, for what good it was—he knew she was in there.

"Mitchell," Lola called.

She thought she heard him groan, but her attention was drawn to the window. She saw Grant running toward it, a green, plastic garden chair in hand. The chair hit the window and bounced off, flying out of Grant's hand and across the garden. Mum had always talked about getting a proper patio set, *a nice one*, but Lola had never been more thankful for cheap plastic furniture. Grant would find something heavier, though; he'd find a weaker window, and he'd be in.

Lola crouched down next to Mitchell and slapped his face. When he started to murmur, she slapped him harder. His eyes crept open.

"Lo…" he muttered. His cheek twitched; the corner of his mouth turned up a little. "I think I've pissed myself."

Despite their dire situation, Lola almost laughed when she looked down and saw the wetness in his legs, wetness she'd caused in trying to rouse him earlier. But no, she didn't have time to make a game of it. "Can you get up?" she said.

There was another bang at the window, and, as she turned, she again saw a garden chair spin off across the garden.

Mitchell lifted his head and took a deep breath.

"Come on, then. We've got to move."

He got as far as one knee before having to stop again. There was no running with him in that state. She helped him to his feet as she considered the best place to hide.

70: TED

The pain in Ted's chest had subsided, but his limbs felt almost too heavy to lift. The speed of his heartbeat had slowed but was erratic with frequent skips and sudden palpitations. There was a familiar scent—the illuminated red dust that stained the air tasted like home, the home he'd come to know over the last seven months. The earthy smell brought calm, and with those two senses, memories returned. He saw a flash of the creatures atop the vicarage, the gargoyles. Yes, but they weren't monsters, not like they were pictured. They'd saved him. They were his guardian angels. And now he had to go back. He held a hand to his chest. He had to go return, or his heart would stop.

He had to get beyond the barrier. His was faintly aware of his mother calling his name, following him, but he didn't belong to her anymore. He longed for his freedom, longed to be back among the others.

"You can't come through here," a police officer yelled when he tried to get round one of the vehicles. "It's dangerous. The ground's sinking."

Ted had an understanding of what was on the other side of the perimeter, beyond the authorities that no doubt looked into it unsure if they were looking upon oblivion or something else entirely. There hadn't been a route out here, previously. Not to Ted's knowledge. The excavations for the new village must have uncovered something, opened a rift. Now the world that Ted was briefly part of, the world that was starting to come back to his memory, would become a part of human knowledge once more, for the creatures had once been known in the world. While they liked to intervene in the lives of humans, only on rare occasions did they allow themselves to be seen, and their likeness was captured and the grand architects, understanding their desire to do good and protect from harm, used this likeness to decorate their buildings. But they were ugly. Grotesque, even. And those that had never seen them or understood their powers considered them to be monstrous and dubbed them gargoyles. Ted didn't know where this knowledge came from–part memory part common knowledge? What he did know was that he desired only to return to them.

Arthur stood beside him, also keen to return to the other side. He turned to Ted, and Ted looked back at him, and suddenly he understood his story, too. The eye was unsavable. He took that out with a shotgun, couldn't take the financial strain anymore or the pressure to sell up, decided to end it all and woke up with a new life in the other place. That's what they did, took those with few chances left and let them live on elsewhere, protected by their benevolence. Julius's story came back to him, too. Struck by a train, his body brutalised, they'd taken him and patched him up, all but his mangled arm which simply refused to stay reattached despite their best efforts.

He felt a hand on his shoulder. Mum stood before him. She looked smaller than before, weak even. In the past, he'd always thought she could look after him, no matter what. After each of the hospital visits, after each of the operations, she was the one holding his hand, helping him through recovery. But her time in that position had passed. He felt the pain in his chest and accepted the reality. To stay with Mum for much longer would eventually lead to a failing he couldn't recover from. Surely it was better to disappear now, back to those that could protect him and save her from the hurt his inevitable death would cause. He knew why he'd been sent back: to say goodbye. He was only supposed to stay for one day, but when he woke by the river, all that had been forgotten.

"Ted, come on," she said, grabbing him.

"No," Ted said. "This is where I belong."

"Your dad's here. He wants to hurt you."

Why would Dad want to hurt him? He remembered feeling unsettled by the way Dad had stared at him, confused by the way he acted, but he never saw his father as someone that would do him harm. Even so, if harm befell him here, they would save him. They wouldn't let him come to harm on their doorstep.

"And your sister's in trouble."

Lola? She was smart and much stronger than anyone gave her credit for. Whatever trouble she was in, surely, she could look after herself? He thought of her as a toddler, struggling to reach a toy on the table. He'd grabbed it for her and she'd kicked up a stink until he put it back and she climbed up to grab it herself. What good could he do? But he thought of the other times, signalling to each other behind their parents' backs while on holiday, making secret plots. No, he might not be able to help Lola, but she deserved a goodbye if nothing else. He let Mum drag him away from the barrier and back toward the car.

Arthur turned to him and nodded. He'd done his job. Ted knew now.

Ted climbed in the passenger seat and Mum hurried around to the driver's side. She kept flexing her hand and pulling at the bandage which looked much too moist to be healthy. She found steering difficult. Even though it wasn't far, at times Ted doubted whether they'd make it home at all.

As they approached Riverview Terrace there was an awful scream. Mum must have seen something in the rear-view mirror. As she yanked the steering wheel to one side, Ted turned his head. First, he saw the dagger, colours gleaming in the handle as it dug into the headrest. Had Mum not thrown Dad off-balance with her sudden turn, the dagger would have been in him.

The car came to a stop when it hit the pavement.

"Run," Mum yelled.

Ted unbuckled his seatbelt and ran from the car.

"Save your sister," he heard Mum cry.

He looked back. You should never look back. Dad had hold of the knife again. He sprung from the backseat and plunged the knife into Mum's shoulder.

Ted turned round, started heading back to the car.

"No," cried Mum. "Get your sister."

71: SIMON

While pulling the dagger from his wife's shoulder, feeling the resistance as the flesh tried to cling on to the blade and seeing the blood pool and then begin to flow as it finally came free, Simon experienced a moment of hyper-reality, a sensory overload in which his brain was hit by myriad impulses from all his senses. The sound was first, sucking, like a boot stuck in mud being pulled free, which caused flashes of memories of walking on a winter's day with Ted and Lola, their tiny legs struggling along a boggy track, but the memory lasted only until Megan's shrill shriek of agony hit him like a punch inside his brain that hit at the same time as the smell, the coppery scent of blood which came so thickly that he could taste it; it filled his mouth causing a reaction in his gut, sending acid sloshing up his gullet and into the back of his throat, a bitter burn he had to swallow back, but at least it had washed away the taste of blood which he could now see gushing, a red beyond the crimson or scarlet normally associated with blood–this shade was grandiose, vermilion, a brilliant, dynamic red. The light that poured in through the car windows had the dual effect of intensifying the colour of the spouting blood and falling onto Simon's body, bathing him in a welcome heat.

The light fell upon his wife's face. Her skin had taken on a whiteness which seemed to shine, and in that second, she was beautiful. The light stripped her of the strain her face had borne since they had become parents, parents with so much weight upon them caused by their children's health issues. After the initial shock of the shriek, Simon had become deaf to his wife's screams and looked at her as an ethereal being.

Colour erupted from his hand, vibrant red, green and purple shone out, reflected from the coloured jewels in the dagger's handle. Something shone on him from above, showing him the way. The dagger had yet to finish its work, the work of the beings of light. Instinctively he looked out of the front window and saw Ted. No, not Ted. This creature wasn't in the light. He walked in shadow. He was one of the creatures from beneath. Memories of Ted showed that he was once a child of the light. Images cycled through his memory of what Ted used to be: building castles in the sand on sunny days at the beach, splashing in the lido with friends, leading the way on family walks using a silver compass that shone in the sunlight.

The creature that came back to them was not like that. He remembered it cowering from the light when they first took it from the hospital. He remembered having to clear the box room, the only one that didn't have natural light. He remembered him clawing around in darkness, trying to worm his way back to the river. He heard Grant's warning: these creatures had come from the place below and were intent on dominating the world, installing a new order with them at the top. He was part of an insidious evil; they would ingrain themselves into the fabric of society and then tear it open from the inside.

Ted carried one of their champions, just as Julius had. He'd seen that boy released from his curse. He knew he could bring Ted peace, too. He could see Ted running in the shadows and knew where he was heading: home. But it wasn't that creature's home. It was Simon's home and if humanity was going to retain its home, he had to stop him.

All of this had happened in mere seconds. Time itself slowed to allow him to compute the plethora of signals fired at him, and as soon as he moved, time raced to catch up. As he reached for the handle to escape the car, Megan turned and clawed at his back. He ignored the raking on his flesh through his shirt, grabbed the door handle and pushed it open, then turned to Megan with the dagger raised. He'd plunged it into her once, but he was a different person then, consumed by madness, a blind fury brought on by his proximity to the hideous subterranean being that had been coughed out of the earth and hid in his son's body. Now he had clarity, and a single purpose: to stop what controlled Ted. But he couldn't hurt Megan. Not his wife. Not the woman he shared so many special memories with. She was the love of his life and she had been bathed in the light. He knew she had the purity to be a valiant soldier in the fight to come. She hadn't seen it with Julius, she'd arrived too late to see that foul being fade away, but when she saw it come out of Ted, she'd understand.

Her grasp was too weak to stop him. He felt her fingers trying to catch hold of his belt loops, but she didn't have the strength. Simon was out of the car. He looked down the road. Ted was out of sight. Those creatures had given him strength. But with the dagger's handle shining in the light, he knew it would be enough to overcome this ancient evil. As he started toward home, he wiped the dagger on his shirt and let the light that shone from the newly-cleaned blade show him the way.

72: LOLA

After Lola helped Mitchell onto Ted's bed, she hurried back into the hall in time to hear the smash of the window and the tinkling of glass as it showered into the kitchen.

He'd be inside in seconds, and Lola needed a plan.

She couldn't very well go out of the front door and leave Mitchell. He'd find him in a matter of minutes and Mitchell would have no chance of fighting Grant off in his semi-comatose state. But she could open the door. She could make him think they'd fled. It might buy her a few minutes. She dashed to the door, pulled it a little way and felt a violent recoil as the chain went taught. She shoved the door closed again, released the chain, threw it open, and then pulled the coat stand down to suggest she'd done so as a barrier on her way out.

She could go upstairs, but he might hear her on the steps, and if she did go up there, she was trapped. Worse, she could imagine going upstairs and then being completely powerless as she watched Grant go into Ted's bedroom. One hundred possibilities hit her in a second and each was easily dismissed due to the risk to Mitchell and her lack of power in comparison to this crazed adult. She saw Grant pulling himself in through the broken window, and in an instant decided on ducking into the living room.

As a younger child, she remembered running in circles through the rooms on the lower floor of the house. They hadn't used the door from the dining room to the living room in some years—ever since her parents had bought a new three-piece suite and not quite got the dimensions right, or at least that's what they said. She suspected it may have been deliberate to put a stop to her endless circling. They never ate in the dining room either, other than at Christmas.

She ran in and leapt over the sofa. From there she could see the front door, could see Grant looking out. Frantic, he, turned one way then the other, pretty much twitching on the spot. Lola gave the sofa a shove, putting her shoulder against it and using the weight of her body to shift it. It didn't need to go far, just enough to be able to pull the door open. But it wouldn't move. She pushed again, but still nothing. To gain purchase, she pushed against the wall with both legs, and the sofa shifted. When she put her feet down, she was aware of the change beneath them and gazed down to see that along with the sofa, she'd shoved the carpet from the floor too. She thought she'd heard a tear, but it didn't matter—it had moved enough.

Grant had heard her movements. He turned and glared with mad eyes, paused to take a deep breath, and then darted into the living room.

She tried to shove the sofa again to give herself a little more room, pushing her hip into it, but it wouldn't budge. The space she'd created would have to be enough. Breathing in and pushing herself against the wall as close as she was able, she scraped the door past her body and toppled over a pile of boxes and into the dining room.

Of course! Dad had piled up most of the junk from what was the office/spare room in there to make room for Ted. But she was out of the living room, that was all that mattered. Now she could think of the next plan. Kitchen and out of the back door was her self-preservation message, but again, what chance would that give Mitchell? She could arm herself in the kitchen, but what hope would a twelve-year-old with a knife have against an adult with a bigger knife and a longer reach? The door behind her slammed shut as Grant crashed into it. Seconds later, it came open again as he tried to get through. He pushed his head through the door, but there was no room for his body. As he tried to push himself through Lola opened a box. Stationery. On top was a stapler. She picked it up and hurled it toward Grant. It struck him on the forehead, and he yelled and then withdrew.

For a few seconds, all was quiet. Where had he gone? No doubt he'd been able to figure out the layout of the house. Was he going around the other way?

Lola stayed quiet and tried to listen for clues. She cursed her poor hearing and fingered her hearing aid. No, it wasn't the disability that was the problem here. If she'd have had the hearing aid serviced, if she'd had her check-up, then there was a chance that her hearing would have been better. Nothing indicated where Grant was. She'd have to risk a look through the door. She poked her head back into the living room. It was clear. Her hearing was good enough to hear his footsteps as he thudded on the kitchen tiles. Yes, he'd gone around the other way. She squeezed back through and hopped over onto the sofa. Seconds later the door opened, and Grant reached through. He shoved against the door, but there was no further movement. Lola looked down at the kink in the carpet and the way the sofa seemed to lean into it. There would be no shoving it out of the way. That gave her some security.

The door slammed shut. Was he going around the other way again? There was the occasional thud against the door, and then it seemed quiet. Surely, he'd return through the hall to the living room? Lola hopped behind the sofa, waiting for Grant. When he appeared, she yanked open the door. Boxes fell toward her. Grant raced across the carpet. Lola squeezed against the door again and pushed against the boxes, sending them tumbling into the dining room. She fell on top of them and turned to see Grant trying to force himself through the gap again. There was too little room for him to squeeze through.

But then he slammed the door shut. Would he be coming back round the other way? She heard a thud. What was he doing? She tried the door. It would only open a few inches. He'd shoved the sofa back in place.

And no doubt he'd be coming for her it just a second. She took off for the kitchen. They reached the opposite entrances at the same time and stared at each other across the room. Grant's body shifted as he took in each breath. His shirt dripped with sweat, and his hair was plastered to the top of his head. In his eyes, madness flared. Lola glanced over her shoulder at the back door. She could head out. It wouldn't be abandoning Mitchell. This guy was crazy, like an animal. He'd give chase. She could come in around the front again, buy herself a little more time, but then their attention was diverted to the voice from the front of the house.

"Lola?"

Ted was home.

73: TED

The front door was wide open and coats were strewn all over the hall. As Ted peered into his house, he could feel his heart hammering in his chest. He'd pushed himself too far, had run too quickly home.

"Lola," he called as he stepped inside. From the kitchen, a man turned to face him, bared his teeth and roared. On one cheek he bore an open gash. His face contorted into an inhuman expression, one controlled entirely by rage. The madman glanced over his shoulder, looking into the kitchen for a second before dismissing whatever was in there and striding toward Ted. In his hand he held a kitchen knife. Ted could tell it had been taken from their kitchen block because of the handle. Dad had warned him in the past how sharp they were, that they weren't to be used for craft activities. He heard his father's voice: *you'll slice your bloody fingers off*. Ted had experienced their sharpness when one had slipped so easily into Larry's throat. Ted thought the one the man held was a carving knife, and from the look on his face he was certain he was the most likely object to be carved.

Ted could have turned and run out the door, but the only reason he was there was because he'd heard his sister was in danger, and now he was confronted by the knife-wielding lunatic who had endangered her; he wasn't about to flee without knowing she was safe.

The man took a step toward him. He walked in a mechanical fashion, as if he had to think about every single function before he carried it out. Jerkily, he lifted the knife into the air and took a step forward. "I know what you are," he said.

He seemed to be looking beyond Ted, through him. Ted swallowed, trying to get enough moisture in his mouth to talk. "Where's my sister?" he said, gruffly, an accidental Batman impression.

"I'm going to slice you open and release this child from your control."

Whoever he was talking to, Ted realised, it wasn't him. He seemed to be talking to something inside of Ted. That was insane. Ted looked into his eyes. Insanity resided there too, multiplied by his different coloured irises, his enormous pupils, and his constantly flickering eyelids.

"Ted," came a shout from the kitchen. Lola! She was alive.

The man took another step toward him, and Ted took a step backwards. He could feel the coat-stand against the bottom of his legs. Lola stepped into view behind him. She signalled to him, pointing outside and then indicating that he should head toward the back.

Ted turned and ran. As soon as he tried to pick up speed, he felt pain explode in his chest, but he couldn't stop. He hurried outside and round the side of the house. Footsteps hammered down behind him, and a second later he heard the front door slam shut. As he reached the back garden, Lola was at the back door beckoning him in. Why hadn't she run, too? It was nuts to go back into the house.

"Come on, Lola," he called. "We've got to get away."

"No," Lola said. "Come inside. Quick."

Ted recognised the desperation in her voice. She was normally the one to acquiesce to his every demand, so her insistence on staying had to be important.

"What are you doing?" Ted asked as Lola tugged him inside and jostled him away from the door, which she quickly locked.

"Mitchell's here. He's been drugged. If we leave, Grant will kill him."

"Who's Grant?"

Lola grabbed plates and cups and positioned them on the counter.

"Some crazy guy Dad knows. When he tries to get in through the window, chuck something at him."

"Dad's gone crazy, too. He tried to stab me in the car."

Lola stared at Ted, open-mouthed.

They waited, Lola armed with a thick, white mug. She picked up the biggest one she could see and didn't acknowledge the slogan WORLD'S BEST FATHER on it. Ted held a plate, ready to Frisbee it toward Grant when he appeared at the window. But that time never came. Instead, Ted heard the key rattling in the lock on the front door. Lola hadn't heard and was still poised with her mug. It wasn't until the door creaked open that she looked at Ted with panic in her eyes.

"Lola, honey," came a shout from the hall. It was Dad.

They couldn't pull against years of instinct and stepped across the kitchen, in view of the hall.

"Nobody's going to hurt you, Lola," Dad called.

The madness Ted had seen in his eyes earlier, when he'd dived at him, dagger in hand, intent on stabbing him through the heart, had gone. The dagger, alas, had not.

From behind Dad, Grant stepped into view. "You get the boy. I'll deal with the girl."

"No," said Dad. "There's nothing wrong with the girl. She's not one of them."

Ted felt as if he'd been stabbed. It was like he had a hook in his gut being pulled downwards. He thought he might vomit. Why did Dad want to kill him? What had he done wrong? He knew he was different. He always had been. He couldn't play in the same way as the other kids, but his family had always helped him feel normal. Dad had made him feel like the champion of the world, but now he was ready to surrender him to some psychopath. He knew it had to do with the place he'd been, the creatures he'd been with, but he understood them now more than ever. They wanted to do no harm, but men like Grant had seen them as a threat, centuries ago, and driven them into hiding. Now they'd go as far as killing kids?

"She is one of them," Grant said, pointing his knife at Lola, "She said so herself."

"Trust me," Dad said. "She's harmless."

Lola looked at Ted, signalled for him to run out of the door.

Ted could already feel the pain in his chest. Running again would do no good. "No one's forcing me out of my home."

"Go round the back, stop them escaping," Grant said.

"Don't touch Lola," Dad said before wandering out.

Lola rushed to the back door and twisted the key a half turn. That way, even if Dad had his key, he wouldn't be able to get in.

Grant moved toward the kitchen.

Ted grabbed a plate and flung it at him, but Grant ducked out of the way and hurried into the middle of the room. He lifted his arm to deflect a mug that Lola hurled, and then he moved at speed and grabbed Lola by her arm as she reached for another projectile. He pulled her to him, his forearm locking around her neck.

The back door handle rattled, but Ted knew it wouldn't open. A second later his father was at the window.

"Grant, I told you, not the girl."

"It's got to be done, Simon, don't you see?"

"Just the boy, Grant, just the boy!"

Each word wielded the dagger and stabbed it into Ted's heart.

"Can't you see it's all part of their plot?" Grant called.

Lola struggled against Grant's grip, and it took all of his effort to keep hold of her and focus on the conversation.

"Ted," Dad called through the window.

"Let me in. You've got to let me in to save Lola."

Ted turned toward his father and flung a plate toward the window where it exploded against the frame.

Ted picked up another and motioned to throw it toward Grant.

"Try it," he said. He lifted the knife in one hand, suggesting how easy it would be to stab Lola.

"Ted," Dad called again, "you have to let me in."

Ted threw the plate down in the middle of the kitchen, an act of teenage petulance. He watched the shards spread across the floor.

"Okay, Dad. Just a sec."

Walking backwards, his eyes on Lola, he took a couple of steps toward the door. He made sure Lola was looking at him, and then focused on his right hand. Lola watched it, too. He scrunched the hand up, and then moved the fist under the flat of his left hand. He nodded at a particularly sharp shard of plate that had come to a stop close to her and made a pointing motion.

Lola understood the signs perfectly. Bite, duck, stab. Even the stabbing implement had been indicated. She sunk her teeth into Grant's arm, and he yelped, releasing his grip on her which allowed her to bend down, grab a shard of porcelain and jab it into Grant's inner thigh. She dragged it down his leg, causing him to buckle over in agony, trying to contain the blood that jetted from his leg.

Ted stepped forward again, grabbing plates and hurling them at Grant. He hadn't seen them coming. The first bounced off his back, but the second caught him on the side of the head, knocking him to the ground.

"Ted!" Lola called as he continued to fling plates at Grant.

Ted turned to see the blade of the dagger flash past him. His father had clambered through the window while their attention was on Grant, and he was intent upon finishing the job.

"Run!" Lola cried.

While Ted had no intention of leaving his sister, he had to escape his father. Dad wouldn't hurt her. He could run for the front door, call out for help, and hope someone nearby would react. Grant was in a sitting position, holding a hand over the gash in his leg to stem the tide of blood and crying out through clenched teeth. The shard of plate sat bloody on the floor. Ted made to move past him, and he reached out a hand, insufficient to stop Ted, but enough to make him stumble. His next step was out of control, his foot hit the coat-stand, rolled off it and sent him tumbling forward. He rolled over, onto his back and saw his father closing on him.

74: MEGAN

There were certain things Megan always kept in her car in case they were required: a bottle of water and a snack in case of getting stuck in bad traffic; a blanket, deodorant and a toothbrush in case of a larger scale emergency; some wrapping paper, a roll of sticky tape and a pair of scissors for those occasions when she bought the present en route to the party. She never thought those implements would come in handy in the situation she found herself in. The badly-bandaged cut on her arm didn't help with the process of patching up her wounded shoulder, but she had to do something to stem the tide of blood. If only she were organised enough to have a proper first aid kit, she thought before dismissing such wishes as futile and fanciful. No, she had to focus on what she had if she was to catch Simon, who was already out of sight.

She cut a patch and a number of strips from the back of her cardigan for dressing. Loose, it would be ineffective. Megan used the roll of tape to hold it in place, fire exploding in the wound every time more pressure was put on it. She'd clearly restricted her movement with the volume of tape, but as movement drew jolts of agony, this was a benefit. Stopping the flow of blood was paramount, for if she lost any more, she feared she would pass out. She couldn't lie there and slip into unconsciousness, not when her children were in danger, not when it was their bloody father who was responsible.

She pushed the car door open, stepped out, and immediately wanted to crash back into the seat. Her head throbbed and her vision blurred. She leaned against the car, letting it take her weight for a moment and then stumbled in the direction of the house. Each footstep sent a wave of vibration up her body and sent those nerve endings reporting pain in her shoulder and hand into frenzy. Worse was the pain in her head. It was like her brain was revolting against her actions, contracting and swelling with each footstep as if alerting her to the madness of the situation. The part that wanted her to stop told her Ted was well ahead of her, that he would have found Lola, and they would be far away by now, somewhere safe. The part of her imagination that kept her plodding on told the opposite story: Ted and Lola remained in danger; their lives would end imminently if she didn't personally stop the madness. The bitch part of her brain chimed in too, telling her she was responsible for this situation. She'd let Simon's drinking get out of control and because of that he'd lost his senses and got involved with some cultish psychopath. She'd let Ted be taken in the first place by not looking after him well enough. And Lola? She'd barely thought of her little problem child for the last seven months. For all they'd done with Lola, for Lola, her brain kept needling her with that momentary agreement of Simon's assessment when they found out about Lola's hearing problems. With every thump on the pavement, accompanying the spike of pain was the mantra. *Problem child. Problem child. Problem child.* Even though she'd only agreed with Simon's words for the briefest of seconds, she'd been punished with a lifetime of guilt, and now, when things seemed to be at their direst it was back at her again.

It wasn't fair! "No!" she cried, willing the voice out of her brain, striding forward with greater purpose. She loved her kids, and she'd do anything for them. Riverview Terrace was in sight. She just had to plod on a little farther and chase down the pain with happy memories: seeing Lola perform in her first school production and remembering her cute little cheek dimples and the way Lola couldn't stop waving at her in the audience every time she looked up; Ted practising guitar, watching his fingers so closely as he strummed his way through his first ever song, Oasis's 'Wonderwall'. Until that moment, she hated that song; after, it filled her with warmth.

Megan's plodding continued, but she snapped out of her reverie when she spotted Grant's yellow Saab. If the car was still there, were the kids there, too? The bitch in her brain told her so, told her she was too late, she was useless and she'd dropped the ball and let a pair or psychos kill her kids—worse, she'd married a psycho in the first place.

This only made Megan move faster. The front door was open. Ted ran toward the door from inside, toward her. He stumbled. She could see the situation slipping out of her control. No. Not this time. Using the pain of each step as a springboard, she drove forward, picking up pace. As Ted crashed to the floor, she was on the drive. As he flipped around, she was on the step.

Simon was closer, and Simon had hold of that damned dagger, closing on Ted. She didn't know which of them would get there first, she only had to hope that the other accessory she'd brought from the car would be enough.

Simon held the dagger in the air. He hesitated, unsure what to do.

"Do it," called Grant.

Megan couldn't afford to suffer the same deliberation, and as Simon moved down with the dagger, she stepped inside the house, swinging the last of the strength in her body up with the fist that held the pair of scissors.

Simon released the dagger. Megan saw it twist, the heavy handle seeking ground first, and she heard Ted yell in pain. It wasn't a scream of agony though, and that was enough. Simon's momentum carried him forward, crashing onto her and she was barely able to roll to one side to let him fall. The way his body crumpled, was as if he were an inflatable that suddenly deflated. The scissors had found a home-sunk to the handles in Simon's chest, protruding between the ribs. He was breathing, but only just—and staring only up at the ceiling. He mumbled something. The only word Megan detected was "dark".

Megan felt the world become distant, too. The edges of her universe were completely white, and her field of vision was shrinking.

She heard Lola's cries. Lola was alive. She'd arrived in time to save her Teddy Bear, and she'd got him home in time to save Lola, too. She'd done enough.

75: TED

"This isn't over, you freaks." Grant had struggled onto one knee, but he couldn't put weight on his other leg.

Ted didn't want to hear him. He didn't want to deal with him, not with his dad lying on one side with a pair of scissors sticking out of his chest and his mother, covered in blood, and, bizarrely, sticky tape, looking like an extra from a low-budget zombie flick.

"I'm calling an ambulance," Lola said, heading for the telephone in the hall.

"Too late," Ted said. He glanced at the dagger on the floor and touched his cheekbone, remembering the sudden pain he'd felt when it fell on his face. Looking at the dagger's point, he realised it could have been a lot worse.

"There are more of us, and we're going to stop this invasion," Grant said. He tried to put weight on his other leg but again collapsed.

Ted thought about what he should do with the dagger. He could think of no better place for it than Grant's back, plunged in deep, striking the heart from the rear, giving him a hole in the heart of his own, a fatal one, but he was no murderer, no matter what had happened with Larry. Regardless of his desires, he didn't have time to do anything about Grant, not if he was going to save Mum. He kicked the dagger into the kitchen. In Grant's condition, there was no way he'd be able to reach it.

He bent down beside Mum. She'd lost consciousness. Shaking her would do no good, nor a light tap on the face. He had to get her up, get her out of there. He pulled one of her arms, so it was over his shoulder and started to drag. He, too, was in no condition for this extra strain.

Lola put the house phone down and turned to Ted. "Shouldn't you leave her where she is? Recovery position or something?"

"No, we've got to get her outside."

"Outside? But the ambulance will be here soon. Less than half-an-hour, they hope."

"No. That's not good enough. Can't you see her? She's lost a lot of blood."

"What good's getting her outside going to do?"

"Help first, I'll explain later."

Lola moved to her mother's side and took some of her weight. Together, they shuffled through the house.

"So, what's the plan?" Lola asked.

"I'm going to send her where I was."

"Where you were?" Lola stopped.

Taking the weight suddenly send another spike into Ted's heart. "They can save her. They're the only ones."

Ted sensed the doubt in his little sister, but as was her habit, she kept moving anyway, and soon, they were out of the back door.

"Whatever people say, no one in our family is to blame for any of this."

"Not Dad?"

"That looney had control over him. He did everything he said."

"Yeah," Lola said, remembering the distant look in her father's eyes.

"He's not going to be okay, is he?"

"No."

"We can't do the same for him?"

"Wouldn't work. Couldn't send him down there with poison inside his mind. He wouldn't make it."

The fresh air outside lifted them and made moving Mum toward the river easier.

"And Lola, you're going to hear that I stabbed Larry, maybe even killed him. Nothing that happened was deliberate. I wanted someone to find him."

"You pulled the fire alarm?" Lola said.

"Yeah. Hopefully, they got to him in time."

Lola remained silent for a moment as they closed on the river. "Are we doing the right thing?"

"Do you trust me?" Ted said, looking Lola in the eyes.

She nodded.

"I'm not going to be around anymore. Mum's going into the water, and I've got to go with her."

"You can't leave me here on my own."

Ted felt the left-hand side of his body tense. A bolt of pain shot up his arm.

"They'll send Mum back. That's what they do, but it might take some time."

At the riverbank, they gazed into the water which sparkled in the bright sunshine.

"But you'll be back too, right?"

Ted reached across and took Lola's hand. He pulled it up to his heart. "I don't think there's any fixing it this time. But they'll let me stay with them, let me look in on you now and again."

Ted could see the tears welling up in Lola's eyes.

"Go back inside. Lock yourself in my room with Mitchell until the ambulance arrives. Call the police, too. You'll be fine. You're strong. I believe in you. I love you."

"I've broken my phone."

Ted reached awkwardly into his pocket, took his phone and handed it to Lola. "Don't say I never gave you anything, okay?"

Lola took the phone, and with the back of her hand wiped away the tears from her face.

"I'm glad I got to come back, just for a little while, to see what an amazing person you're growing into."

"Don't go," Lola said. "You don't have to."

"There's no other way. If we stay, you lose us both."

Lola let go of her mother, let Ted take all of the weight.

"Get back inside, quick, while it's safe."

Ted waited for Lola to be back inside before he did anything. Finally, he could draw in the deep breaths he needed to. He didn't want Lola to see how much he struggled to breathe, didn't want her to know that he too felt like he was slipping away. And most of all he didn't want her to know that he had absolutely no idea whether this would be successful. For all he knew, they'd fall into the water, and nothing would happen. With the breach in Fenmore, it was possible the beings no longer possessed the capability to help them. But when the memories had come back to him of his time in that place, more than anything he was convinced they would save him; they would save them both. He took one last look at his home knowing he'd never return, and, holding on to Mum, plunged them both into the water, and into instant blackness.

76: LOLA

Upon returning to the house, Lola discovered that Grant had disappeared. He'd left a trail of blood behind him. She looked out of the door and saw his car in the drive with the passenger door open. Part of her hoped he'd bleed out right there. She closed the front door. Dad lay on the floor, still struggling to breathe, still trying to speak, but making no sense.

"Ted says it's not your fault, Dad," Lola said, squeezing his hand. She had no idea if he heard her or not. She'd heard what he said, how he tried to stick up for her against Grant. But she'd also heard what he said about Ted. Maybe Ted was right about poison in his mind. He hadn't always been like that; she refused to remember him like that.

Maybe Grant was in his car calling in reinforcements, maybe he wasn't. Either way, she wasn't about to sit there and wait for them. She closed the front door and returned to Ted's room. Mitchell still slept, hopefully overcoming the effects of whatever he'd been drugged with. He was breathing steadily, and the paramedics would surely know what to do with him.

She lay on the bed next to him, looking around the room at Ted's things, the things he'd never use again, never set his eyes upon again. She looked at his guitar and smiled, remembering the silly birthday song he'd made up for her when she was eleven. She looked at his movie collection and remembered a hundred nights watching films together, nights full of laughter. And eventually, when the ambulance did arrive, she was so lost in her memories that at first, she didn't hear them knocking on the door.

After that moment everything happened so quickly that Lola barely had time to understand what was going on. Obviously, when she'd called the emergency services, she'd mentioned her mother, and her absence at the scene caused confusion which Lola claimed to be unable to explain. But unexplained occurrences were plentiful. Her father didn't make it. As devastating as the loss was, she couldn't have accepted him back if he'd lived.

Mitchell suffered little more than a terrible headache when he woke, but the vague memory of having wet himself troubled him until Lola revealed the truth. Later Lola learned that Larry had survived being stabbed in the neck. He'd told everyone Ted had done it, and the police were willing to believe the story that he'd run away after the incident to avoid getting into trouble.

Lola read a number of news articles and blog posts about the cause of the sinkhole. They blamed poorly dug foundations, the changing of the course of the river, and the shrinking of the peat. Thorough geological surveys of the area found no evidence of subterranean passageways. Those who claimed something more lived beneath the ground were ridiculed and no one reported on the glut of people seemingly missing for years who turned up in Fenmore that day.

With her father dead, and her mother missing, Lola fell into the care of her aunt, Claire. She lived in a nearby village, Little Mosswick, which was also in the catchment area for Fenland Village Academy, so after some time to mourn, some time to adjust, Lola returned to school.

Every day she thought of her brother's promise, that Mum would be back even if he wouldn't be, and every day she checked in with the police and scanned social media and websites for news of missing persons or unknown people turning up out of the blue. Heimlich grew tired of her constant calls but remained patient.

One afternoon in early December, Heimlich called on Lola. She'd finished her maths homework and was in the middle of some research for English when Aunt Claire told her she had a visitor.

"Now Miss Wallace, I don't want you to get too excited, but I have some news."

If this ended badly, that was okay, for at least, for a time, there was hope. "What is it?"

"We've had a call from the hospital. A woman who fits your mother's description has been brought in."

Lola felt as if someone had attached helium balloons to her inside, lifting her up. Could it be? Ted had promised she'd be back. "Is she okay?"

"Physically, yes. She's not saying much. She's unable to confirm her identity."

Lola stood up. "Can we see her?"

"I'm going to take you as part of the identification process, but listen, I don't want to get your hopes up. Even if it is her, she may not be the same as before."

"I understand."

For the whole journey, Lola held on to hope. Ted had promised her it would be fine. Ted had promised he'd take Mum to where he went, and they'd fix her. It had to be her. It had to be.

What used to seem like a relatively quick journey to the hospital now took an eternity, and once they'd arrived, it didn't improve. Each metre they walked down the corridor felt like a kilometre until they came to a stop outside one of the rooms.

"Wait outside one moment," Heimlich said. He knocked on the door and entered.

For a second, Lola heard a voice. It could have been her mother's, but the words made no sense. It might not have even been a voice, only sounds: *Teh-teh-teh.*

With the door closed, Lola again suffered in silence. It might have been for only a minute she waited, but it felt much longer. Heimlich opened the door, and beckoned her in.

Teh-teh-teh. Teh-teh-teh.

The voice continued: three syllables while inhaling, three while exhaling. Lola crept toward the head of the bed. Her first thought was that the woman in front of her was too thin to be her mother, the grey hair belonged to a much older woman, but when she turned her head to Lola and looked into her eyes, Lola knew.

Her mother's breathing slowed. *Teh. Teh. Teh.*

Her pupils shrunk and her focus fixed on Lola. The pattern of her breathing changed. She stopped trying to speak and started taking shallow, panicked breaths.

One of the doctors pushed in front of Lola. "Excuse me," he said. "I'm sorry, but you'll have to leave."

Lola stepped away from the bed and felt Heimlich place his hand on her shoulder, ushering her outside.

But then her mother's breathing slowed as she calmed and started to make sounds again. Not *Teh* anymore, but *Luhluh*.

Yes, it was Mum. She was trying to call her name. Lola took hold of Mum's hand.

It might take time for her to fully recover, it might be difficult, but that didn't matter. Ted had kept his promise. Ted had sent Mum back, and Lola would be alone no more.

THE END?

Not if you want to dive into more of Crystal Lake Publishing's Tales from the Darkest Depths!

Check out our amazing website and online store or download our latest catalog here:
https://geni.us/CLPCatalog

Looking for award-winning Dark Fiction?
Download our latest catalog.

Includes our anthologies, novels, novellas, collections, poetry, non-fiction, and specialty projects.

TALES FROM THE DARKEST DEPTHS

We always have great new projects and content on the website to dive into, as well as a newsletter, behind the scenes options, social media platforms, our own dark fiction shared-world series and our very own webstore. Our webstore even has categories specifically for KU books, non-fiction, anthologies, and of course more novels and novellas.

AUTHOR BIOGRAPHY

Benjamin Langley has been writing since he could hold a pen and has always been drawn to dark tales. He has had short stories published in over a dozen publications including *Crescendo of Darkness*, *Deadman's Tome*, and *The Manchester Review*. He has also written Sherlock Holmes adventures that have featured in *Adventures in the Realm of H.G. Wells*, *Adventures Beyond the Canon*, and *Adventures in the Realm of Steampunk*. Benjamin has also written comedy sketches that have been performed on stage, radio and television.

He lives, writes, and teaches in Cambridgeshire, UK, where he also studied at Anglia Ruskin University. He was awarded the prize for best Major Writing Project while studying for his BA in Writing and English. *Normal* is his third novel after *Dead Branches* and *Is She Dead in Your Dreams?* His novella, *The Fen Witch of GooseFeather Split*, is also available. Alongside his works of quiet horror, Benjamin Langley is also the author of the very noisy alternative history trilogy, *Guy Fawkes: Demon Hunter*.

Readers…

Thank you for reading *Normal*. We hope you enjoyed this novel.

Help other readers by telling them why you enjoyed this book. No need to write an in-depth discussion. Even a single sentence will be greatly appreciated. Reviews go a long way to helping a book sell, and is great for an author's career. It'll also help us to continue publishing quality books.

Thank you again for taking the time to journey with Crystal Lake Publishing.

You will find links to all our social media platforms on our Linktree page:
https://linktr.ee/CrystalLakePublishing.

MISSION STATEMENT

Since its founding in August 2012, Crystal Lake Publishing has quickly become one of the world's leading publishers of Dark Fiction and Horror books in print, eBook, and audio formats.

While we strive to present only the highest quality fiction and entertainment, we also endeavour to support authors along their writing journey. We offer our time and experience in non-fiction projects, as well as author mentoring and services, at competitive prices.

With several Bram Stoker Award wins and many other wins and nominations (including the HWA's Specialty Press Award), Crystal Lake Publishing puts integrity, honor, and respect at the forefront of our publishing operations.

We strive for each book and outreach program we spearhead to not only entertain and touch or comment on issues that affect our readers, but also to strengthen and support the Dark Fiction field and its authors.

Not only do we find and publish authors we believe are destined for greatness, but we strive to work with men and woman who endeavour to be decent human beings who care more for others than themselves, while still being hard working, driven, and passionate artists and storytellers.

Crystal Lake Publishing is and will always be a beacon of what passion and dedication, combined with overwhelming teamwork and respect, can accomplish. We endeavour to know each and every one of our readers, while building personal relationships with our authors, reviewers, bloggers, podcasters, bookstores, and libraries.

We will be as trustworthy, forthright, and transparent as any business can be, while also keeping most of the headaches away from our authors, since it's our job to solve the problems so they can stay in a creative mind. Which of course also means paying our authors.

We do not just publish books, we present to you worlds within your world, doors within your mind, from talented authors who sacrifice so much for a moment of your time.

There are some amazing small presses out there, and through collaboration and open forums we will continue to support other presses in the goal of helping authors and showing the world what quality small presses are capable of accomplishing. No one wins when a small press goes down, so we will always be there to support hardworking, legitimate presses and their authors. We don't see Crystal Lake as the best press out there, but we will always strive to be the best, strive to be the most interactive and grateful, and even blessed press around. No matter what happens over time, we will also take our mission very seriously while appreciating where we are and enjoying the journey.

What do we offer our authors that they can't do for themselves through self-publishing?

We are big supporters of self-publishing (especially hybrid publishing), if done with care, patience, and planning. However, not every author has the time or inclination to do market research, advertise, and set up book launch strategies. Although a lot of authors are successful in doing it all, strong small presses will always be there for the authors who just want to do what they do best: write.

What we offer is experience, industry knowledge, contacts and trust built up over years. And due to our strong brand and trusting fanbase, every Crystal Lake Publishing book comes with weight of respect. In time our fans begin to trust our judgment and will try a new author purely based on our support of said author.

With each launch we strive to fine-tune our approach, learn from our mistakes, and increase our reach. We continue to assure our authors that we're here for them and that we'll carry the weight of the launch and dealing with third parties while they focus on their strengths—be it writing, interviews, blogs, signings, etc.

We also offer several mentoring packages to authors that include knowledge and skills they can use in both traditional and self-publishing endeavours.

We look forward to launching many new careers.

This is what we believe in. What we stand for. This will be our legacy.

Welcome to Crystal Lake Publishing—Tales from the Darkest Depths.

THANK YOU FOR PURCHASING THIS BOOK

Printed in Great Britain
by Amazon